Reprisal

by

Douglas Mitchell

ISBN: 9798645899813

For Jane

Foreword

Isabelle de Bonnefoix reached desperately into her bedside table and pulled out an old chamber pot. She retched and heaved into it then lay back exhausted. She was sure now. She had noticed her missed period but had not paid it much attention – she had always been a bit irregular. But the last two mornings she had been sick. The first time she put it down to something she had eaten. Today she had no such excuse. As she recovered, she could not help the smile starting to spread over her face. It would create a terrible scandal of course, but she would go away for a trip when she started to show, and come back with "an orphan" - there would be many after the war. She hoped it would be a boy and a boy like Alan – strong and gentle and good – and beautiful.

She thought back to the night she had conceived and her smile spread. She rose, pulled on her dressing gown, and made her way downstairs to her study. She opened her desk and took out a piece of paper, then sat down and picked up her pen.

She hesitated, and stared at the paper for a moment blankly. Then her eyes cleared and she seemed to resolve a dilemma. She smiled, and started to write.

" My darling Alan…….."

CHAPTER ONE

On the first day McGill reappeared at Scotland Yard after his return from France he was unsure what to do or where to go.

When he had left in early November, he had been a Detective Constable. Now, just about a month later, he was an Inspector. At the front entrance he paused, then made his way to Superintendent Truman's office.

McGill entered the outer office where a Sergeant was reading files. It was the same man who had been resentful of him the last time he had been here. Now, he stood up immediately, and there was a new respect in his eyes.

" Welcome back sir. Superintendent Truman is expecting you."

McGill nodded and followed the sergeant as he made his way to the inner door, knocked and opened it.

" Inspector McGill, Sir."

Truman was behind his desk surrounded by a mountain of paperwork. He glanced up as McGill came in, threw his pen down, and reached across to shake McGill's hand.

" McGill, my boy! I'm really glad to have you back!"

" Thank you sir. I'm really glad to be back. There were a few moments when I wasn't certain I would be."

" Well you're here now. I've had sight of a very commendatory letter from Field Marshall Haig – Sir Giles showed it to me yesterday. I may say I'm delighted."

" Thank you again sir"

" Millager's eyes nearly popped out of his head when Sir Giles turned up here. And I'd be willing to bet he listened at the keyhole as to what we discussed."

" I had noticed a change in his attitude sir."

" As well he might! Now, what are we going to do with you, eh? The simplest would be for you to slot into poor Brown's shoes. We'd have to reassign the sergeant that was there, and your old position would be taken over by a new constable, but I think that would all work perfectly well, don't you?"

" Yes sir, if you say so sir."

" Yes I do McGill. Between you and me I'm glad Brown has gone. I've no idea how he ever got to be an Inspector in the first place – he was there when I took over this post. Leave it to me, I'll arrange it. In the meantime you better finalise your report then go and sort out whatever is lying about on Brown's desk. We organised some of the more urgent things to be taken over, but there are a few that have just been left. Better get on and get them sorted."

" Yes sir, very good sir." McGill turned to go.

" Oh and McGill – you've to see Sir Giles at noon."

" Sir Giles sir? Really?" Truman nodded.

" Oh yes. He wants to thank you for your work."

As McGill crossed the outer office, Millager had leapt to his feet once more. He had clearly been listening at the door, because his face betrayed his curiosity and astonishment that somebody who was a constable only a few weeks ago was now suddenly hobnobbing with the Commissioner. Millager raced to open the door to the corridor.

" Just let me know if there's anything I can do for you sir."

"Thank you Millager, I will."

McGill made his way to his old office. No one was sitting in it, and there was no sergeant in the office on the other side of what had been Brown's office. Feeling rather like an interloper, McGill walked behind the desk and sat in the chair that had been Brown's. He held the desk with both hands. He opened one drawer then another. There were files but nothing personal. Everything that had been Brown's had been taken away – given back to his family, McGill supposed. He opened the rest of the drawers and methodically piled all the files on top of the desk. He arranged them with the oldest on the top and the newest at the bottom.

He knew he would know what they contained. After all be had been working with Brown for some months before they had left for France, and there would be nothing new. He settled himself more comfortably in the seat, pulled the oldest file towards him and started to read.

After an hour or so the outer door opened, followed by steps across the floor. McGill heard them stop outside the inner door, and shortly thereafter there was a knock at McGill's open door.

McGill looked up from his reading, and waved the newcomer in.

" Good morning, sir, Superintendent Truman said I was to report here."

" Ah, yes, I see. And you are?"

" Croker, sir"

McGill took his watch from his pocket.

" I've an appointment to see the Commissioner at twelve noon, but I'd say a cup of tea wouldn't go amiss."

Croker appeared to smile slightly, his light brown hair and brown eyes taking on an almost festive air.

" Yes, sir, I had heard that. I'll get us a pot." No wonder, thought McGill. The news of his meeting with the Commissioner would have flashed around the Yard in less time than it took to say it. Millager had clearly made sure everyone knew immediately. Maybe being back as an Inspector wouldn't be so bad after all, thought McGill.

Croker turned and went out, and McGill picked up another file. He didn't think any of them really deserved very much attention – mostly petty thefts and requests for information that were now out of date. He sighed. He didn't suppose even his new found status would get him some interesting cases. After all, his superiors had never paid much attention to him before.

At one minute to twelve noon, McGill was standing outside the grand doors that led into the suite of offices that the Commissioner, Sir Giles Compston, occupied. A Constable sat at a desk to one side, and McGill presented himself there.

" Yes, sir, I'll show you in." The Constable rose and opened the double doors. McGill passed through into an anteroom that, although it had several desks and various people working at them, remained quiet and ordered.

It reminded McGill of the offices that Generals occupied in France, but much less busy and more subdued. Once inside, he was collected by a sergeant and moved towards the other end of the room, where another set of doors stood. The sergeant knocked on the door, opened it and ushered McGill inside.

He found himself standing in an anteroom, where two female secretaries sat at desks, both with typewriters. There was another desk that looked suspiciously clear, but McGill could see that it was actually occupied. One of the secretaries was busily flicking through a shorthand notepad, whilst the other, older, woman picked up her pad and a pencil, and pointed McGill towards the inner door.

" I'll be taking notes," she said flatly. She knocked, waited for a "Come!" then opened the door and stepped through. Even before McGill had stepped through the doorway, she had announced " Detective Inspector McGill, sir." That's really strange thought McGill. I've never heard it said that way before.

Compston rose from behind his desk, where he and another man, who was standing, had been scanning some papers.

" McGill – come in and sit down." McGill looked at Compston and saw the bright eyes and high forehead that he had come to recognise as meaning intelligence. The hair was thinning somewhat, but Compston's handshake was firm and robust.

McGill took one of the two chairs in front of the desk, whilst the man who had been standing took the other. Compston waved a hand at him.

" This is Simonds from the Home Office. He can sit in on our discussion. And, Miss Howard will be taking notes."

" Yes Sir."

Compston resumed his seat then leant forward and folded his hands in front of him on the desk.

" Now McGill, I've read your report, and very good it is too. If I know Douglas Haig you had to give it to him first?"

" Indeed sir." McGill wondered how much Compston knew. He thought he would elucidate a little. " In fact, I doubt I could have got out of the area if I hadn't!" Both Compston and Simonds chuckled slightly.

" Ah yes, that's Douglas all right. But straight as a die. Well, I'm delighted we put one over on the Military, even if you didn't manage to find the murderer." Compston glanced up and his eyes appeared to burn through McGill. "Hmmm, yes well, it remains to be seen what we are going to have you working on. Can't have you wasting your time on petty thefts, what?"

" No sir. I'd be happy to be dealing with more serious cases."

" Quite right. I've got enough ninnies dealing with old ladies teaspoons as it is, eh Simonds?"

" Yes, Sir Giles" Simonds had a rasping voice that sounded like sandpaper on rough wood. McGill wasn't sure if it was smoking or something else that had caused it.

" Anyway," Compston went on, " I've assigned a Sergeant Farr to you. Good man with some of your disrespect". McGill made to protest, but Compston held his hand up. " Don't say anything, we both know how you feel about your superiors here, and Farr is very much of the same mind. You'll have met young Croker already. I'd almost go so far as to say you are all well suited and irreverent enough between you to make even the Archbishop of Canterbury have apoplexy."

Compston glanced at Simonds.

" I've been discussing you with Simonds here, and we've come up with a plan".

Compston stood up and started pacing the floor behind his desk.

"You see, the thing is too much of what I get to see and hear gets filtered. People only tell me what they think I want to hear. And that's bad. I need to know the truth, however unpalatable, and I especially need to know if one of my men is either not pulling his weight or having problems of one sort or another he doesn't want to talk about." Compston stopped pacing, and looked directly at McGill. " Can you do that?"

McGill was quiet for a moment, then rubbed his chin.

" A sort of spy sir?" he said quietly.

Compston considered for a moment. " Not really. If something goes wrong I want an independent assessment of what and how. I'm not asking you to spy, just report the exact truth. I know you can do that."

McGill nodded slowly. " Yes I can do that for you sir. If Farr and Croker are of a like mind to myself, we will almost certainly be ostracised by all and sundry."

Compston laughed. " Would that be so bad?"

McGill smiled grimly. " Actually sir, in many ways I wouldn't mind that at all!"

"That's settled then. You and your men will be my terriers when there's something fishy going on. On an everyday basis, you'll only deal with the more serious crimes as well. You'll have a separate team that can take over when I need you to do something for me."

Compston extended his hand again, and McGill rose and shook it.

" Thank you sir. I appreciate your confidence in me."

" You will only report to me on matters that I brief you about, but you will continue to report to Truman on all other matters. Any problems at any time you come directly to me. Is that all understood?"

"Yes sir. And thank you again." Compston nodded, glanced at Miss Howard and nodded. She rose and indicated the door.

" This way sir" McGill nodded to Simonds, who nodded back, and followed the secretary through the doorway.

Once the door had closed, there was silence for a few moments, then Simonds spoke.

" I think he'll do." Compston nodded.

" Yes I'm sure he will, Major. Not sure how long he may last, but at least we've got someone who's prepared to take risks, and who we can rely on."

CHAPTER TWO

McGill made his way slowly back to his office. When he opened the outer door, young Croker came to his feet, and another, dark, swarthy man, sitting at another desk did likewise. McGill glanced from one to the other.

" Well, I know you're Croker," he said pointing at the constable, " And unless I'm very much mistaken, you are Sergeant Farr."

Farr nodded, and McGill took note of the dark, seemingly dead eyes that stared back at him. Cold but clever, thought McGill. He extended his hand and Farr, after a moment's hesitation, took it.

"Welcome to the party," said McGill. He turned and shut the outer door, then indicated his private office. " Right, you two, in there with me."

Slightly puzzled, the two police officers followed McGill through the doorway, and turned, surprised as he held back as they entered the room. Without saying a word, McGill shut the door behind them.

" I expect you're both wondering what this is all about." They nodded, and McGill went on. " From now on we will have two masters. Firstly, Superintendent Truman will be our superior officer for day to day matters and we will only deal with more serious crimes. And secondly, we will report direct to the Commissioner on… on other matters." Both Farr and Croker looked astonished. Farr cleared his throat.

" Other matters sir?"

" Yes, Farr, other matters."

" What kind of matters sir, if I may ask?" McGill scratched his head.

"Let's just say on matters that are of concern to the Commissioner." There was a silence. Farr scratched *his* head and looked straight at McGill.

" Do we know what concerns him just now sir?" McGill grinned.

" He didn't say, but I get the impression we'll all know soon enough. Suffice to say he called us his bulldogs!" Sounded better than terriers, thought McGill.

Farr looked sharply at McGill. " I'd heard Sir Giles was perturbed by some slackness in the force, sir." McGill grinned again.

" You could say that. I'd say we are going to be very unpopular in lots of quarters." Farr barked a derisory laugh.

"I hope so sir. There's nothing I hate more than officers who are untrustworthy." Croker nodded.

" I agree with you, though that's not necessarily the word I would use – and not that I've had any particular cause to think about such things until now. We might pool our present knowledge to begin with and see what we can come up with. I might then take that to Sir Giles and see what interest he has in it. And Croker.."

"Yes sir?"

"I think tea is called for." Croker grinned.

"Definitely sir!" I like him thought McGill. Not sure about Farr yet, but it will come, I suppose.

For the next few weeks the three detectives settled down to the usual round of checking statements and investigating crimes of a more serious nature. To be fair, the criminal fraternity was still holding off from their activities, as part of their own contribution to the war effort. McGill had an affinity with those on the other side of the law. He always felt they were badly treated. Not that he thought they should be treated softly, but simply that they should be fairly treated. Farr and Croker appeared to be of like mind. McGill reflected that Brown – his since-deceased superior – had a completely different view. He regarded lawbreakers as scum, and treated them as such with a disdain and sneering attitude that meant he had always had great difficulty even getting facts from them, even those that were not incriminating. McGill, with his somewhat more amiable disposition, was frequently able to get to the bottom of things, and had built up a sort of trust amongst many of the gangs and crimps that he dealt with.

The rapport between the three men had grown as time went on and the list that they had come up with, once they went through the details, only came down to questions about three serving officers. Sir Giles had confirmed that he would deal with matters, and had taken the papers McGill gave him not so much with sadness but with a grim determination.

Christmas came and, as everywhere, events slowed down and took on a mantle of their own. McGill had gone to his father's cousin's house and taken gifts for the children and grandchildren. McGill Brothers car business had done very well, particularly since McGill's father had died and his cousin had bought out his father's share. McGill always smiled ruefully about that. Why the business was called McGill Brothers, McGill could never understand. The two partners had both been named McGill, but only cousins, not brothers. McGill had no interest in the business, and didn't begrudge his relatives their good fortune. Their new house was large enough to house all the family that was in London, along with the servants and staff. His second cousin's wife often opined McGill should have been married by now, and appeared to want to introduce him to a young lady who just happened to drop in on Boxing Day.

McGill was scrupulously polite, but he felt none of the spark that had been between himself and Isabelle de Bonnefoix. He felt a pang when her memory sprang into his mind. He wondered how she was, and wistfully remembered his time recuperating in her house in Amiens. As he thought about their last night together, his cheeks reddened and he turned away from the company.

McGill's second cousin James clapped him on the shoulder.

"Well, Alan, how do you like being an Inspector?"

McGill thought for a moment. " Well enough. I get my tea made for me now!"

" Ha! Well that's progress I suppose! Come and see my new car." The pair went outside. McGill had seen and admired the gleaming new vehicle sitting in the drive. He didn't recognise the make.

" I thought production was virtually stopped for the duration," said McGill.

" Indeed! But there are still some being built and of course the spare parts business has grown enormously. I put this one together for myself. I might do a few more. It would certainly pay!"

McGill nodded. James had always been the business brain, his father the mechanic.

" I want to expand, Alan, and I'd like you to come in with me. Blood is always thicker than water."

McGill shook his head. " It's very kind of you, but I've never wanted to go into commerce. Maybe if I get invalided out or something!"

" Ah well, you know the offer's there."

They turned to re-enter the house, but James put a hand on McGill's arm.

McGill glanced at the older man.

" Alan, I'd like your advice about something." McGill turned to face him.

"Of course."

James rubbed his chin. " I've been wondering whether I should tell you or not. It's a bit tricky. I've been approached by a man who has suggested I might want to turn a blind eye if one of my cars disappears for a day or two." McGill looked astonished.

" How do you mean, someone borrowing it for a few days?"

" I'm not really sure. It sounded pretty strange. What was even stranger was I was told if I wanted to check it out I should talk to one of your lot."

McGill was even more astonished. " That *does* sound very strange. I don't suppose you got any names?"

James shook his head. " No, but the man did say I might do myself some good. He said he'd let me think about it over Christmas, and he would come back before the New Year. If I was on for it, he'd tell me all I needed to know."

"Hmmm, that could be a threat or a bribe. No idea when he's actually coming back?" James shook his head. " No, none."

McGill thought for a moment. " Right, I'll send someone over in the morning who'll keep an eye out. When he comes back, just let my man know and we'll see about it. You'll need to work out a set of signals between you. Tell him you'll go along with his plan and see if he'll tell you who the policeman is that's involved. And how much you'll get out of it."

James nodded. " Thanks, Alan. I feel better about it now."

" Just be careful. If they're really up to no good, they won't be best pleased that you've involved me."

The next day, back in his office, McGill sent Croker off to find the man he wanted. He was a watcher, one of the best, instantly forgettable and almost invisible. Within a few minutes, Croker returned, followed by a somewhat shabby looking man. The man flicked his right forefinger to his bowler, and shuffled into McGill's office. He was small and stocky, with a scrubby little moustache. He looked as if he spent most of his life outdoors. Which indeed he did.

"Thanks for coming Cole. I've got a job for you." Cole's droopy eyes crinkled, and his moustache twitched. Cole and McGill had been involved in a couple of cases when McGill was a mere constable. They liked each other and McGill knew he could rely on Cole absolutely.

" I'm your man, Inspector. What do you need me to do?"

Briefly McGill explained what his second cousin had told him, as Cole looked lugubriously serious.

" At the moment, I just want to know who is doing the asking and what exactly is going on. Once you know, report back directly to me."

" Right you are sir, leave it to me." Cole turned and made his way out of the office. It was almost as if he hadn't even parted the air to get to the corridor. McGill shook his head. Since he'd met Gunner Crowall – Crowie to all and sundry - in the battlefield mud of the Somme, he had had a profound respect for men who had a gift. Crowall's was a sixth sense, Cole's of invisibility.

McGill thought for a moment then made his way out of the office and along the interminable corridors towards the office of the Commissioner. When he got there, he asked the constable on duty if he could see Sir Giles. A few minutes later Miss Howard, Sir Giles' very private secretary came out.

" He'll see you now, but he only has a few minutes," she said severely. McGill nodded and followed the muscular woman into the presence.

Compston was just closing a file as McGill entered.

" Inspector! To what do I owe this pleasure?" Quickly McGill explained, and Compston's face grew darker and more sombre.

"One of us? A policeman? Don't like that at all. Are you sure?"

" I'm only repeating what I was told sir. I wanted to check if you knew anything about it, but I've set Cole onto it, so we'll know a lot more in a short while."

"Hmmm not good. I know nothing about it, and if it's police business I jolly well should! Well we shall see. Don't tell anyone else in the meantime. Carry on."

"Thank you sir."

CHAPTER THREE

McGill waited impatiently for information from Cole. The more he thought about it the more strange the whole thing seemed to be. He could see "borrowing" a car for a day would be helpful, but why would a detective be involved? He could simply requisition one. That said, the local criminals probably knew all the cars at Scotland Yard's disposal, and they would soon be spotted if they were sitting waiting somewhere.

So perhaps it was for surveillance, but in that case, McGill was certain the Commissioner would have known. He had denied all knowledge. So whoever the policeman was who was involved in it, he had to be acting for himself. And McGill knew the Commissioner wouldn't like that at all.

It was two days later when Cole reappeared, just as McGill was getting ready to go home. He had sent Farr and Croker away earlier. He had been overwhelmed by a longing for Isabelle de Bonnefoix which had almost rendered him weak, and he didn't want his men to see him like that.

There was a knock on the door and Cole came in quickly.

"Thought I'd wait until you were alone sir."

"Thank you Cole. Sir Giles doesn't want anyone else knowing at the moment." Cole smiled slightly.

"My thoughts exactly sir."

"So what do we know?"

"The man who turned up was known to me sir. Nasty piece of work by the name of Watt."

"It's crooked then?"

"Almost certainly. Your relative told him he wanted to meet with the Policeman, and about an hour later a detective by the name of Low appeared."

"Don't know him,"said McGill.

"No reason why you should sir, not that he has a great reputation anyway. He's a sergeant in the river police." McGill frowned.

"So what does he want the car for?"

"Your relative asked him that. He said for surveillance." McGill's frown deepened.

"That would actually make sense, and it would be why Sir Giles knows nothing about it anyway. The river police have their own establishment."

"Still doesn't smell right to me sir – not with Watt involved."

"No, I suppose not. Thanks Cole, I'll tell himself what we have found out."

With Cole disappeared once more, McGill sat and thought for a minute or two.

It better wait until the morning, he thought. Shaking his head, he stood and opened the door to his outer office. He gathered his coat and hat and left for his home. As he waited for the omnibus, a pretty girl walked past and smiled at him. It was quite suddenly as if he had been punched in the stomach. The girl transformed into Isabelle de Bonnefoix. McGill shook his head. I keep seeing her, he thought bitterly. She won't be thinking of me.

The next morning Croker was in the office before McGill. As McGill opened the door, Croker was there laboriously writing in a file and he leapt to his feet.

"I wish you'd stop doing that when there's only us here," said McGill peevishly. "I'm sure it ruins your penmanship, apart from anything else." Croker grinned sheepishly.

"Can't help it sir."

"Well never mind. I'm off to see the Commissioner." Croker was used to McGill taking off to see Sir Giles, and merely nodded. McGill shut the door again and turned back along the corridor. It wasn't that far to the Commissioner's office, but McGill always felt as if he was on the way to see the headmaster. His feet always seemed to drag. Ridiculous, he thought as he arrived in front of the door to Compston's secretariat. The constable on duty knew him and opened the door for him, with a crisp salute. McGill walked in and looked around for Miss Howard. He couldn't see her, so he supposed she was in with the great man. One of the other younger ladies approached him clutching a file.

"It's Inspector McGill isn't it?"

"I am yes, thank you. I'm after a few minutes of Sir Giles' time."

"He's with Miss Howard at the moment, but I doubt she will be much longer. Could I get you a tea while you wait?" She smiled shyly at him.

"No don't trouble yourself. It's most kind." And McGill smiled back.

The girl's smile widened. She knew half the girls in Scotland Yard had a crush on the lovely Inspector McGill. And the other half had designs on him of a more permanent nature. Apart from Miss Howard she thought, and giggled to herself.

McGill took a seat and waited patiently for Miss Howard to appear. It didn't take long, and as soon as she saw him, she waved him forward.

"Don't be long" she scolded him. Yes thought McGill. Just like being in front of the headmaster.

Compston was behind his desk with a file open. McGill didn't think he had ever seen him without one. He glanced up, then back to his papers.

"Sit down McGill, I won't be long." True to his word a minute later Compston sighed and closed the file.

"Damn all politicians," he said.

"Can't say I disagree there sir." Compston harrumphed.

"Don't tell anyone I said that! Well what have you got?" McGill quickly explained what Cole had told him.

"So, if I read this right, it's not impossible it's on the level?"

"Not impossible sir, but the involvement of Watt would tend to suggest otherwise. And Cole doesn't seem to think Low is a shining beacon of rectitude either." Compston thought for moment, fingering his chin.

"Well I suppose I better have words with Morrison at the River Police. It's a bit of a trek to Wapping, though."

"I live not very far from there sir. If you wish I could call in one evening. Keep it under wraps as it were." Compston brightened considerably.

"That's a very good idea, McGill. If we keep this low level for now there won't be any people wondering what I was doing in Wapping – or Morrison over here. I can call him up and tell him to expect you."

"I can go this evening if that helps sir."

"Good idea, let's clear this away quickly, one way or the other."

McGill returned to his office. Farr was back and looked askance at him. Croker would have told Farr that McGill had gone to see the Commissioner. Nothing was said and Farr respected the "need to know" that existed because of McGill's relationship with Compston. Within half an hour a young constable handed in a note addressed to McGill. He opened it and read:

"Five O'Clock"

McGill took out his Hunter and saw it was time for a cup of tea.

"Croker do you...."

"Yes sir, I know", grinned Croker, interrupting. "Do I think we should have some tea? Absolutely." Even Farr almost chuckled at McGill's discomfiture.

Just after four o'clock, McGill was already waiting for the omnibus that would take him to Wapping High Street and the headquarters of the Thames River Police. It had been their headquarters since their founding in 1798. McGill knew they did sterling work but had not so far had a reason to be involved with them. He arrived in the High Street with ten minutes to spare and he walked briskly into the building that housed the division.

He introduced himself to the Sergeant on the front desk and stated he had an appointment with Superintendent Morrison at five o'clock. With no more ado the Sergeant called for a constable who promptly led McGill through a door behind the desk and along a corridor. At the end the constable knocked on the door and opened it. He ushered McGill through and shut the door.

Morrison was standing looking out of a window onto the Thames. It was clearly low tide and therefore pretty muddy and messy but it was very busy with all sorts of vessels churning up and down the river. He turned and walked towards McGill, hand outstretched.

"McGill – how do you do? Sir Giles has only praise for you." McGill instantly picked up the slight burr of a Scottish voice. His own had long ago flattened into a non-descript English.

"Very good to meet you too sir. And very good of you to take time to see me at such short notice." Morrison waved his hand. "Crime never sleeps. Sit down."

McGill sat on one of the two chairs in front of Morrison's desk. He quickly told Morrison what he knew, and asked if in fact Low was acting under his, Morrison's, instructions. McGill could tell as he talked that Morrison knew nothing about any of it, as his brows knitted together more and more. When McGill had finished, Morrison let out a sort of bark which startled McGill.

"Inspector, I know nothing of this, and I am very unhappy about it, too. What's your opinion on all this?"

"Well sir, if you don't know about it then there is definitely something not right, as otherwise why would it be hidden from you? There's one thing I didn't say in the first instance is that my man said Sergeant Low had an unsavoury reputation. If that's true, then I believe that strengthens my opinion that there's some illegal activity planned." Morrison nodded.

"My thoughts precisely. And Inspector, you would be right about Low. We've never proved anything but there are straws in the wind. I don't like 'im. So what do we do now?"

"I suppose we can only watch and wait. I can certainly arrange that. We'd need to track the car to see where it goes. That might be tricky but once the car is handed over, we will have the make and model, the colour and the registration number. We can pretty quickly get that out to the beat police in what will not be a particularly large area I suppose."

They settled some communication issues and McGill left feeling satisfied that matters were properly in hand.

The next day Cole was called for and appeared an hour or so later.

"It definitely looks "off"" said McGill. "The river police know nothing about it and friend Low is not well regarded in that force." Cole nodded.

"Yes as I told you sir. Will I keep an eye on it?" McGill thought for a moment.

"Yes, we will need to know when things start happening. What I'd really like is if we could keep an eye on the car once it's collected, but I suppose we will just have to do as best we can. You might find out if Watt or Low have a small warehouse anywhere. It's not impossible they could take the car there and change the registration plates."

"Indeed they could sir, my thoughts exactly. Might need a little help on this one, I'll get my mate Charlie to give me a hand."

"Is he as good as you?" McGill asked innocently. Cole looked hurt.

" Mister McGill, you knows there 'ent no one as good as me!" McGill laughed.

"That I do, David, that I do." With a happy grin on his face, Cole did his disappearing act.

McGill called Farr and Croker into his room and explained the situation to them. Farr's face became even darker, if that was remotely possible.

"Don't like policemen doing things like that," he said.

"Nor do I, and neither does the Commissioner nor Superintendent Morrison."

"What's the plan sir?"

"We need to get the local police to up their patrols in the general area – we can think of some excuse – and only tell them about the car when we have definite information. Cole is keeping an eye out and will let us know as soon as there is anything to report. I imagine there will be a visit to tell cousin James to get the car ready and then the pickup so we should have at least an hour to lay our plans."

"I'll get it set up sir," said Farr.

New Year came and went, quietly as far as McGill was concerned, though he did take a beer or two in his local pub. Before, as a constable, he had frequently had too much to drink because he hated his work and he hated the condescension with which Brown, his Inspector, treated him. Now, everyone treated him with respect and deferred to him and he felt no need for the drink. He grinned to himself as midnight struck. If only he had had someone to share it with, he thought – and Isabelle appeared without warning in his head. He shook his head to clear it, but she only smiled and sparkled at him, then faded.

On New Year's Day, a call came through from Cole.

"It's on sir. Watt just appeared and your cousin gave me the sign. I have the registration of the car they will be taking," and he passed it across. "It's a Minerva sir, dark blue." McGill wrote down the information then bellowed for Farr and passed the details to him. McGill knew the local police station would have the details almost immediately and it would be out with the beat bobbies within a very short space of time.

Within half an hour Cole was on the phone again. "Watt and another man collected the car – I don't know who the second man is but he looks a shifty character. I'll keep after them."

"Thanks Cole." Farr had joined McGill as soon as he had heard the telephone ring. As McGill replaced the earpiece, he wondered what the criminals plan was.

"They must want the car to collect something," he said. "But where does Low come in? They must be going to change the registration plates – it won't work otherwise."

"I agree sir. What's Low's job in the river police?"

"He's a sergeant." They both thought about this for a moment.

"I should tell Morrison," said McGill, and he reached for the telephone. Quite quickly he was put through.

"It's on." Morrison was quiet for a moment.

"What do you want me to do?"

"Nothing sir. If it's with *you* we don't need any of your people knowing. By the way what job does your man have?"

"He's on rotas today." It all became clear to McGill.

"Thank you sir, I'll be in touch."

He turned to Farr. "Good thought, Don. He's on rotas today." Farr's eyes widened marginally.

"So he can keep patrols away from given areas."

"Exactly. That's why it will only be from time to time he wants the car. It's only when he is doing rotas. And it presupposes something worth lifting. We need to know where he is keeping people away from and what ships are in that area. We don't need to risk any followers being spotted. Come on we're off to Wapping. Croker!"

"Sir"

"I need you to take a message to the Super and another to the Commissioner." Croker nearly fainted. The Super was fine – he knew Millager, his sergeant – but the Commissioner? McGIll was already dashing off a few lines and then took another sheet and wrote almost the same thing. He addressed two envelopes, placed the letters inside, and sealed them. He left them on the desk telling Croker to pick them up and deliver them. Farr and he almost ran out of the door and out to the street. There was a hansom cab passing and McGill hailed it. He gave the address in Wapping and settled back in the seat as the horse picked up its pace.

Once in Wapping the pair made their way straight to Morrison's office who was somewhat surprised to see them arrive so precipitously. McGill explained his theory, and Morrison rifled through some papers on his desk. He came up with the rota list for that day. He pored over it for a moment then looked at McGill.

"There's a gap tonight between nine and ten at the Albert." He searched again and produced a huge number of papers held together with a Bulldog clip. He waved it.

"Every ship in the docks, where they are and what cargo they are carrying."

Morrison flicked through the pages, working through until he got to Albert Dock. " There's only a handful of ships there at the moment." Morrison read quickly through the information. Then he shook his head and passed the papers to McGill.

"There's nothing worth stealing there – at least, not what would fit in a car." McGill read through then handed the papers to Farr. He looked askance at Morrison who nodded. The two men looked at each other whilst Farr read through.

"If it's not on the manifest it's contraband," said Morrison. McGill nodded

" Or a person."

Farr looked up. "There's a ship here from the Baltic sir. The Hun can access that area." McGill read over what Farr was pointing to.

Morrison looked over McGill's shoulder then reached for the papers.

"Indeed they can. Should we concentrate on that one?" McGill shook his head.

"We don't know exactly what they are up to so it could be any of them. There's a ship from France as well as others. I think if we just watch that whole dock for the car arriving and have some men stationed at the gate, we can cover it all."

"There's two gates," said Morrison. " One at either end."

"Fine, we'll cover both."

McGill and Farr left Morrison and headed towards the local police station that covered the Albert dock. It was further away than they had thought so took another hansom. As they walked into the building, the desk Sergeant saluted.

"Good afternoon sir. Can I help you?"

"Yes please. I'm Detective Inspector McGill from Scotland Yard and this is my sergeant, Detective Farr. We'd like to see your senior officer." The desk sergeant stiffened. McGill was known to be in thick with the Commissioner, and his exploits in France had gone before him. Respect was mingled with caution as a result. The sergeant immediately opened a door to one side of the desk and waved the detectives through. Once inside the gloomy building, a constable appeared and McGill repeated his request. They were taken up a flight of stairs and into a room that housed just one man – an Inspector. McGill introduced himself again and the Inspector shook hands.

"My name is Raslin. What can I do for you Inspector?" Quickly McGill explained what was happening and asked that Raslin would use his men to keep the gates to the dock under observation. Once the expected car was inside, they were to seal both ends and arrest anyone in the car. Raslin rubbed his chin.

" We'll need something to block the access. We have some heavy chains we use but they are a bit unwieldy, and certainly not for a fast set up. Any ideas?"

"The easiest would be a truck or even some market barrows – can you arrange that?" Raslin nodded.

"I'll get that done right away. I'll put a patrol at either end and keep them out of sight just now."

"I'll send you one of my men who will know the car so you will have a warning. He won't come into your station."

"How will my men know him?" McGill grinned.

"Believe me he will get the information across to them without a problem."

McGill and Farr left Raslin to organise his men and they made their way towards the Albert Dock. They scouted both ends. It was a secure area with two large and heavy gates. At least they wouldn't need anything else to stop a car. McGill did wonder if his second cousin's car was going to require repaired.

The day wore on and the detectives stationed themselves in a small pub. Suddenly Cole was standing beside them. He had a superior grin on his face.

"Hello sir." McGill nearly dropped his drink.

"Cole! How did you find us?" Cole pointed to one side and McGill and Farr saw another man who looked almost identical to Cole.

Cole laughed. " My mate Charlie. He's followed you all day and let me know where you were." McGill touched his hairline in acknowledgement of Charlie's expertise. A brief grin crossed Charlie's lugubrious face before his features settled back into nonentity.

"The car didn't have its plates changed, at least not while I had it in view. So they must be pretty confident." McGill nodded and looked at the clock behind the bar. Six o'clock. They probably had at least two hours if not a little more before they needed to get back to the dock.

"How are we going to co-ordinate the closing of the gates?" asked Farr. McGill looked at Cole.

"I thought I'd be sort of half way along. Then whichever way the car comes, I can nip off the other way and get the other gates shut."

"Good,"said McGill." We better have something to eat. Will they do us something here?"

Farr got up and went to the bar. He returned shortly to say the Landlord's wife would do sandwiches. McGill ordered them all another round of beers as they waited quietly for the food to arrive. Cole said Charlie wouldn't have anything and indeed when McGill looked towards where he had been there was nothing to see.

Ten minutes later thick ham sandwiches were placed on the table by a cheery girl. McGill decided she was the Landlord's daughter. The three munched their way contentedly through the food. By the time they had finished Raslin was standing beside their table, shaking water from his hat and coat.

"How did you know we were here?" asked McGill as he sent Farr off to get Raslin a beer.

"A message was left for me at the front desk." McGill glanced at Cole, whose face betrayed a small satisfaction. The man's a genius, thought McGill. Somehow he must have told Charlie to leave that message. I should have done that.

Not long after Farr returned with the beer for Raslin, Cole simply disappeared. Raslin seemed taken aback when he noticed, but McGill and Farr, who knew Coles' gift, accepted it. McGill kept glancing at the clock and by the time seven forty five had come round, he felt the time had come to move.

The three policemen sauntered along to the main gate of the dock. McGill was pleased to see that there were no police uniforms visible, but Raslin ducked into a building just inside the gates where a sergeant and five burly constables where waiting. Cole had already told them the details of the car and McGill was sure he would have done the same at the other end of the dock. Raslin pointed at his men.

"There's another seven at the other end, so we are sixteen strong in total."

"If the car comes in this end Cole will go to the other end and tell them. Likewise if it comes in at the *other* end he'll come here and tell us."

The policemen waited quietly, some smoking, cupping the glow with their hands. There were no lights on in the building. The dockside was bright from a variety of different sources, and that gave them enough to see what was going on. As nine o'clock came and went, the tension palpably rose, and cigarettes were extinguished. McGill and Raslin were standing beside the front window, when the lights of a car flashed across the gateway, and the two policemen ducked down below the windowsill.

"Was that it?" asked Raslin in a whisper. McGill nodded and all the men instantly clustered closer to the door of the building. By now the car had moved along the dock a little way. McGill strained to see its progress. It stopped. By now McGill had eased the door open and was cautiously watching the car. Two men got out carrying torches. They flashed these around for a moment or two, looking at the ships tied up. They got back into the car and continued down the dock.

"Sergeant" said Raslin quietly. " Get those gates locked!" The sergeant and five constables moved past McGill and towards the gates. Three ran to the other side of the gate and the sergeant and two men ran to the gate nearest the small building. The gates were heavy but with three men on either side they were soon shut. A couple of heavy carts were pulled across to reinforce the barrier.

"Right sergeant you stay here with two men. You three come with me."

Walking deliberately in a line and using what cover there was, the two Inspectors, Farr and three constables cautiously walked towards where the car could be seen some hundred yards away. When they were within forty yards, McGill raised his hand to halt the advance. There was no sign of the two men who had been in the car. McGill waved his hand indicating they should move forward. The men walked even more carefully towards the car. McGill could see policemen approaching from the other side and he held his hand up to indicate they should pause. Looking about, he could see there were some boxes and other cargo scattered about. Pointing at these, he ducked behind a mound covered with a tarpaulin. He saw the other policemen looking for hiding places as well. The car was well surrounded, but there was still no sign of life anywhere.

Suddenly a stream of light broke across the deck of the ship closest to the car as a door was opened. Instinctively McGill ducked further down. He could hear the voices of three or four men. He took off his hat and lifted his head to be able to see what was happening on the ship. The men appeared to be shaking hands. McGill thought he picked up a French accent and another which he didn't recognise. He could see one of the men was sporting a cap. Must be the Captain thought McGill. The other three moved to the gangplank and set off along it. The moment they were all on land with space between them and the ship, McGill jumped to his feet and shouted "STAND WHERE YOU ARE! POLICE!" Two of the men did exactly that, but the third, without even waiting for McGill to finish speaking, had turned and raced back onto the ship. Not even pausing he dodged to the left and ran the length of the deck before taking a flying leap from the bow onto the dock. The policemen from the local station had surrounded the two who had not moved, and McGill and Farr set off along the dock after the third man. He appeared to have the hounds of hell after him and McGill realised they would never catch him. At least the men we left at the gate will get him, he thought as his lungs gasped for air. The fugitive ran on and McGill could see he was fast closing on the three police who had been left to guard the gate. McGill saw the man pick up something as he raced to what would be certain capture. The sergeant and two constables moved to intercept the man. He suddenly swung at the lead policeman, who went down like an ox. The sergeant and the second policeman were only a couple of yards behind, but the man jabbed forward at one and swung again at the second, and they both went down. Without a moment's hesitation the man dropped what he was holding and with one bound leapt onto the cart. He took another leap and scrambled to the top of the gates. McGill saw him perched on the top for a moment. A light from somewhere suddenly flashed across his face as McGill saw a well-built man with longish hair. It was a cruel face sporting a look of disdain. As suddenly as he had been illuminated the light disappeared, and the man dropped over the other side. Hell! Thought McGill we'll never get him now. It'll take too long to get these carts away and the gates open. He pulled up beside the first constable who had gone down. His helmet had been knocked ten yards away, but the man was coming to. The sergeant and the other constable were equally reviving, even though the constable was still badly winded. McGill looked about and saw the weapon. It looked like a wooden spar. At least we have the other two and the ship, he thought.

Still breathing heavily but satisfied the downed policemen were all right, McGill told them to get the gates opened again. He and Farr made their way back to the ship and the car where

Raslin had sent men to get the gates at the other end opened. The two miscreants from the car were handcuffed and bracketed by two constables each. Raslin and the remaining men were trailing onto the ship where the Captain hadn't moved. McGill and Farr followed them.

CHAPTER FOUR

When they were all on the deck, Raslin took charge. "Right" he said. "What's the story here?" The Captain shrugged.

In a strong French accent he said, " I am ask to bring zis man. I am tell 'e will be collect. Voila!" Raslin guffawed.

"Right men, search the ship." McGill drew Raslin to one side.

"We should get the river police men involved. They will know more than us about all this sort of thing."

"You're right" said Raslin. He turned to one of the constables. "You! Get a message through to the river police at Wapping. Tell them we need some men here right away. And if you see any wandering about let them know!" The constable turned to go but just then a speaking trumpet boomed across the water.

"Inspector McGill are you there?" McGill recognised Morrison's voice. He cupped his hands to his mouth. "HERE!" he bellowed. Moments later a small vessel bumped alongside the ship and grappling irons snaked up onto the railing. There was a scraping and screeching noise and then Morrison and two other policemen were standing on the deck. He had a wide grin on his face.

"Haven't done that in years! You didn'y think I was going to get left out did you?" McGill laughed.

"Very unlikely sir. Unfortunately we think this man's passenger escaped, but we got the other two as you can see." Morrison nodded.

"Well we can help search the ship but I doubt we'll find anything. I think this was a strictly human transport." The Captain still hadn't moved and Morrison told him they would go to his cabin to check the manifest. The Captain shrugged again and led the way through the door that the four men had emerged from.

"We better get these two back to the station. We need to get them interviewed and charged. I've got a prison van nearby, we can all get a lift back." McGill nodded and followed Morrison through the doorway.

"Sir, we are going to the local station with the prisoners. Will you deal with Low?"

"Oh yes, we lifted him very shortly after the car was collected. He's busy denying everything, but of course we have witnesses and statements. He won't escape this time."

"Very good sir. I'll get away then." The men shook hands and McGill turned back to regain the deck. By the time he got there, the barred van with its two horses had arrived and the two prisoners were being bundled inside. McGill, Farr and Raslin joined the driver up front, and two of the policemen got in the van itself. The door was then locked. It wasn't long before they were drawing into the courtyard of the police station. The van door was unlocked and the four men inside were let out and into the station. Raslin and the two detectives followed the little group but then peeled off up the stairs to Raslin's office.

"Well, at least a two thirds success," said Raslin.

" No, I'd say seventy five percent. Morrison has Low dead to rights as well." Raslin nodded.

"I don't suppose they will be able to pin anything on the Captain of that ship."

"I doubt it," said McGill. "He'll likely have some paperwork saying Mr.Bloggs had booked a passage. After all, if the man who ran was legitimate, he would only have to report to the dock authorities to declare his presence. He'll have had papers to cover himself. No, I think our friend the Captain will be away again tomorrow. Though I would be pretty sure if he turned up here again, Morrison would be onto him."

There was a knock on the door followed by the sergeant who had been at the dock. He was sporting the beginnings of a fair bruise on the side of his face.

"That looks sore" said Raslin.

"Just a touch sir. Did you want to interview the prisoners now sir?" Raslin looked at McGill, who nodded.

"No time like the present," said Raslin. "We'll be with you shortly." Once the sergeant had gone, Raslin turned to McGill. "What exactly do we want out of these two?"

"Ideally,we would like them to give us Low, though that might be a lot to ask. Cole says Watt is a nasty bit of work and won't crack. They might know who the bloke is who laid out three of your men and what he is doing here. But I doubt that as well. Why would they know anything? As far as they were concerned, they were just picking someone up and dropping him off. They might have an address we could look at, but if it was me I would have them drop me off away from where I was actually going." Raslin sighed.

"You're telling me there might be nothing we can charge them with?" McGill shrugged.

"Not impossible, but see what they say. By the way I got a pretty good look at the ship's passenger when he was on top of the gate. I would definitely recognise him again."

"That's something. Come on then, let's see what we can wring out of them."

It was quickly obvious that Watt was going to say nothing to Raslin. The other man, Barker, was voluble in what he said, but was revealing nothing to Raslin's sergeant. McGill motioned to Raslin to come out of the room. Raslin was clearly cross, but McGill said "Let Farr and me have a word with friend Barker. I've an idea which might make him more co-operative." Raslin harumphed but stood aside to let McGill and Farr take the two seats on the other side of the table from Barker.

McGill smiled slightly. "Well, Mr. Barker, let me tell you a little story." Barker waved a hand and said "Feel free."

"As you know there is a war being fought on the other side of the Channel. Now because of that, certain people would want to get into England without being noticed. Do you know what those kind of people are called?" Barker looked mystified. "I'm going to tell you. They are called spies." A look of alarm flashed across Barker's face.

"What's that to do with me?"

"I have a question for you first, before I answer yours. Do you know what happens to spies?" Barker said nothing but looked even more uncomfortable.

"They are shot out of hand, Mr. Barker. There is no trial, no evidence presented, they are just shot." McGill paused. "Dead." Barker was squirming in his seat.

"Now I'm going to answer *your* question. What does it have to do with you? Very simply you were meeting a man who entered our country illegally and then ran away. We have evidence he was a spy." Although Farr's face never changed, McGill could feel him stiffen. Barker had broken out into a sweat and his mouth was working.

"I never…..," he started.

"Oh yes you did," said McGill in a quiet and reasonable voice. There was a silence as Barker passed his hand over his eyes.

" I never.." he started again.

McGill leapt to his feet and leaned across the table, his face nearly into Barker's.

"YES YOU BLOODY DID!"

"All right all right! I'll tell you what I knows!" McGill sat down again.

"From the beginning, please." Farr flexed his writing hand and started to make notes.

After Barker explained all that had taken place, and had implicated Low, McGill was able to get an address where they were to take the man. He was sure it would lead to nothing, but Farr scrupulously wrote it down anyway.

At the very end, with Barker now more than eager to tell all, McGill asked what he knew about the ship's passenger. Did he know where he was picked up for instance?

"Honest, I 'ent got a clue. We was only supposed to collect 'im from the dock."

"But you heard his voice, what was the accent?"

" 'E were a Paddy."

"Irish,"said McGill

"Yers, definite." McGill thought about that for a moment or two then nodded to himself. It was an Irish face he had seen on top of the gate.

With Barker broken, Watt was not far behind and the two men were led off to the cells to await the magistrate's court in the morning.

Raslin was delighted with the outcome. "You've got all you came for, but what am I going to charge them with?"

"Aiding and abetting illegal entry to England and conspiracy so to do," said McGill. "It's not huge but it will get them away for a bit. In reality they haven't done much. We've got Low which was our primary target. Morrison will have his eyes on a particular French ship. And we can get a description circulated of our Irishman. I very much doubt if he will be seen again though. We'll check out the address, but if I were a betting man, I'd say he was heading in a completely different direction."

" Put like that, it's not the worst night's work!" Raslin rose and shook McGill's hand then did the same with Farr. I like that, thought McGill. Haig was right about things changing.

The next day, the address Barker had given was searched but there was nothing incriminating there. The elderly landlady denied all knowledge of an Irishman, or even that she had any empty rooms or even an Irishman due to arrive – none of which surprised McGill. He cursed himself for not seeing the possibility of the race along the ship's deck. He cursed the policemen who had been floored – then thought in all probability the same thing would have happened to himself. A lesson learned .

CHAPTER FIVE

A few days later, McGill was sitting in his office in Scotland Yard. He was looking out at the drab grey morning, and into the courtyard at the centre of the building.

As an Inspector, he had a Sergeant and a Constable to do his bidding, but even after a few months, ordering people about did not sit well with him. He did rather want a cup of tea though, so he stood up and opened the door to his outer office. McGill knew he could not make himself a cup. Not if he wanted to retain his authority. It just was NOT done.

His Constable, Croker, was going through some reports, but looked up as McGill came through the door.

" Do you fancy a cuppa?" asked McGill.

Croker put the reports down and stood up.

" I'll make a pot, will I sir?"

" Excellent! Thank you! By the way, where's Sergeant Farr?"

" He's gone to take a statement from that witness in the jewel robbery sir"

McGill nodded. He rather missed taking statements. He'd always enjoyed talking to witnesses and victims and digging for what the facts really were. So much of Police work was filtering out people's prejudices and perceptions to reach the truth. As an Inspector, he spent more time reading what other people had elicited in interviews and cross checking statements than he did in the field.

He sighed to himself as he went back to the window and looked out once more. He realised his thoughts were on Isabelle again as he saw her sitting opposite him at dinner.

There was a knock on the door and Croker put his head in.

"Gentleman to see you sir. A Major Simonds." McGill turned and there stood Simonds.

"Major. To what do I owe the pleasure?"

"Your operation at the Albert the other night."

"In what way."

"There's been a drawing of a man circulated who was involved, but he escaped."

"Ah the Irishman. What is your interest in him?"

"We are looking for him in connection with crimes against the State in Ireland."

"I see. Do you have a name?"

"The problem is we have several. We are not at all sure which is his real name. Or even if any of them are."

"And why do you want to talk to me?"

"I just want to be sure it's the same man." McGill indicated a chair and Simonds sat. Croker appeared with tea, and quietly closed the door.

McGill talked Simonds through the whole episode, and although no notes were taken, McGill was sure everything he said was memorised.

"So,"said Simonds. "What we have is a French ship's Captain who we can't do anything with, as he has a man on his manifest. It's not his job to make him report to the dock authorities. We have two lowlife crooks who are told to pick up a man whose name they don't know, to an address which turns out to be not connected either to the Irishman or the crooks. They've done nothing totally illegal, just a bit naïve. We have our sergeant in the river police who was contacted anonymously by a mysterious character, told to organise transport, told to keep the river police away from a dock at a particular time, was paid to do that but never met either the mystery man, nor the Irishman. We don't know much, do we?"

McGill shifted uncomfortably. "No sir, we don't." Simonds sighed.

"There's nothing we can do about it. Had we caught our Paddy there might be something to be pleased about from my point of view. At least we *think* he may be in this country, but we have no idea what he is doing here, or where he is. And we have no leads to let us know either of these things. That drawing you had done of him is better than the one we've already got so that's one thing in our favour, I suppose. All we can do is keep an eye out for him. He's a Will o' the Wisp though. I wouldn't be surprised if he isn't back in Ireland or even France, rather than here in England." McGill nodded.

"Yes, I'd be surprised if he stayed here after nearly getting caught. As you say we can only watch for him. The only thing that might give him away is his accent. Nobody heard him say much, but they agreed his accent was Irish." There was little more to be said and Simonds left in a few minutes.

There was a knock on the door and Farr came into the room.

"I heard some of that sir. Bit unfair I'd say." McGill grinned ruefully.

"Perhaps. Have I just had a dressing down or a pat on the back for getting close to our man? I don't know! I'd know him again, but the chances are that'll be the last we see of him."

Farr turned and left the room. He and the Inspector had other crimes to attend to.

CHAPTER SIX

Some weeks later, McGill was pondering the situation again, and longing for Isabelle de Bonnefoix.

In the early months of 1918 the War was still dragging on. McGill had seen what the reality was, and he hated it. He knew both sides were close to exhaustion, and he fervently hoped that Field Marshall Haig's comments to him at the end of 1917 would prove prescient.

Haig had said that the Germans would make one final huge effort, but it would be thwarted, and thereafter the war would not last long. He was also relying on the many more troops that America would send, and the industrial capacity that she could bring to bear against the Hun.

McGill knew that the Germans had effectively knocked the Russians out of the war, and that dozens of divisions were being transferred to the Western Front. Not only was it more men, it was seasoned soldiers, most of them younger than those that had fought to a stalemate over the previous three and a half years. The news from Russia was very confusing, but clearly there appeared to be a civil war in the offing which would give the Germans a free hand in the West. He could see the logic of what Haig had said, and shook his head again at how that man had manipulated him. I won't fall for that again, he thought. I've learned a bit since last year.

There was a knock on the open door, and McGill turned to see Croker bearing a tray with tea pot, milk jug and sugar. There was only one cup on the tray, and as Croker put it down on McGill's desk, he pulled open the right-hand top drawer. Reaching in, he pulled out a battered enamel mug and put it beside the teacup.

Croker shook his head. "Still using your old mug I see sir."

" Indeed. You have no idea how often it saved my life!" McGill had been given the mug whilst in France at the end of 1917. It had come from a dead soldier. It had only saved his life in so far as there was no other way to get a drink of tea. No china teacups at the front.

Croker filled the mug and the teacup, poured some milk in both and put one spoonful of sugar in McGill's mug. Lifting his cup, he ladled two overflowing spoonfuls into it, then turned and made his way back to his desk, leaving the connecting door open.

Absentmindedly, McGill stirred his mug, then sat down and pulled a file towards him. A picture of Isabelle de Bonnefoix appeared on the front of the file. He shook his head. Would he ever forget her? He hadn't even been able to say goodbye. He smiled a sad smile. Someone like her would never want a plain policeman like him. No wonder her maid had dismissed him.

Sighing, he worked steadily for an hour until he heard the outer door open and he saw Don Farr, his sergeant, enter the outer office. Gratefully, McGill sat back in his chair as Farr took off his coat and hat, and hung them on the stand in the corner. McGill stood and walked to the doorway.

" How did it go?"

Farr smoothed his hair with both hands. He was a dark man, dark in complexion and in temperament. His moustache always looked as if it had been applied with a black crayon, but McGill knew he was a thorough detective who, like himself, was not satisfied until the last question had been answered.

" Well, sir,.." He never got any further, as there was a knock at the door, and Sergeant Millager appeared.

" Sorry to bother you, sir, but the Super would like to see you right away." McGill sighed. No one ever seemed to want to see him tomorrow or even later, it was ALWAYS " Right away". He nodded at Millager and rose to his feet.

"Sorry, Don, it'll have to be later."

" Don't worry, sir, it'll keep!"

McGill followed Millager along the corridors and up the stairs to Superintendent Truman's office. Millager knocked briefly, and ushered McGill in.

As ever, Truman was sitting behind piles of paperwork, with an intense scowling concentration, but looked up at McGill as he came into the room. His face cleared.

"McGill, my boy, thank you for popping in!" Hmmm, thought McGill, as if it wasn't an order!

" Sit down, sit down! How do you fancy going back to France?"

" Well sir, quite frankly, I'm not that keen but I daresay you have a good reason for asking!"

" Oh, I do, McGill, I do. I'm sure you know who I mean by Sir Terence Blythe-Hill?"

" Do you mean the rather loud troublemaker who is an MP?"

"Indeed. He has been in touch about his younger brother, Gerald. Not with me in the first instance but with Haig himself. Gerald's a Monsignor." Truman paused to let that sink in. He cleared his throat. " I should say, was." He cleared his throat again.

"Yes, well, there it is. So, somehow he managed to get himself stabbed to death whilst he was in Amiens."

" Really sir? Some sort of bar fight?"

" Oh no, he was taking confessions in the cathedral, and someone shoved a British Army bayonet through the side and straight through him."

McGill looked surprised.

" That would take some strength, sir."

" Not necessarily. Apparently it was the person doing the confessing. And these confessionals only have a flimsy divider between priest and penitent."

" I see sir. So where do we come in?"

"The problem is it's not a Military matter. Indeed, it appears the Adjutant General's office jumped on it immediately and said they would have nothing to do with it. The French police don't want to get involved with an Englishman's murder, and the Church want the whole thing hushed up. Doesn't look very good a Monsignor being murdered in a Cathedral! That's why Sir Terence has been stirring things. Can't say I entirely blame him. If my brother had been stabbed to death, I'd want to know all about it!

So your friend Sir Douglas asked for you to nip over and see what you could dig up."

McGill groaned. "Bloody Haig again! I knew he'd want his pound of flesh!" Truman laughed.

" It's your own fault for being good! If you'd bungled that Braintree business, no one would ever have heard of you again!"

" True enough sir, but I'm not sure that's a comforting remark! If I'd bungled it as you say, I could very well be dead."

" Well, possibly I suppose. Anyway, Blythe-Hill is annoying enough to make our political masters wish to make the problem go away, and if that means you wasting a bit of your time, that's a small price to pay."

McGill thought for a moment, raised his arms, then slapped his hands down onto the arms of his chair.

" I assume I can take Farr, sir?"

" Absolutely. I'll have your tickets and travel documents drawn up immediately. Millager will drop them off with what files I have presently and you can catch the afternoon train to the coast."

McGill stood up.

" Does Sir Giles know about this?"

" The order to send you out there came directly from him."

McGill nodded and sighed.

" No reprieve then!" Truman laughed.

"No, I'm afraid not!"

Truman rose and came round the desk and held his hand out to McGill.

" Take care, Inspector. I want you back here in one piece – and your Sergeant too. The last time I sent an Inspector over he was dead within a few days".

McGill thought back to his previous trip and poor Inspector Brown. McGill hadn't liked the man, but still felt for his family.

" I'll have everything I've got sent round to you."

McGill shook Truman's hand, then turned and made his way out and back to his office. He walked slowly, thinking deeply. He couldn't think why a soldier would kill a Monsignor. Was it a moment of anger, something that happened whilst in the confessional? Was it something from the past – or even the present?

By the time he reached his office, a Constable was just coming out. He saluted smartly and turned away. McGill entered and found Farr just opening the first of several folders. Farr stood up and waved his hand at his desk.

"A French mystery, sir"

" Sorry, Don, we're going on a trip." Farr's deadpan face betrayed nothing, but his eyes, normally impenetrable, seemed to McGill to gleam just a tiny bit.

Farr lifted the first page in the folder that was open and waved it at McGill.

" This is politics sir. That Sir Terence is a bloody nuisance."

McGill nodded. "I agree, but it's an order. And you and I both know we don't like people going around being killed for no apparent reason."

" No I suppose not sir." Farr closed the file. "I expect we're due to leave this afternoon sir."

" We most certainly are. Nip off home and get a bag sorted. I'll meet you at Victoria. I'll get word to you when I know what time the train is."

Farr reached across and plucked his coat and hat from the hook behind his desk, donned both, and made his way out of the room.

" Croker get me Cole would you?"

" Sir." Croker popped out.

McGill went into his room and sat down. He quickly checked the files lying there. He knew his files would be taken over by Team 2 as they were known. He started flicking through them. A few minutes later Croker reappeared with Cole. He was closely followed by Millager, clutching a sheaf of papers. Croker took them from him. McGill waved at the small man who had materialised behind Millager.

" Thank you Millager. In here, Cole." Millager saluted and disappeared through the door.

McGill scribbled a few lines and handed Cole the note.

" Take that to Mrs. Wolfe at my house and wait whilst she packs a bag, then bring it back here."

" Right you are sir, shouldn't be more than an hour." McGill knew Cole had almost every distance in London tabulated in his head, and you could rely on his timings absolutely. Cole's main occupation was trailing suspects. No one had ever spotted him.

Complete nonentity, thought McGill. No one would look at him once, never mind twice.

A few minutes later another inspector and sergeant came into the outer office. Croker, who knew them from their previous appearances, stood and saluted.

" Welcome back sir."

" Thank you Croker. I can see the boss is in. Would you just brief Sergeant Starston on what's happening?"

" Certainly sir"

Inspector Needham waved nonchalantly and made his way into McGill's office.

" Hello George. Sorry about this." Needham laughed.

" My dear Alan, I couldn't be more delighted! Getting you out of everyone's hair for a week or two will raise my stock no end!"

McGill shook his head. " Yes I know we're not the most popular on the block."

" And I know it's not your fault! It's perfectly fine, I'll take care of all this until you get back."

McGill nodded and stood. " There's nothing much that needs a lot doing with just now, but it's all in order." Needham nodded.

" Of course it is Alan. You wouldn't have it any other way."

McGill turned to get his hat and coat, then stopped, and moved back behind his desk just as Needham was moving behind it from the other side. McGill reached across and pulled open his top right-hand drawer. He reached in and pulled out his old battered enamel mug. He gestured with it at Needham.

" Can't go to France without this."

Needham laughed.

" Your talisman! May it keep you safe!" McGill nodded and stuck the mug in his coat pocket.

" I'll let you get on. I'll wait for Cole outside." Needham waved his hand again and sat down. As McGill crossed to the outer door, Croker and Starston half stood but McGill waved them down.

Croker would remain with Team 2 – it meant he could answer any questions, and brief McGill and Farr when they got back.

McGill crossed to the main door and opened it. He turned back and with a wave of his hand stepped out into the corridor. He made his way towards the back entrance of the building. He knew that was the way Cole would return, in keeping with his invisible status. He was greeted with salutes and hard faces. His job as Sir Giles' terrier didn't endear him to his colleagues. Even so, they respected his scrupulous adherence to the truth, which, indeed, was what made him so valuable to the Commissioner.

McGill didn't have long to wait. Cole's estimate of time was spot on, and, even though McGill was looking for him, it wasn't until Cole was almost beside him that McGill became aware of him.

" Good grief! How do you do that?" he asked, taking the bag from his hand.

Cole smiled wanly. " It's just a gift, sir! By the way, Mrs. Wolfe said the neighbour wasn't too pleased handing over this 'ere bag."

McGill laughed. " The last one got blown up in France! This is the replacement I bought for her."

McGill was about to turn away, when a thought struck him. He rummaged in his trouser pocket and came up with two sovereigns.

"Look here, David, I'll probably need to use a bag more in the future. Could you buy one like this and give it to my neighbour? At least there won't be any fuss in future. And get a hold of Don Farr and tell him to be at Victoria at two sharp."

" Righto, sir, take it as done."

CHAPTER SIX

McGill had no sooner left the Yard, than a constable knocked on the outer door to McGill's office. Croker rose from his desk and opened the door.

" 'Ere you go, Crokey. Letter for his nibs."

Croker took the proffered letter and turned it over.

" From France," he said.

" Yers, and from some tart, I'll be bound. Look at that writing! And unless I'm mistaken there's a whiff of some perfume still on it."

Croker raised the letter to his nose and sniffed. There was indeed a slight scent, though what it was he could not say. Waving the letter, he dismissed the constable. He placed it carefully on his desk. Taking his time, he laid it squarely on the blotter, then repositioned it. He stood back, took a couple of paces, then turned back and looked at the letter again. He pondered a moment, quickly took two paces back to his desk, snatched it up and almost ran out of the room. Within minutes he had made his way to the offices of Superintendent Truman, and knocked on the door. It was opened by Millager.

" Hello Croker, what brings you here?"

" It's a letter, Sarge, for my Inspector."

" Is it now? And why would you be bringing it here?"

" Well, Sarge the Inspector and Sergeant Farr just left for France, and as this letter is from there, I thought it might be important."

" Did you indeed?"

Millager took the letter and turned it round, reading the address carefully.

"Detective Inspector Alan McGill, Scotland Yard, London, England," it read.

"Hmmm," said Millager. " I think you did right, son, I'll see the Super gets it. He'll know what to do."

" Thanks Sarge."

"Well done lad, off you go now." Croker disappeared, basking in the glow of praise. Millager tapped the letter a couple of times against his thumbnail. He glanced towards Truman's door, then sat back behind his desk. He studied the front of the letter intently, and turned it over. He held it up to the light but could see nothing. He was about to put it to one side when the door of Truman's office opened and the Superintendent stuck his head out.

"Millager, see if you can find…." But he never got any further, as he saw Millager holding the letter.

" What's that?"

" It's a letter for Inspector McGill, sir."

" Really? What's it doing here?"

" Well sir, seeing as how the Inspector just left for France, young Croker thought it might be important, and brought it here."

By now Truman had moved the rest of his body into the outer office and was looking at the letter in Millager's hand.

" And why would it be important?"

" Because it's from France, sir."

" From France? Let me see it." Truman held his hand out and Millager hurried to place the letter in it. Truman peered at it, reading the address carefully.

" It's for McGill, all right. I can't think it can have anything to do with why Sir Giles sent him off." Truman stared into the distance, thinking.

" Very well, Millager. Tea, I think." So saying, he spun on his heel, entered his room, and shut the door to his office behind him.

Settled once more behind his desk, he carefully placed the letter in the middle, and stared thoughtfully at it. Could it have anything to do with the case McGill had been sent on? Truman couldn't think it did, but there was no way of telling. A moment or two later, Millager appeared with a chunky mug of industrial strength tea, and placed it to the left side of the desk. Truman mumbled his thanks, still staring at the letter as Millager retreated.

There was only one way to find out. He reached for his letter opener.

CHAPTER SEVEN

McGill and Farr had arranged to meet again at Victoria Station by two p.m. McGill's neighbour's wife had been none too pleased to lend him the valise again - despite the fact it was a new one that McGill had bought for her – but reluctantly agreed. McGill thought of his previous trip to France, when he had lost everything, ending up with just the clothes he stood in. As he entered the station, he glanced up at the sun which had managed to break through the clouds, and was now casting a wan light over London. Seems to brighten the place up, thought McGill, and guffawed slightly at the thought.

Farr was waiting for him beside the platform where the trains for France came and went. McGill looked Farr up and down. He liked the man, but he never had a hint of light about him. He could have been one of the devil's disciples, with his dark dead eyes and black clothes.

"Well, Don, ready for the adventure?"

" Absolutely sir. What do you think our chances are?"

McGill shrugged. " About zero I'd say. According to the reports no one saw or heard anything. We'll need to do quite a bit of digging to get anywhere."

Farr nodded. " Do you think it's got anything to do with him being a Catholic, sir? Something to do with the Church?"

" Can't see it myself. There's lots of Catholic Monsignors, why pick him? No it has to be something in his background or because of his family. That Sir Terence is a complete nuisance, as you say. I would have been less surprised if someone had stabbed *him*! And I'd have bet on it being another politician!"

Farr nodded, smiling grimly. "Yes, I could see that, sir."

McGill checked the station clock. Their train was due to leave at half past two, and the mass of troops had been filing onto the platform for some time. He and Farr had tickets and passes for the officers' compartments, and they now joined the stream of other ranks. They slowly made their way to where a group of officers were standing. McGill and Farr stood out like black crows on a snow-covered landscape, amidst the solid khaki.

The officers looked at them curiously, but stood aside to let them into the compartment. The soldiers split into smaller groups and started clambering on board the train. Six of them got into the compartment with McGill and Farr, joking and chattering, glancing sideways at the detectives.

The last time McGill had made this trip with Brown, he had been a brand new Sergeant. A few days later, Brown had died when an enemy aircraft shot at the car he was in. McGill remembered Brown had been the third man to light his cigarette on a train, and had been chided by one of the other passengers. McGill didn't smoke, but the memory of the event made him shiver. With a crash of doors and a cacophony of whistles, the train started to move, steam billowing all around in the enclosed area of the station.

By the time they reached Folkestone, the officers in the compartment with them had fallen silent, thinking, McGill supposed, of what awaited them. He had seen first-hand the horrors and senselessness of the Western Front, and he wouldn't wish any of it on any man.

Don Farr had never been to France. McGill could see, even though he betrayed no apparent emotion, that inside he was fizzing with curiosity and excitement. It was only because McGill had got to know him over the last few months that he recognised that there was something going on behind the absolutely set face.

When the train drew into the quay, there was a sudden crescendo of noise as the troops surged out of the carriages and onto the platform. There were hundreds more troops waiting to get onto the train who all bantered and shouted at the arrivals.

Farr never blinked but turned to McGill.

" Blimey, is it always like this?" he yelled.

McGill nodded and shouted back. "Yes, but usually worse!" Farr shook his head as they joined the serpent winding its way towards the boat, whilst Redcap MPs and Sergeants shouted and shoved the troops towards the waiting troopship.

Once on board, McGill led the way to the area reserved for officers and purloined a couple of chairs. Farr and he sat and awaited departure amidst the chaos and noise that typified soldiers on the move. The sirens screamed and the ship began to move away from its berth. McGill passed a folder to Farr.

" Have a proper look at that. It's pretty much just background on Gerald and the Blythe-Hill family. See if there's anything you think we should be following up."

McGill had merely perused the folder, but he trusted Farr to spot anything worth commenting on. He smiled to himself. He had slipped easily enough into the ways of Inspectors. He thought how his old boss, Brown, had always given him folders to read and asked what they should be checking. He smiled again. Being an Inspector was pretty good. In fact, he would have to say that having risen to his present giddy height, his view on his job had changed completely!

After twenty minutes or so of turning pages back and forth, Farr passed the folder back. McGill opened it and was met by the picture of a very handsome man.

The hair was brushed back behind the ears, with a touch of grey showing at the temples. It was a strong face with a sharp nose, a high raking, intelligent forehead and eyes that held a look of sharpness and superiority. This was Gerald Blythe-Hill. McGill turned the photograph over and beneath it was a picture of the older brother, Sir Terence. Where Gerald was intelligent and handsome, Terence had a grumpiness, a disdain and an arrogance in his look. What little McGill knew of him fitted that description. He glanced up at Farr.

" Well?"

Farr shrugged. " Nothing much to go on sir. He did well at school and university, got a first in divinity, then decided to go for the Church. You could say his rise was meteoric, but he's been stuck for a while now. I expect him being English doesn't help matters in Rome.

He's been in France for nearly three years, always close to the fiercest fighting. He moves about a lot, but recently he's been pretty much based in Amiens. By all accounts a good man. He doesn't seem to be attached to any Army Group, but he ministers to anyone who asks."

McGill stroked his chin. "So a good man gets butchered and there's no apparent motive or witnesses. No one gets murdered for nothing, Don. There's always a reason and there's always someone who has seen something. We just have to find them." Farr nodded and sat back.

" So what do we do sir?"

"Well we have three or four lots of people to call on. There's the Church and its representatives. There's the Redcaps – they won't be much use, they mainly want to beat people up who they think have stepped out of line. There will be the Army itself, and the French police. None of them want anything to do with it. Not surprising really. Doesn't look good for the Church or the French with a Monsignor being murdered. The Redcaps don't care and the Army has clearly disowned him if he isn't directly attached to a particular Army Group. My guess is we are on a fool's errand to cover backsides, just because Sir Terence is an embarrassment to the government. The only thing that worries me is it appears Sir Terence approached Haig directly, who then asked for me specifically. I had dealings with him once before, and had hoped I'd never need to meet him again. Let's hope we can get away sharpish without getting shot or arrested!" Farr's expression changed for almost the first time since McGill had known him.

" They can't arrest us sir! We're the Police."

"My dear Sergeant Farr, they most certainly can. We are entering an area under military rule. We have no standing at all. They can arrest us and shoot us as spies if they feel like it. In fact, Sir Douglas said as much the last time I met him. So we need to take them with us at all times."

Farr appeared shaken, but held his peace.

When they got off the boat, the scene that had enacted at Folkestone was repeated with thousands of soldiers moving to and fro, and an indescribable babble of noise hanging over everything. As they moved off from the dockside, McGill felt a hand on his shoulder. He turned and looked straight into the grinning face of yet another man he had hoped never to see again.

" Inspector, how good of you to come." McGill groaned inwardly.

" Colonel, I'd say it was a pleasure, but it isn't."

The Colonel laughed." No, I don't suppose it is. But my master wants to see you." McGill groaned inwardly again. The other man he didn't want to see, Sir Douglas Haig. The Colonel was his amanuensis. McGill had never learned his name, but knew he had been trailed by him as he had moved around the Western Front the previous November and early December. It wasn't that he disliked Haig. He just didn't like the way Haig had manipulated and used him. With a sinking heart, McGill wondered if the same was going to happen again.

" Come along, " said the Colonel, " I've a car and driver waiting". The policemen followed the Colonel to a quieter part of the dock, where a mud-spattered vehicle sat, complete with driver. The Colonel opened the door and the three men squeezed into the back. There were rugs and blankets piled on the floor, and the Colonel pointed at them.

" You better wrap up, we've about a hundred and sixty miles to go and it'll be damn cold by the time we get there." McGill and Farr draped themselves, and McGill immediately felt warmer.

" How long will it take?" he asked.

" Around five and a half hours – at least that's what it took coming. We should be there by around eleven thirty."

" Are we seeing him in the morning?" The Colonel shook his head.

" My instructions are to take you straight in to Sir Douglas, then you'll be put up for the night and taken to Amiens."

" Sounds important." The Colonel looked at McGill.

" You could say that," he said quietly. "Apart from anything else we think the Huns are building up for a huge attack, and Sir Douglas is making all possible preparations. But I'll let him tell you all about it." The Colonel settled back in his seat and wrapped himself in the remaining blankets. He pulled his cap down across his eyes, folded his arms and appeared to be trying to sleep.

McGill settled back too, but Farr looked out at everything passing by. The troops thinned out as the car wound its way out of the town and onto the country roads that would lead to Haig's headquarters.

It was the night of 19th. of March, 1918

CHAPTER EIGHT

The car made reasonable time as it wended its way towards British Army Headquarters. McGill remembered his last visit here which had ended well with mutual respect between McGill and Haig. He still felt a shiver pass through him as he thought of the absolute power of life and death that Haig wielded. That particular meeting hadn't started well at all.

As they drew up outside the Chateau it was as if it was midday rather than nearly midnight. Officers were striding quickly up and down the steps and guards were busy saluting and checking papers.

The Colonel led the way up and waved away any enquiries. Once inside they headed up the grand staircase to the familiar door that McGill remembered. They passed easily enough through the anteroom, the Colonel clearly not to be questioned at any time. He marched straight to the door at the end, knocked twice and entered the room that was Sir Douglas Haig's operations room.

McGill's immediate reaction on seeing Haig was that he was exhausted. The piercing blue eyes were dull and strained and the fierce thrust of his personality was blunted.

Haig straightened up from looking at maps spread out on a table, and came across the room to greet McGill, hand outstretched.

"Good to see you again McGill."

" And you too sir. This is my sergeant, Detective Farr."

Slightly to McGill's surprise, Haig stretched across and shook Farr's hand. He reflected that he had not been dealt with like that when *he* was a sergeant. Haig turned and sat back behind his desk, hands on the arms of his chair, eyes staring into the middle of nowhere.

" Sergeant Farr," he said. " Please don't take this the wrong way, but I'd like a few minutes alone with the Inspector." Farr turned and made his way to the door . Raising his voice slightly, Haig went on " Colonel, would you be kind and see we are not disturbed."

The Colonel nodded and the other people in the room made their way out. The last person out was the Colonel, who shut the door. McGill heard the snick of a lock being turned, and steps moving away.

Haig rose and made his way to a side table. He poured two good measures of whisky from a decanter, and passed one to McGill. They raised their glasses to each other and both savoured their drinks.

McGill remembered the last time he had tasted it, around three months previously, when last he had been in Haig's presence. The man has aged and shrunk in that time, thought McGill.

Haig carefully put his glass on his desk, and sat heavily.

"I'm sorry about this McGill, but I need your help again." McGill groaned inwardly. At least he's letting me in on what he knows, thought McGill. I'm seeing him before I get to work rather than after. He sighed.

" I rather thought that was why you had asked the Colonel to pick us up the minute we landed in France. By the way, what is his name – I've never heard."

Haig chuckled and a modicum of his old verve returned.

" He doesn't like anyone to know, but I think in this case we can say it's Colonel Julius – Nigel Julius."

McGill nodded. " And I suppose he's going to follow me around again in a Captain's uniform?" Haig threw his head back and laughed properly.

" Oh, you worked all that out did you? No wonder Sir Giles thinks so highly of you!" He took another sip of the whisky, thoughtfully. " No, I don't think that will be necessary this time, but you will need to liaise with him for me. I doubt I'll have time to keep up with this for the next few weeks."

" Why's that sir? What does the Monsignor's death have to do with you that you need Julius to keep a watching brief?" Haig thought again, then leant forward, arms on his desk.

" Do you remember me telling you about the Huns great offensive that was coming?"

" Yes sir, I do."

"Well it will have to be very soon, perhaps even in the next few days. I have been working night and day to discover where and when they will attack and I'm fairly sure I know where. What I don't know is when.

The point is, as I told you before, if they wait longer the Americans will really start to make a difference. The Germans simply don't have the manpower any more, nor the resources, but they are superb fighting men, and will throw everything into one last great gamble." Haig leaned back and took another sip of his whisky.

"There have been straws in the wind. Some of our reconnaissance flights have spotted what look like replicas of some of our trench systems, but well *behind* the German lines. Why? It can only be because they are practicing against some of our positions. Then there was the battle at Caporetto. Brilliant on all fronts – for the Germans. They used a completely new method, a sort of storming attack. Once they punched a hole through the lines they simply went hell for leather forwards, effectively rolling up the Italians on either side. The Italians had to run or be cut off. So it's not a battle along forty miles of front, it's just a few miles and they throw absolutely everything at it." He paused again.

" I'm pretty sure they will attack where we have just taken over from the French, about another 30 miles of trenches. Bloody awful they are too, not properly maintained or supported. We've got everyone doing their best to get them into shape, but it's not something that can be done overnight. I need time to get them right again, and the sheer amount of work required is leaving my men exhausted. I wanted an extra six hundred thousand men this year and I've only got one hundred thousand, so I'm doing everything I can to make the Hun think I've got my full complement." Haig walked to the window and looked out, hands behind his back, thinking. McGill sat quietly, waiting.

Haig suddenly swung round.

" I didn't tell you everything I knew last year, and I should have done. I'm sorry. Now I know you, and I know you can be trusted." Haig walked across the room and stood in front of McGill, who looked up at him from his chair.

"Blythe-Hill was a spy." McGill blinked and recoiled. " Yes, as well you might. And not for us either, for the Germans." McGill was dumbfounded.

" The brother of an English Member of Parliament? Spying for the other side?" Haig nodded.

" Yes, it really doesn't bear thinking about. And before you ask, no, I did *not* order him killed. He had his uses. We were able to feed him false information, which we could be fairly sure was getting back to Ludendorff. In fact, he was a big part of my deception campaign, little did he know it. The problem, of course, is I MUST know why and by whom he was killed. If it was merely some random lunatic, that's fine, but if it was some German assassin then we could be in serious trouble. If they did it because they knew he was feeding them false information, then I'm effectively naked in terms of my strategy. At least if I KNOW they know I can take some steps. But I can't take those steps without effectively signalling that Blythe-Hill was misleading them." Haig was silent. McGill sipped his whisky again and thought about the situation.

" So, what you are saying, sir, is that Blythe-Hill was feeding the Germans false information from you, in the hope that they would either hold off or alter their planned attack." Haig nodded.

" Exactly. He was not my only method of disinformation, but he was a very important part of it. I simply MUST know what happened."

McGill stretched forward and carefully placed his now empty glass on Haig's desk. "With due respect sir, why would they kill him if they found out? Knowing that what he was telling them was false, they could simply have used that information for their own ends. I would have thought getting false information which they knew was false would be a huge plus. And you say the attack is imminent. What if I don't find out anything in time?"

Haig shook his head. " I couldn't blame you, it's a damned tall order." He paused, then resumed. " I have done some redeployment over this winter past. We have the same number of men in the field in total, but I have changed the structure and numbers within groups. In other words, there are more newly created divisions in the field, and I've been able to put together some extra divisions as reserves. I'm taking the more experienced and fitter men into those reserves and resting them as much as possible. The Huns will think they are facing more men in a larger number of divisions. That's part of what we have fed them. Hopefully, we will be able to stem the grey tide when the attack comes and then push them back again with the reserves. But it'll be a close thing. If everything goes to plan for the Germans we may not be able to hold them. If they make a few mistakes we should just manage."

McGill stood up. " Any idea where I should start?"

" Colonel Julius has a list of everyone who was in the Cathedral around the time of the murder. We've had a look at them, of course, but we don't have your eye for detail. He'll also give you some connections we think Blythe-Hill had, and to whom he might have been passing our doctored information. Can't give you any more than that, I'm afraid."

Haig was looking directly at McGill, and the latter stared hard at him.

"You haven't held anything back, have you sir? Things could go badly wrong and I want to be prepared." Haig shook his head sadly.

" I just wish there was more I *could* tell you. Julius is more up to date than me. I'd prefer if you keep all this between yourself, myself and Julius." McGill thought for a moment.

" I may have to tell my sergeant more than you might care for, but I trust him absolutely. I'll keep it to a minimum. He's very good, and will probably realise there's more to this affair than meets the eye even if I tell him nothing. I would much rather his keen brain was focussed on what we want to know rather than feeling resentful about my not keeping him informed."

Haig stood pensively for a moment, then nodded.

"I trust your judgement McGill. Do as you think fit."

McGill grinned.

" And you won't have us shot as spies?" Haig put his head back and roared with laughter, looking like the Haig McGill remembered from their previous meeting.

" That was only ever a sideshow. But you have to admit it got your attention!"

" It certainly did, sir." Haig thrust his hand out and McGill shook it.

" Let me call Julius back, he'll have all the details ready." Haig reached across his desk and pressed a button on the side. McGill heard rapid steps and then the lock being turned. Julius appeared clutching a sheaf of papers.

" Ah, Colonel, you have the papers for Inspector McGill. He'll be leaving now. Please see that he and Sergeant Farr are comfortably housed then taken to Amiens in the morning. I've alerted Major Watkins they will be there."

" Watkins, sir?" said McGill. Haig nodded. " He's one of us," he said.

"I thought he might be when he accompanied me here last year. So I take it he's my direct liaison." Haig nodded again.

" And he was keeping an eye on Blythe-Hill and his contacts. Good luck, McGill." McGill nodded.

" Thank you sir. I've a feeling I'll need it!"

CHAPTER NINE

McGill took the papers from Julius who led him through the ante-room. Farr fell in beside him.

"Can we get something to eat, Colonel?"

Julius smiled. " You'll be back where we ate together last time."

" And are you going to lock me in again?" McGill saw Farr stiffen out of the corner of his eye.

Julius laughed. " No need this time."

They made their way out of the Chateau, and down the steps. McGill noted all the smart salutes and stampings to attention as Julius passed. As Haig's amanuensis, McGill supposed Julius was worth the extra smartness.

Farr was used to the deference paid to senior police officers, but was clearly impressed with the saluting and general demeanour of the men they were passing. He said nothing but McGill could see his eyes darting everywhere, taking everything in.

The car took them to the small hotel and the weary police officers were shown to their rooms. It was very late, but Julius appeared as fresh as if he had just arisen after a long sleep.

" I'll see you in the morning, McGill. There's food ordered for you downstairs – and a whisky each. Sleep well." Julius turned and walked away.

McGill and Farr dropped their bags in their rooms and made their way back down the stairs. As they entered the dining room, the door to the kitchen opened and a well-padded Madame came in bearing a steaming toureen.

"Messieurs – sit sit sit!" The soup was put on a table set for two, where bread was already sitting in a basket. There was a flask of wine and another of water. The lady bustled out and McGill and Farr sat. McGill took the ladle and put a healthy portion into Farr's bowl, then another into his own. They both set to with a will, tearing chunks of bread from the baguette on the table. McGill poured some wine into their glasses, and took a swig. He grimaced.

"Give me a beer any day."

" Me too sir, I'll just drink water." The door to the kitchen opened again and the lady appeared once more, clutching two plates of steaming food held with cloths. McGill hastily removed the bowls and the plates were placed on the table. The woman surveyed the table then bobbed her head. "Ah!" she exclaimed and went through another door. Moments later she was back holding two whiskies.

"Bon. I go now – Bon nuit." She turned and headed out through the kitchen once more.

McGill and Farr worked their way steadily through the food, not speaking. Farr could tell that McGill had much on his mind and left him to ponder matters. Farr finished first, as McGill seemed to be slowed down by his thoughts.

"This could be quite dangerous, Don. We may be dealing with desperate men who will not hesitate to kill us."

" I had thought that sir. I don't believe this is an ordinary murder. It's a bizarre way to kill someone. It's as if a message was being sent. And what's the significance of the British bayonet? Is it supposed to make us think it was a British soldier?"

" I would have to say it's a bit too trite, don't you think? But on the other hand surely someone would have noticed a sword or heard a gunshot. It could, after all, be a soldier who didn't like what he was hearing." McGill was silent for a moment, reaching for his glass and taking a sip of whisky. Nothing like Haig's, he thought. I'll have to let Don in on the secret, he thought. He considered his next words carefully.

"If I was a betting man, I'd have to say something in the background of the Blythe-Hill family is the reason for this. Why would anyone kill a Monsignor? Another jealous priest? What's the significance of the bayonet? And why through the eye? It makes no sense. Haig thinks it might be some German spy, but I don't buy that."

Farr thought for a moment.

"Why a spy?" Mcgill took a breath and plunged on.

"It seems our esteemed Monsignor was a double agent. He was feeding the Germans false information." Farr's face hardly changed, but he was clearly thinking through the implications. Then he shook his head.

"No sir, I just don't believe the Germans killed him. Why would they? If they found out it was false information he was giving them, the last thing they should do is tell everyone they knew by killing him. They should have kept taking the false information and using it for their own ends."

McGill grinned. "Don, it's no wonder we get on. My thoughts exactly! Come on, let's turn in. Maybe something will occur to us overnight!" The pair trudged up the stairs and into their rooms.

McGill locked the door behind him and slumped into a chair. Damn these people, he thought. Give me a good old straight forward murder any time. McGill sighed, then reached for the folder with the information that Julius had given him.

Next morning Julius was downstairs having a cup of coffee as McGill made his way into the dining room. Julius looked at McGill.

"Do you have everything you need?"

"Apart from a motive and a murderer? I would say so, yes." Julius snorted.

"Sir Douglas is particularly keen on the motive."

"Yes, he told me. Farr and I actually think he has nothing to worry about in respect of the Germans killing him. That makes no sense. From the papers you gave me we have practically nothing to go on. No one saw anything. Blythe-Hill was only found when the priest due to take the next lot of confessions turned up. And that was well over an hour after he was killed by the look of it. There's a list of twelve people who were seen before the time of death – seven priests, two ladies, one elderly, one young, an Englishman and a Frenchman, and then the Duchess of Lincolnshire. I'd say we can rule out the Duchess and the ladies, and almost certainly the priests, which just leaves us with the Englishman and the Frenchman. So why was he killed? And why in the manner he was?"

"If we knew that we would know who…"

"We would. Who put these names together?"

"It was the Church officials originally. French Gendarmes next. Of course we then had our own people go over them, but nothing popped up. The MPs turned up, took one look, turned around and walked out. The Army never even deigned to turn up! I think by that time Sir Douglas had decided he wanted you here, and then the letter from Sir Terence turned up. Perfect cover!" McGill shook his head.

"I just don't believe any of these people were involved. There must have been someone else hanging about who escaped notice." Julius shrugged.

"Up to you to find out." He finished his coffee just as Farr came into the room. No sooner had he entered than the lady from the night before appeared with bread and tea on a tray, and placed them on the table where McGill and Julius were sitting. Farr joined them, instantly starting to pour the tea for himself and McGill.

"Once you've finished I've to take you to Amiens. It's only about 50 miles. You'll be in the barracks I'm afraid, there simply isn't anywhere else to put you."

"Wonderful," said McGill.

CHAPTER TEN

Breakfast finished, McGill and Farr collected their belongings and stepped out into the street where Julius was waiting for them with the car. They were quickly on their way. In daylight the countryside was already beginning to shake off winter and Farr watched the passing scene avidly.

"It's a beautiful country sir," he murmured to McGill, who nodded. As he gazed out over the countryside, he remembered a walk he and Isabelle had taken in the wintertime.

As they drove, the closer they got to Amiens the more the roads had lorries and troops moving about. By the time they reached the outskirts of Amiens the roads were clogged and the car moved slowly with a tide of khaki around it. They finally arrived at a large wire fence with guards and watch towers either side of a gap. The car drove into the compound and headed for a larger building a bit further on. Once there, Julius jumped down as the guards on the building snapped to attention and saluted.

"Come on," said Julius, "Let's get you sorted." McGill and Farr followed him into the building. Julius marched straight to a door at one side of the building, opened it without knocking and walked in. There was a Captain at a desk who looked up from papers he was reading and leapt to his feet with a smart salute.

"Stand easy Newham. These are the detectives I was telling you about. Where are you putting them?" Newham was clearly flustered in Julius' presence but reached across his desk and plucked a paper from a pile and handed it to him. Julius took and looked at it. "Have you got someone who can show them where this is?"

" Ye –ye-yess, sssir," stammered Newham, and raised his voice. "JONES!" Moments later there was a knock on the door. "COME!"

A short wiry man with a small moustache entered, spotted Julius and came smartly to attention. "Sir."

" T-take these g-g-gentlemen to their b-billets p-p-please." Julius handed over the paper which Jones took. He glanced at it, then swung towards McGill and Farr.

"This way please gents."

"I'll leave you to it then,"said Julius."If you need me I'll be at Amiens HQ until this is over." He flicked his right hand to his cap and strode through the door.

McGill could feel the tension subside in the room, and Newham in particular appeared to relax as he let out a breath. "Carry on Jones."

" Thank you" said McGill as he followed Jones.

As they made their way across the lobby, a figure waved an envelope at Jones.

"'Ere! Jonesy! Letter for you!" Jones reached across and took it. He glanced at the writing, and popped it in his pocket.

" Sweetheart?" asked McGill.

" I 'opes so," said Jones fervently. " 'er dad owns the butchers shop where I worked before the war, and 'e 'ent got no other children! There's no other young men 'oo could nip in neither!"

Jones led them to a sort of beach hut amidst other beach huts. He opened the door for them, and pointed them to the two camp beds.

"You get someone with hot water in the morning, though I don't expects you'll be here much. I'm always around the Captain if you need anything."

"Thanks Corporal. I appreciate your help."

Jones saluted and turned on his heel.

They didn't have much settling in to do and within ten minutes they were ready to set off into town.

There were trucks coming and going all the time and it seemed to be the convention that if you needed to go somewhere you simply flagged one down. McGill wanted to check in with Watkins and see if he had anything to add to what they already knew. It took a little while but they eventually found someone who was going to HQ, and they jumped into the back of the truck as the front bench was already full. It took about fifteen minutes, and they were dropped near the centre. McGill recognised where he was. The pair set off towards

Amiens HQ, making their way through the crowded and bustling streets. They were soon standing at the bottom of the steps of British Army, Divisional HQ, Amiens. McGill stared up, remembering the last time he had seen them. His reverie was broken by Farr.

"So who is this Watkins, sir?"

"He was someone I worked with last November. He's a Military Policeman, but I suspect he has links to our secret service. Sir Douglas mentioned I should look him up. He might be able to give us names of people Blythe-Hill was involved with."

McGill expected to see some of the same guards that had been there three and a half months previously, but he recognised no one. He had been looking forward to seeing the man who had helped him, Private Murgatroyd – better known as Nobby. McGill now knew that Nobby was in fact related to Sir Douglas Haig and was enraged he was on guard duty behind the lines rather than at the front getting shot at.

As they approached the steps, a young soldier barred the way with his rifle held across his chest.

"Off limits sir"

" I'm Detective Inspector McGill from Scotland Yard, here to see Major Watkins." The young man eyed McGill dubiously.

"Sarge!" A whippet of a man came out of the wooden hut that did duty as a shelter for those on guard. He didn't look happy. Probably had had his tea break interrupted, thought McGill.

" What is it?"

"This 'ere gennleman is wantin' Major Watkins." The sergeant eyed both McGill and Farr. "'E says 'e is Detective McGill from Scotland Yard." The sergeant nodded.

"Oh yes, I knows about you. You were 'ere last year, causing trouble." McGill fixed the sergeant with a piercing look.

"Sergeant, whatever you think or believe, I'm sure Major Watkins will be interested to hear your thoughts – if I choose to tell him. Can't help but think that might be the end of your cushy job here." The sergeant reddened, swung around and set off up the stairs.

"Follow me!" The young soldier stood aside, wondering at the audacity of someone prepared to speak to the sergeant in such a manner.

Once inside the building, the sergeant marched up to a desk with a Captain sitting behind it. Throwing a smart salute, the sergeant stamped to attention. McGill sighed inwardly. What *is* the point of this rubbish, he thought.

"Sir! A Detective Inspector McGill to see Major Watkins, sir." The Captain glanced up and looked McGill and Farr up and down. Nodding towards Farr he said " And you are?"

"Detective Sergeant Farr." The Captain continued to look at the detectives, then, without looking away, called "Emsworth!" A well set corporal detached himself from a group across the hall, and stamped to attention in front of the Captain.

"Sir!"

" Take these gentlemen to Major Watkins."

"Sir!" He spun round. "Follow me please gentlemen." They set off up the wide staircase, buffeted by officers and NCOs running up and down, mostly clutching papers. McGill recalled the large room they were ushered into and there, sitting exactly where he had been in November, sat Watkins. As the group advanced on him, Watkins glanced up, but then raised his head properly and watched as they came towards him. When they reached the desk, he rose and extended his hand to McGill.

" Good to see you again – though I daresay you don't feel the same way!" McGill shook Watkin's hand.

"You could say that! I've been sent here by Sir Douglas." Watkins nodded.

"Indeed and by Colonel Julius I understand. THAT speaks volumes."

"It does, and I can't say I'm happy about it. This is my Sergeant, Don Farr." Watkins acknowledged Farr, and started to open drawers in the desk. After a couple of tries, he extracted a folder with the red stripe of top secret emblazoned across it.

" I can't let you take it away, but we can go somewhere quiet and you can read it." Watkins stood and led the way towards the back of the room, where a narrow door, looking unloved and bereft, stood awaiting its fate. Watkins opened it and ushered them through into a corridor. He turned right and walked along until he came to a narrow set of stairs. He quickly climbed them two at a time, tugging a set of keys out of his pocket. At the top of the stairs was another door, which Watkins unlocked and stood back to allow McGill and Farr to enter the room. Entering himself, he shut and locked the door behind him.

McGill glanced around the room. It was a not overly large circular room, presumably some sort of turret. The back of the door they had come through was heavily padded, and the hinges and the opposite side of it were all covered with heavy flaps. Watkins made sure everything was in place, and sat on one of the chairs. He placed the file on the table, untied the ribbon around it and flipped it open.

"This is the most highly confidential document you are ever likely to see. I cannot stress enough that its contents must never – I repeat NEVER – be revealed to anyone."

"I'm more than aware that this is both dangerous and potentially damaging. However, we need the information to reach a conclusion."

McGill passed the file to Farr, who took his notepad and pencil from his pocket and started to read.

" I can give you an overview," said Watkins. "In essence, we caught Blythe-Hill with compromising information on him about two and a half years ago, and he had no good explanation as to why. He didn't hesitate for a moment and confessed he was spying for the Boche, even though it would mean him being shot as a spy. But he then went on to say he was disillusioned, and wanted to spy for us. He would feed his contacts false information, doctored information, which we would give him."

"That would tie in with him being close to or in Amiens in the recent past."

"Yes that's right. We wanted to keep an eye on him. He did tell us who he was passing information to and we have been able to keep a discreet watch on him. It's an Irishman called O'Leary. Nasty piece of work, supposedly here as a contact for the Irish soldiers. There's a picture of him in that file. We haven't particularly found out where he goes – he's very cautious and would quickly spot anyone following him. In a sense, though, we don't mind where he goes. We are sure what we have been telling Blythe-Hill has found its way back to the Germans, as a few things have happened to confirm our fabrications. The problem we have *now* is, did someone on the other side twig what was going on? If they did and murdered the Monsignor, not only do we not have what information he was able to give us anymore, but we can't feed his spymasters anymore disinformation. And if they *did* kill him, they will disregard all we have already fed them. We need to know."

McGill nodded as Farr read on, making a note here and there. "Yes I can see all that. Do you think this O'Leary might lead us to his masters?"

Watkins shook his head. "He's a cagey one. I'd say it would be luck that got us home against him. The house he lives in has numerous rooms and more than two exits, so it would be a large operation to cover and follow him. There's a picture of him in that file."

McGill thought for a moment. "Was Blythe-Hill followed at all? For example, after he had been fed information that you wanted to get to the Germans?"

"What are you getting at?"

"Well, where would he have gone to pass the information across."

"He was a Monsignor, he could go anywhere."

"Yes, but do you know where he DID go?" Farr looked up from the folder.

"It says here he always went back to the Cathedral – at least the couple of times he was followed." Watkins nodded.

"Yes, the first few times we had him followed. He certainly went back to the Cathedral." Farr had been rummaging through the file. He pulled out a picture and passed it to McGill. "That's O'Leary," said Farr.

McGill had frozen. "Do you recognise him, Don?" Farr took the photograph back and studied it briefly before handing it back.

"Looks familiar, but no sir, I don't. Should I?"

McGill studied the picture again.

"Yes," he said quietly. "From the Albert dock." Farr almost snatched the picture, looking earnestly at it.

"If it's not him it's a damn fine likeness!"

"It's him," said McGill. "Now we know for sure what he was up to." Watkins had been sitting mystified.

"What are you two talking about?"

McGill passed the picture to Watkins. "Your man O'Leary tried – no, he didn't just try, he actually *did* get into England nearly three months ago. We were tipped off about something happening at the docks in London but we didn't know what it was to be. In the event it turned out to be this man" McGill tapped the photograph " trying to smuggle himself into London. And very sadly he succeeded. We never managed to trace him after he escaped. What can you tell me about him?"

Watkins blew his cheeks out. "Well, he might have been away at the time you are talking about. He's been around here for at least two years, possibly more. We only got on to him after Blythe-Hill started working for us and told us he was his contact."

"So a careful man, if you didn't know about him. I'm wondering if we should pick him up. The problem is the same one we have all along. If we do, the Germans will know we are on to them, and that Blythe-Hill was feeding them rubbish. How else would we know about O'Leary unless the Monsignor told us? I don't like leaving him wandering about, but I think we have to at the moment." Watkins nodded.

"I agree. We can keep a closer watch on him but that might be counterproductive too."

" Can you see a copy of this picture gets to a Major Simonds in London? The best place to send it is via the Commissioner, Sir Giles Compston. I've actually no idea where Simonds works." Watkins nodded and took the picture. McGill was glancing at a couple of the pages from the folder, as Farr scribbled notes.

"You do know it makes no sense that it was the Germans who killed Blythe-Hill? They wouldn't want to show their hand if they DID find out." Watkins shrugged.

"There's nothing to say he immediately passed the information along. But it would be good cover if he regularly took confessions. The information could be passed to him under the confession, then forwarded on in the same way."

All three were silent for a moment, thinking about it. McGill frowned then looked across at Farr briefly. Farr nodded almost imperceptibly and McGill turned to Watkins.

"We need to know who has been visiting him to confess. Have we any information on that?" Farr riffled through the papers in front of him and extracted one.

"O'Leary definitely according to this. But there's a list of others too."

"How do you know about O'Leary?" asked McGill.

"We had no information about him before Blythe-Hill told us about him. We've since managed to put a few things together. He's no friend of the English."

McGill turned to Farr. "Is there a list of other people who were known associates of Blythe-Hill?" Farr pulled out another sheet and handed it to McGill. He read through it. There were more than 20 people on the list, mostly French by the sound of them, although one or two had English names. McGill passed it back.

"I'm not sure that gets us very much further. If Blythe-Hill was passing information to O'Leary, they must have had some way of getting it across the lines and into German hands."

"Might be homing pigeons,"said Watkins. "However, we think there were a number of No Man's Land slopers who would take information. The only problem would be if they were spotted by either side. They'd likely be shot by the Germans as they went towards them and by us as they came back." McGill thought for a moment.

"What if they didn't need to come back the same way? How often was there information to be smuggled out?" Watkins shrugged.

"Probably about every ten days or so."

"All right, so there was time to get across and then get back some other way. Let's think about the return first. Suppose they made it through the German lines and wanted to come back. What could they do?"

"Well, a fishing boat could bring them back I suppose via the Channel, or they could come back in through Switzerland. But it would take longer than what we are talking about."

"There could be two or three couriers. That would cover it. So that's the return. And they might approach the German lines showing a red light or something to stop them getting shot. Thinking about the crossing from here to there, I know a man who could do it almost blindfold. Thankfully, he's on our side."

"I take it you met him last time you were here."

"I did indeed. Gunner Crowall. He was around Albert when I was here before. It would be worth getting a hold of him to see what his thoughts on this were."

"Could be tricky. The Huns are very active in that area at the moment."

"See what you can do please. It's not critical, but at least it might prove our theory."

"What about these other names sir," asked Farr. Watkins held his hand out for the list and scanned it. Then he shook his head.

"We had a look at them but nothing very much came out of it. I would say the French are extremely unlikely to be involved. The antipathy to their big neighbour is almost tangible. It's always possible there's a rum 'un, but I'd say these three other names are more likely."

Farr noted the names and addresses and placed the sheet back in the file.

"The one thing clear from this file, sir, is there is a ring working here in Amiens. Blythe-Hill was just one of the enemy agents, and it looks as if O'Leary is the handler. What we really need to know is if there are others."

"Agreed. The problem is if we round them up they will know we are on to them and the head men might be able to get away. In any case we don't know the full extent of the ring nor who its members actually are. If we are to smash the ring and close it down, we have to get everyone at the same time – and all the way to the top."

"And we don't even know if the people on this list are even involved – they could just be friends or acquaintances." McGill sighed.

"Well we better start interviewing them. Have you got addresses and places of work, Don?"

"Yes sir." McGill rose, followed by Farr and Watkins, who gathered the papers together, put them back in the file and carefully tied it. He unlocked the door, ushered the detectives onto the landing, and locked the door on his way out.

They made their way down the stairs back to Watkins' desk. There was a safe behind it that McGill had not noticed before, and only saw it now as Watkins opened it, placed the file on top of a pile of similar files. He swung the door shut and locked it.

"I'll be back when I have something to report," said McGill. Watkins nodded.

"Yes please – Julius will be rampaging about wanting answers. And I'll try to get a hold of Gunner Crowall."

McGill laughed bitterly. "Of course. And we don't look as if we are going to have anything to tell the Colonel in quick time." The three men stood for a moment contemplating the position. Then Watkins shrugged.

"Because of the situation with Blythe-Hill, we rather discouraged anyone else from looking too closely. We wouldn't want the Frenchies finding out we had a traitor on our books. The animosity between commanders and the politicians is bad enough! In any event, if there's nothing to tell, there's nothing to tell. You better get off and start those interviews!" McGill and Watkins shook hands, as Farr started to walk away. Watkins stretched across and held his hand out. Farr was slightly taken aback but took the hand and shook it.

"By the way," said Watkins, rummaging in a desk drawer. "You'll need some money." He produced a wad of grubby papers. McGill took it and frowned.

"Looks like old newspaper." Watkins laughed.

"Yes and not worth much more!"

McGill and Farr walked down the staircase and then the steps back to street level. The sergeant and the private who had met them when they arrived watched them go with ill-disguised distaste.

Once out on the street again, McGill led Farr to a café. He ordered the dish of the day and a couple of beers. Farr eyed the food when it came with some misgivings, but started to eat and quickly became more enthusiastic. McGill grinned to himself. He knew what French food was like. The thought brought a recollection of dinner with Isabelle de Bonnefoix and the extraordinary service of the two one armed servants. A pang lanced through him as he saw her face again. He shook his head to clear it. Farr finished first and took a long swig from the beer. Putting the glass back on the table, he wiped his moustache, and sat back. He pulled his notebook from his pocket, and flicked a few pages back.

"Where do we start sir?"

"Scene of the crime? Not sure it will tell us anything but at least we might get a feel of why no one saw anything. We can probably interview those priests in short order which would be a good start." He paused for a moment. "Even the dead ends may tell us something when we know nothing!" Farr nodded.

McGill paid, proffering some of the paper he had been given, which the waitress gratefully triaged and removed some. McGill wondered how much she had pocketed herself but decided it didn't matter. Before she removed herself, McGill placed a hand on her arm and said " Cathedral?"

"Un moment," and she walked back to the bar and spoke to an older woman who was pouring a glass of wine. She glanced across at McGill and Farr then nodded. She finished pouring the wine and handed it to the French soldier in front of her, swiftly pocketing the coins he gave in exchange. Wiping her hands on her apron she lifted the flap at the end of the bar and came to the table where McGill and Farr were sitting.

"Messieurs – you wish ze Catedrale?"

" We do," said McGill. "Is it far from here?" She shook her head.

" Non, it ees Parc de L'Eveque. Notre Dame d'Amiens." She raised both hands fingers extended upwards.

"Dix minutes," and then walked her fingers across the table. McGill nodded. She pulled a pad from her pocket and a pencil and started to draw. Within a few moments, an easily followed map showed the detectives where they were and where they wanted to go. McGill thanked her, took the paper and he and Farr left the café.

By the time they had taken the first couple of turnings, they could see the Cathedral soaring ahead of them. It was a magnificent building and once inside they were even more impressed. The black and white marble floor proclaimed its wealth and the three tier interior spoke of its age. The rood screen was magnificently carved. The detectives stood taking in the sight and the soaring roof. Farr, who seldom appeared impressed, whistled under his breath.

"Quite something sir"

"Indeed it is Don. I never saw it when I was here before. I was too busy getting shot at and having artillery shells explode near me!"

There were black attired priests walking about and McGill stopped one. He did his usual introduction and the young man nodded.

"I will fetch Monsignor Moulin." He scurried away and McGill and Farr stood taking in the magnificence all around them. Within a few minutes a small rotund priest stood in front of them.

"I am Monsignor Moulin. It is I who is charged with dealing with this terrible murder." The accent was clearly French but with a slight lilt to it. McGill shook Moulin's hand.

"You speak good English, Monsignor." Moulin smiled.

"I was fortunate to be in Ireland for a number of years. Now I am back in my home town." Ah thought McGill that's where the lilt comes from.

"How nice for you. Now – could you show us the confessional where the Monsignor died?" Moulin shook his head.

"No, I cannot. I can show you where it *was* but we have removed it and burned the wood." Oh great thought McGill. Nothing like destroying evidence.

"Well, I suppose that will have to do." Moulin pointed to one side of the Cathedral and led off down the aisle that divided the outer wall and the massive row of pillars that towered over the central nave.

As they walked, Farr was consulting his notes. "Were you here when the murder took place Monsignor?"

"No I was not. I was on an errand for the Bishop." They had walked almost the whole distance of the aisle when Moulin stopped in an open space.

He pointed to an area which looked somewhat cleaner than elsewhere.

"Here." McGill and Farr stared at the space. Absolutely useless thought McGill. He turned away and looked towards the centre of the building, then to the left and right. There were a set of pews immediately in front of the space. McGill pointed.

"Would this be where penitents would sit to wait for a priest to hear their confession?" Moulin bowed.

"Indeed." Looking about him again, McGill noted the enormous pillars to right and left, blanking out large areas from sight. Farr was walking backwards and forwards, notebook in hand. He backed away from the area first to the right, keeping the centre of the space within sight. He drew a line on his notebook then did the same to the left. McGill said nothing but let Farr draw his map. Once complete, Farr returned to where McGill was standing.

"Despite the size of this place, you can't see where the confessional was very well, and only from a very restricted angle." McGill nodded.

"No wonder no one saw anything." He walked to the other side of the pillars and was then able to look all the way to the altar in one direction and the main entrance in the other. Walking back towards Farr, the view in either direction suddenly disappeared to be replaced by the massive pillars. He shook his head. He cut off to one side and raised his voice to Farr.

"Don go and stand on the other side so you can just see the area." Farr strode away in the other direction, and a few moments later the two detectives were the fulcrums at the outer angles of a triangle, the sides of which ended where the confessional had stood. McGill counted how many places there were on the seats within his line of vision.

"No more than twenty" he grunted and Farr nodded. He paced off the distances and added them to his drawing. Moulin stood quietly watching.

"Can you get the seven priests who were here to come so we can interview them please?" Moulin bowed and indicated the detectives should follow him. He led them to a side door which opened into a small room. Must be a robing room thought

McGill, as he saw all the vestments hanging everywhere. Moulin indicated they should sit, and disappeared through another door.

Over the next couple of hours a steady stream of priests of all ages came to see the detectives. None had anything to tell. It was almost as if they were blind. McGill decided that priests paid no attention to anything or anyone about them. True, they had not been within the triangle McGill and Farr had delineated, and so could not really have been expected to see very much. But something – anything – would have been a help. The last priest was a youngish man who had discovered the body. There had been no one waiting to confess and, indeed, he had thought that the Monsignor had left. It was only when he opened the door to the confessional that he had seen the gruesome sight. He had quickly shut the door and informed the nearest senior priest. Gendarmes had arrived quickly and the statement the young priest had given at the time was entirely consistent with him knowing absolutely nothing.

Once he had left, Farr consulted his notebook again.

"That leaves five. Three women and two men. Where to now sir?"

"What do we know about the women?"

"There's two ladies and the Duchess of Lincolnshire." McGill snorted.

" I can just see me telling Haig that a Duchess killed the Monsignor. I'd have less chance of getting away than I did last time."

"They've got to be talked to sir."

"I know I know. I just wish this was a good old gangland killing. At least you know where you are!" A ghost of a smile crossed Farr's dark face.

"Be careful what you wish for sir!" Farr closed his notebook. Moulin suddenly reappeared through the door and asked if they had finished.

"Yes thank you Monsignor," said McGill. "We will leave you in peace." Moulin bowed his head and appeared to say a small prayer as McGill and Farr stood and walked to the door beside him. Moulin raised his eyes and looked from one man to the other.

"Have you learned anything?"

"Sadly not, but we have more people to interview. There may be something… By the way, what have your own investigations revealed?"

Moulin looked startled and stammered slightly. "Why nothing, Inspector. No one saw anything."

"Where did the body get taken?"

"We had an undertaker take it away. Such a tragedy."

"Give me the name of the undertaker."

" It was LeClerq. He is just the other side of the square."

"Thank you. We will go and see him"

"I wish you luck." Moulin led them to the main door then hurried to find the bishop in order to tell him what was happening.

Farr dug out the address of one of the two women, and McGill asked passers-by if they knew it. Within a few minutes they were heading in the direction of the street.

As they walked, McGill spoke softly to Farr "The only reason the Germans would kill him is if he knew of an imminent attack and they wanted to stop him telling us. But *if* he knew he would hardly have been taking confessions. He would have taken the information immediately to Watkins. By then it would be too late to kill him and it would tip our hands about it all." McGill thought a moment.

"But if that was the case it might well add weight to what Blythe-Hill would have said. Killing him would show he had information that the Germans did not want to reach us." There was silence then McGill shook his head. "No it's too far-fetched. It makes no sense. If he had only just obtained the information he would NOT have gone off to take confession. And if he had had it for some time, and they knew that, what was the point of killing him? It would tend to confirm what he had said." Farr nodded.

"I agree sir. We may think bad things about the Hun, but not that they are stupid. If anything they are ahead of us in many ways."

McGill suddenly stopped. Farr took a couple more steps then turned and looked at McGill.

"Sir?"

"Wait a minute Don. There's something we're missing. When was the last time Blythe-Hill was given information to pass on? We only know he was given something every ten days or so. What we *don't* know is when was the last time he was passed something for the Germans. It might be relevant."

"You're right sir. If it was a week or so before his death and he had passed it, it's not impossible the Germans knew it was false. On the other hand if it was only hours before perhaps a German agent had come to get the information just before he was killed. In either case it's extremely unlikely the Germans killed him." McGill was walking backwards and forwards along a very short number of steps, face screwed up in concentration.

"Correct. If we can rule the Germans out there's a completely different motive and a completely different set of possibilities. Come on! We need to get back to Watkins." The pair set off striding out quickly back the way they had come earlier in the day. This time there was no delay with being allowed access to HQ and the pair found Watkins reading papers behind his desk. He looked up as they approached, a look of surprise as he saw how eagerly they were coming towards him.

"My, somebody's keen!"

" Major tell me.." and then he stopped. He could hardly ask out loud if false information had been passed to the Germans – even in a British HQ. Leaning across the desk, he grabbed a pen and a piece of paper and quickly wrote his question, spinning the paper round for Watkins to read it. Watkins eyebrows shot up as he read the words, and quickly covered the note with other papers.

"Are you mad? I can't talk to you about that with other people around!"

"You don't have to. Just write the date and time on a piece of paper. No one will hear and no one would know what it was." Watkins looked at McGill then tore a bit of paper from the bottom of the note and hastily scribbled a date and time. He handed it to McGill. It read 9a.m. on the morning of Blythe-Hill's murder. McGill grabbed another piece of paper and dashed off a second note.

It read " And how did you get the information to him?" Watkins turned the note over and wrote: " I sent someone to confess." And as he wrote it, Watkins suddenly realised the implications. He continued writing: " It was all spoken, nothing written down." McGill read the note then looked up at Watkins.

"So no incriminating papers anywhere. Very good."

McGill wrote a final note.

"It wasn't the Germans." Watkins nodded.

"Yes I see that now. I will tell Julius. Do you have anything to go on?

"Not really" said McGill. "But now that is out of the way we can concentrate on a good old fashioned murder without political overtones. Hallelujah!"

McGill and Farr went back towards the address they had been given for the penitent they wished to interview. Watkins put a match to the paper on which he and McGill had written. He got some strange looks, but he stared them down.

As the detectives walked, McGill decided they would cross off the other bodies with an interest in the murder first.

"Don, I think we should talk to the Army first about all this. I assume they have no interest and did nothing to investigate. We know Watkins' lot were discouraging all and sundry, but it might be worth talking to them." Turning on their heels, the pair soon found themselves back where they started.

They climbed the stairs to Watkins again, who was even more astonished to see them than before.

"Do I have some strange attraction I don't know about?" McGill laughed.

"Not really. We just thought we would try to cross off the army and the French before we got to the penitents. I'm assuming I don't need to talk to your lot." Watkins shook his head.

"No, we are focussed on the ring rather than anything else. And as you have seen, we don't have anything much. The person you need to talk to is in the Provost Marshall's office. His name is Colonel Reid. He is my liaison. He'll be able to tell you anything they came up with. I wouldn't hold my breath though. The man at the French Police is Commissaire Lemuel. He is definitely not interested in the least, but you better see for yourselves." Watkins scribbled an address and handed it over. "That's the French. Reid is in this building on the third floor." McGill thanked him and he and Farr set off to climb the additional flights to the third floor.

Once there, it was clear that security was even tighter than lower down. The policeman's warrant cards were minutely inspected and details written down. These were then passed to another MP who took them into the Provost Marshall's office. A message was eventually passed back that they might enter. Farr raised his eyes at McGill who shrugged imperceptibly. Only then were they allowed to proceed, albeit escorted by two very stone-faced MPs. They were ushered into Reid's office and the two MPs remained standing behind the policemen.

Reid was very much in the mould of a Colonel who would brook no nonsense. He sat ram-rod straight on his chair and glowered at McGill and Farr. "Which of you is the Inspector?" rasped Reid.

"I am sir," said McGill. No handshake here, thought McGill. Nor even acknowledgement of Don.

"What do you want?"

"We are here because Field Marshal Haig has asked us to investigate the murder of Monsignor Blythe-Hill in Amiens Cathedral. We have been told your section undertook some enquiries." Reid looked hard at McGill.

"We have no interest in this. Blythe-Hill was a Catholic priest. He was murdered in a Cathedral. It's a Church matter."

"I understand that sir, but did your people not even take a look at the body or the confessional?"

"No. That's all I have to say. Goodbye."

The two soldiers made way and opened the door to allow McGill and Farr space to get out. There was nothing they could do bar leave, which they did.

Once safely out of earshot, McGill turned to Farr. "I told you no one would want to have anything to do with this."

"Too right sir. Are we going to see Lemuel?" McGill sighed.

"I suppose we better. There's absolutely nothing to go on. And we better see that undertaker."

Without more ado, the pair set off back to the square beside the Cathedral to find LeClerq.

Moulin was as good as his word. "Pompes Funebres LeClerq" was opposite the Cathedral. It was quite a grand shop, all painted with a very high black gloss. McGill and Farr pushed the door open and a tinkling bell announced their presence. A lugubrious man of about forty appeared from the back of the shop, holding his hands together in an obsequious manner.

"Messieurs."

" Are you Monsieur LeClerq?" The man bowed his head with his eyes shut.

"I am he."

"We have been given your name by Monsignor Moulin as the person to talk to about the body of Monsignor Blythe-Hill." LeClerq's eyes snapped open wide then settled on McGill.

"And you are?"

"I am Detective Inspector McGill of Scotland Yard and this is my sergeant, Detective Farr." LeClerq nodded and spread his hands wide.

"I see. What would you wish to know?"

"Do you still have the body?"

"I do. It is here under the command of the Church. They will tell me when it is to be released. I presume that as it was a murder, the Gendarmerie will decide when it can be buried."

"We may not need to see the body if you can answer some questions for us. Can you tell us anything about the body? Was there anything strange about it?" LeClerq shook his head.

"Apart from the bayonet sticking out of his right eye, no."

"What did you do with the bayonet?"

" I removed it with great difficulty and was told to return it to a Major Watkins at British Amiens Headquarters." McGill was surprised that Watkins had not told them.

"Have you done that? Who told you to return it to him?"

"Not yet. I have been busy and I didn't think it would matter very much. It was Monsignor Moulin who told me to give it back."

"How did you know to give it to Watkins?" asked McGill. "Did Moulin tell you?"

"He did, but so did an English Officer and a French Gendarme." McGill was surprised, but as the overlapping uninterested parties would want to have nothing to do with it – yet seem to be involved – dealing with the murder weapon was a good diversionary tactic.

"Would you have any idea whether it was a man or woman who stabbed the Monsignor? Was it pushed in all the way? Or only part way?"

"It was right the way through to the back of his head."

"So considerable strength?" LeClerq shrugged.

"The eye is soft and there is no bone behind it until the back of the skull. Strength yes, but not enormous."

"So it could be either a man or a woman?" mused McGill. Farr caught McGill's eye and McGill nodded.

"Monsieur LeLerq – if the bayonet was only stopped by the skull, was there much still sticking out?"

"Why yes. The human skull is only some nineteen centimetres from front to back. The bayonet was some forty centimetres long."

"So there was no possibility of the bayonet not penetrating the brain and killing the Monsignor?"

"Mais non. In effect there was still half the bayonet that could have been pushed through and out of the skull had enough force been used." That's horrible thought McGill. There must have been overwhelming hate pushing that blade to do that.

"Do we need to see the body sir?" asked Farr. McGill thought for a moment then shook his head.

"I can't see it would help very much. We know what he died of. His body can't tell us much more." McGill turned to LeClerq. "Thank you for making time to see us. You have been very helpful." LeClerq performed his obsequious bow again, and extended his arm to show the detectives out of the door. It tinkled twice – once as it was opened and again when it was shut.

Once outside, the pair wandered into the park. They found a bench and sat down.

"What have we got so far, Don?"

"We know what killed him and very roughly when. We don't have any plausible motive or suspect. The confessional could only be seen by a very limited number of people. We don't know the order in which the people confessed, so we don't know who the last one was who saw him. And we don't know for sure that he wasn't killed earlier and somebody else took his place for taking confessions."

"That's a good point Don. We've been assuming all along the last person into the confessional was the person who killed him. But he could have been killed at any time and the killer take over the confessions." McGill blew out his cheeks. "This keeps getting worse," he muttered.

"I don't feel up to talking to an old French lady. Let's see if we can find the Duchess of Lincolnshire."

Farr pulled out his notebook and flicked through until he got to the page with the names of the penitents in the Cathedral.

"It says here she works in a hospital in Rue des Anges." McGill looked about for an estaminet and led off towards it.

Once inside he enquired as to the whereabouts of Rue des Anges. As he had expected, it wasn't far from the Cathedral. He and Farr set off to find the hospital.

CHAPTER ELEVEN

The hospital was relatively easy to find, as it was the building with the ambulances outside and filthy, benighted, bandaged creatures limping or being stretchered into it. It was obvious from the traffic that the main centre of operations was in fact in the basement. It appeared the access was a hastily constructed set of steps down what could have been a coal chute. The detectives pushed their way down past beings whose eyes were bewildered and vacant, many of them needing to be led by kindly nurses.

From the moment McGill walked into the ward, the overwhelming feeling he had was of suffocation and horror. He had seen it before, but here, away from the front, it seemed so much worse. The wounded lay groaning and screaming, with hardly anything to alleviate their suffering. There were those blinded by the gas, men with no arms and legs, and some with the whole side of their faces blown off. It was as much as McGill could do to avoid retching. He made his way through the moaning mass with Farr behind, whose usually blank face had gone white, making his dark eyes even more prominent in his head. McGill heard him whisper " Jesus" behind him, but kept going. He accosted a nurse who told him where "Miladee" could be found.

When he finally got to the end of the stinking beds, there was a small door leading out. McGill opened it and stepped through, holding it open for Farr, who glanced back over his shoulder then stumbled through and stood, panting slightly.

" Jesus" he said again

" Not a pretty sight is it? " said McGill. " And this could be multiplied by thousands." Farr shook his head and made a conscious effort to pull himself together.

In front of them was an ancient desk, behind which sat the woman they were looking for.

She sat, perfectly calm and erect, her eyes watching McGill and Farr with a slightly amused look. Anne Grey-Lennox, Duchess of Lincolnshire, was a Duchess through and through.

Even sitting as she was behind the desk, McGill could see she wasn't tall, though perfectly proportioned. He knew she had long hair that in the photograph had sat perfectly around her shoulders, framing her face, and setting off a pair of enticing lips. Her outfit, definitely not standard issue nurses uniform, had been tailored. Not for her the standard issue sack which made all the ladies shapeless. There was nothing shapeless about her, as she brushed a stray lock from her forehead.

" Your Grace, " began McGill, only to be interrupted by an imperious hand held up .

" Stuff and nonsense, you must call me Anne. Everyone else does!" So saying she stood, turning slightly to one side so she could stretch her hand across to shake McGill's. He couldn't fail to notice her figure as she did so, and felt himself awkward and stupid.

He shook the outstretched hand. " I'm Detective Inspector McGill from Scotland yard, and this is Detective Sergeant Farr." McGill stopped, unsure how to go on.

" And what can I do for you Inspector?" the Duchess prompted. " Do sit down, both of you." McGill gave himself a mental shake and took the straight-back chair nearest him. Farr took the other, and began to look as if he was getting the better of himself. The Duchess subsided gracefully onto her own chair.

"It's a dreadful sight, isn't it? Have you been to France before?" she asked.

McGill cleared his throat. " Yes I have been before – I was here in November and early December. I was around Albert so there were plenty of casualties there." Anne nodded. "I'm sorry to have to intrude on your work here, but I understand you were in the Cathedral the day Monsignor Blythe-Hill was murdered." McGill caught a small stiffening in her demeanour, but nothing else.

" I believe so. What can I help you with?" She appears very calm, thought McGill. Maybe she's just too superior to believe she should be bothered by such things.

" I wonder if you could tell me anything about that day?"

The Duchess lowered her head for a moment, then looked hard at McGill.

" I was there alone to make my confession."

McGill nodded. "That's not quite true is it? There were other people there to confess as well."

"Ah I understand. Yes there were other people I saw. What I meant was I was alone with my God."

"I see. And what time did you get there?" The Duchess looked at McGill distractedly, almost vacantly, as if she was making her mind up about something.

" It was in the morning." McGill nodded again.

" What time might that have been?" She was silent for so long McGill thought she might not have heard the question.

"Time?" she eventually said. " I'm not sure, but I think I heard a clock chiming. It might have been ten. I know I got back around noon. We were just starting to try to feed those who couldn't help themselves."

McGill thought for a moment. " So let me take you through the morning. What time would you have got up?"

The Duchess waved a hand. " I normally rise at six, but it might have been a touch later."

"And what did you do then?"

" Really,Inspector, I fail to see this has anything to do with anything."

" Oh, I can assure you it does, er... Anne. I'm trying to place everyone who was there that morning. If I can get a fix on timings, then I might be able to find someone who saw something."

Anne laughed. " Oh Inspector, I can assure you I saw nothing!"

McGill smiled slightly. " I appreciate that, but there may be something you saw subconsciously, but have dismissed. So tell me, did you have breakfast?"

Anne nodded. " Yes, very quickly. I wanted to check on the overnight intake."

" It is very commendable that you have taken on this charge. What made you come here?"

McGill noted the slight hesitation, but then felt her gather herself.

" My son was near here. A mother wants to be near her son, Inspector. I offered my services and was allowed to come." She paused, and lowered her head. " My son was killed in February. I have stayed on to do what I can, and to try to keep his memory alive."

"I'm sorry. I didn't know."

Anne smiled grimly. " There's no reason that you should. He was enlisted under a false name to avoid fingers pointing."

"Did he do that himself?"

" He did," she said bitterly. " He went to the recruiting centre and did it all himself. He could have been an officer, but he chose to be a private." She paused again. Her voice took on a different tone, one of pride. " He had already been made up to Corporal and was destined to be a Sergeant. But it was not to be."

There was silence for a moment, allowing McGill to gather his thoughts.

" Did you see him before he died?"

" Oh yes, twice." She shook herself slightly, and looked straight at McGill again.

" But he can have nothing to do with this. To satisfy your curiosity, I suggest you speak to Sister Barker. I would have handed over to her when I left the ward, and she, bless her, would have noted when I left and when I got back."

"Thank you, we'll have a word with her on our way out. In the meantime, what else can you tell us about when you were in the Cathedral?"

" I hadn't actually made up my mind to make my confession. Since my son was killed I go as often as I can, just to be nearer him, but I've been unable to actually face making confession. I know that sounds strange, but I do feel closer to him there. And it's the right place to be to rage against the fates that took my son from me. I probably prayed for over an hour, and then I thought I *would* make my confession. Even once I had made my mind up, I still waited, letting others who had come in after me go into the confessional. It allowed me to pray quietly, reflecting."

" Did you have many sins to confess?" McGill could feel Farr stiffening slightly, as if such a question should not be asked of a Duchess.

Anne laughed. "Inspector, I take it you are not a Catholic? You have no idea of how many sins a completely blameless woman can be guilty!"

McGill pondered what she had said, then glanced at Farr. He had recovered himself and was leaning forward slightly, rather like a small dog ready to attack.

" Sergeant, would you mind finding Sister Barker and try to verify her Grace's timings?"

" Very good, sir." Farr rose and made for the door. McGill saw him hesitate, then draw himself up, grasp the door knob, and stride purposefully through. He turned back to the Duchess.

" I'm afraid my Sergeant has been somewhat overcome with the sights and sounds here."

Anne laughed. " Yes it takes a bit of getting used to. But I can assure you, after a while the awfulness just becomes normal. You'd hardly credit it, but it does."

McGill nodded, thinking. If her timings were anywhere near right, she would have been gone when Blythe-Hill was killed, and certainly at least an hour before he was discovered. McGill's difficulty was not having any kind of exact time of death.

" Did you by any mischance confess to the Monsignor?"

Anne laughed again. " Inspector, I assure you I did not. I made no confession in the end. Besides, had I known it was him on the other side of the partition I would have got up and left!"

McGill's senses prickled. " Oh? And why would that be?"

The Duchess looked up at the ceiling with a faraway look in her eyes. Then she looked back at McGill.

" I may as well tell you, as I'm sure you will make further enquiries. Many years ago, I was very friendly with the Monsignor – in the days before he became a priest. I was very young – only eighteen – and he was a divinity student at Oxford. He was already destined for great things, and passed with a first. Our families lived near each other, and the summer after his graduation we were much in each other's company. I'm – I'm sure he regarded me as a silly little girl. He could certainly have had the pick of the young ladies in the whole of England. You will have seen his picture, I'm sure, and know how good looking he was. That was only a part of it, of course.

He was charming and debonair, and everyone, even older people, deferred to his views. I will admit I was madly in love with him. By the end of the summer, at the point where I was sure he would propose, he disposed of me like a soiled napkin. It broke my heart. As you know, love can easily turn to hate. I hated him. I suppose after all these years I shouldn't care anymore. I made a good marriage and had my son, despite him. But I can't say I'm sorry at his death."

McGill was quiet for a moment. "Did you think he would marry someone else? Or was he set on the Church even then?"

Anne thought for a moment. "I think when he left me I thought it would be for another woman, but he entered the priesthood shortly thereafter. He certainly didn't appear to have any other lady friends." McGill noted the bitterness in her voice.

McGill tried to recall details from her file. He supposed she wasn't much more than forty now, and she had had a son of fighting age. She must have married not long after Blythe-Hill dropped her, he thought. He wondered whether he should ask. Why not? he thought.

" This is rather an impertinent question, but I'd be most obliged if you would answer." Anne shrugged. " How long after the break with Blythe-Hill did you marry the Duke?" McGill caught the slight hesitation, then the firm reply as she looked straight at him. " Within two months."

He wasn't sure what to make of that. He came at it from another angle.

" Had the Duke been courting you at the same time?" She hesitated slightly once more, and went on in a lower voice.

" Archie was an old family friend. Much older of course – he was nearly forty when we married. I remember him saying when I was six or seven that he would wait to marry me. Of course, everyone treated that as a huge joke, but it's what happened. I truly believe he always loved me. He had loved my mother, but she loved my father, so I was second best, I suppose. When Gerald dropped me, Archie was there to help me back on my feet. I remember his hang-dog expression throughout that summer, as Gerald and I cut a swathe through County society. And I remember the gleam in his eyes the first time he came to visit after Gerald left. It was almost triumphant." She was silent for a moment. " I married him to still the wagging tongues I suppose, and because he was such a rock. I didn't realise how lonely I was after Gerald left, until Archie took the loneliness away. We went away after the wedding, and didn't come back for over a year." McGill felt a tingle again, but could not put a finger on it. " By that time I had my son, James, and we took up our rather grand lives. Partly, I suppose, because of Archie's age, we lived quietly."

McGill could still feel the tingle, but the door opened and a somewhat pale Farr came back in, shutting the door firmly behind him. McGill cocked an eyebrow, and Farr nodded.

"Sister Barker says she reckons her Grace left just before 10 and was back here just after twelve." McGill turned to Anne again.

" That's a great help." He thought for a moment. "If you were in the area beside the confessional by say ten or quarter past ten, how did it take so long for you to come back here?"

The Duchess laughed. " Inspector, you clearly know nothing of our religion. One has to do one's penance. I admit I did not actually make a confession but the penance cleanses one's soul. And I was angry with God and the Church for taking my son away from me. I chose to remain in the Cathedral whilst I recited quite a large number of Hail Marys and other prayers. When I went outside it was almost warm, so I sat in the park by the Cathedral for a while."

"Did you have so much to confess?"

She laughed again. " Unburdening one's soul is not a race, Inspector. It's a cleansing".

McGill thought for a moment. " Did you notice anyone else, or recognise anyone?"

Anne shook her head. " I can't say I did. In fact, the Cathedral seemed unusually empty. When I left there was no one else waiting to confess. I didn't recognise any of the people waiting whilst I was praying."

"So after there was no one else waiting to confess – you sat on? The Monsignor did not leave the confessional and no one else came in?"

Anne shook her head. "No Inspector. I was quite alone."

McGill nodded. He still had questions he wanted answers to, but he didn't feel the Duchess would answer them. He stood up.

"Thank you. We won't take up any more of your time." Farr stood too, and the pair made towards the door. Anne, Duchess of Lincolnshire, rose and leaned against her desk.

" Taking up my time is a luxury I enjoy, Inspector," she said quietly, with a sad, gentle smile.

McGill smiled back at her and then hesitated. "Why did you go to that particular place to pray when you went to the Cathedral – if you didn't intend to confess?" Anne shrugged.

"It's probably the quietest place in the whole Cathedral. It's a long way from the entrance." McGill nodded and followed Farr out into the cellar that passed as a ward. There were stretchers coming in and others going out, with doctors and nurses going about their work in a stolid fashion. I can see what she meant about becoming inured to all this, thought McGill.

Once he and Farr had regained the street, McGill looked about for somewhere to get a drink. Farr still looked rather pale, and the thought of a brandy gave McGill a lift to his spirit.

" Come on Don, I'll buy you a brandy. I need one myself!" Farr nodded.

" I'd no idea it was like that, sir. I suppose I never thought about it. I've seen a few of the wounded back in town, but they're usually patched up by then, and it don't seem so bad."

" I know, we sort of paint them out of the picture. The dead are dead, but the living are dead to us as well."

A short walk took them to a café that was already doing a roaring trade. McGill pushed his way to the bar and ordered two brandies. He handed one to Farr, raised his own in a universal salute, and downed it in one. Farr did likewise, swallowing hard. A touch of colour came back to his cheeks and McGill nodded.

" Good! Now, what do you make of all that?"

"Well, sir, her timings could mean she killed him. Doesn't seem likely though. Strange to go to make a confession and then not do it."

" I'd agree, except I twice got the impression there were things she wasn't telling us. The first time was about her son and his death. The second time was about her son as well, but about his birth. Strange that it should be that both times that made my brain tingle.”

Farr smiled slightly and carefully put his glass down. He cleared his throat. “Your famous tingles, sir! Well, it seems to me we should make some enquiries about the son in that case. I’ll get on to the Yard and have them send us what they can.”

“ And while you’re at it, Don, find out about the Duke and anything else about when they were married. It’s probably nothing, but she did admit to hating our Monsignor. Murder is nearly always to do with love or money – or love gone wrong.” McGill thought back to the last time he had been in Amiens, listening to a General tell him about his anguished love. He nodded to himself. Yes, murder was always about love or money.

CHAPTER TWELVE

McGill and Farr walked away from the hospital area, moving aside for stretchers and handcarts with wounded men on them. Farr's head moved from side to side taking in the blood soaked bandages, the missing limbs and the strange air of relief from the wounded men. McGill looked straight ahead. He had seen this all before. He didn't like it any better but he knew there was no use dwelling on it. It was a fact of the present stalemate. Even with no attacks, there remained those blown up every day by the continual bombardments. In the end, he supposed it would come down to who had more men. With the United States now in the war, the balance had finally tipped towards the Allies. McGill thought about what Haig had said to him about the world after the war. It would be utterly different, with none of the old certainties to cling to. He sensed rather than knew that his country, his Great Britain, might no longer be so great. Already America was flexing her industrial muscle. He knew that everything in Britain was working flat out on war related work. He also knew that America had merely diverted a small percentage of her might towards the war. Britain and France, if they were the victors, would be utterly exhausted, their industries played out. America would have no such problem.

As they finally cleared the immediate vicinity of the hospital, Farr breathed a sigh of relief.

" It's terrible, sir. I had no idea it was like this."

"Terrible it is. When I was here in November last year, everyone was laughing at me because I was trying to solve a murder when every day there were thousands dead or wounded. I can feel the desperation here now. Something must give one way or the other soon. It cannot continue as it is."

Farr nodded. " I don't suppose it can, sir," he said quietly.

They walked in silence for a few minutes. Unbidden, McGill suddenly thought of Isabelle de Bonnefoix, and of their last night together. In quiet moments she appeared. He thought of his dismissal by the maid, Marie, the following morning. He couldn't believe there was such a cold hearted attitude after the joy they had both experienced. Well, he was after all only a lowly English policeman, and she was a rich and beautiful widow. He decided if he had the chance he would visit her again, if only to lay her ghost.

Farr cleared his throat. " Where to now sir?" McGill hadn't been aware that he was simply walking as things churned through his mind. He looked about him.

"Shall we go and see the French?"

"Why not sir? I don't suppose for a moment they will tell us anything, but we've got to do it."

Within ten minutes the pair arrived at Amiens police headquarters. A few enquiries had them directed up the stairs to a busy open office where people came and went all the time. They were directed to a harassed man sitting at a desk near the back of the room. McGill stood in front of the desk and waited patiently for the man to look up. He was a small plump man with pince-nez, held round his neck by a cord. It was only a moment before he looked up, still holding the papers

"Oui?"

"My name is Detective Inspector McGill, and this is Detective Sergeant Farr. We are from Scotland Yard and we have been sent to find out the murderer of Monsignor Blythe.." The Frenchman's hand shot up, palm towards McGill.

"One moment, Inspector. My Superior is the correct person for you to see. Follow me." He placed his papers carefully in the centre of his desk and rose, removing his pince-nez and letting them drop to hang round his neck. He extended his right arm in the universal gesture of "This way please" and led off towards a door in the corner. Once they were all through, he turned and knocked on a door just to one side of where they stood. There was a shout of "Entrez!" and McGill's guide turned the door knob, ushering the Scotland Yard men into a bright room, overlooking the courtyard of the building. There was a large desk with a small man behind it, moustache perfectly groomed. His desk was orderly and tidy, and he was sitting opposite a policeman in uniform. The man looked up.

"Quesquia Dupont?"

Dupont spoke rapidly, and the man behind the desk registered no change to his demeanour or face. When Dupont finished, the man rose and extended his hand to McGill.

" I am Commissaire Lemuel. I believe you are from Scotland Yard?"

McGill was surprised at the excellent English, even though it was somewhat accented.

As he shook the proffered hand he repeated the introduction he had made to Dupont. " I was told to ask for you by Major Watkins,"said McGill

"Please Inspector, be seated. Yes I have had dealings with Major Watkins." Lemuel spoke to the man sitting in front of him, who stood and left the room. McGill and Farr took the two remaining seats and Dupont stayed standing at the door.

" I believe Monsieur le Commissaire your people were called by the Cathedral authorities and you made a list of everyone who was there at the time – or shortly before."

Lemuel inclined his head. "True Inspector."

"Could you or one of your people please just confirm this is a complete list?" Lemuel glanced at the list and handed it back.

"You have twelve, there were twelve."

" Did you take statements from any of the people? I suppose they might be called witnesses. It certainly looks as if no one saw anything but I have no sense of what actually happened. I wondered if you could tell me what you think happened – and more importantly who it might have been who killed the Monsignor."

Lemuel let a ghost of a smile escape, and threw his hands in the air dramatically.

" My dear Inspector, I probably have less idea of who might have killed him than you do! He was, after all, English! But as to what happened, we know he started taking confessions around nine thirty, and he was discovered dead just after one. We took very brief statements from three people but we did not undertake any more interviews. There seemed no point. The penitents were, as you may have seen, seated in front of the confessional, the last entering it at about a quarter past or half past eleven. So he was still alive then. I have to assume that the next person entering the confessional killed him. But why no one saw that he was dead between then and the time his body was discovered…” Lemuel shrugged. “ Strange too that there were not more penitents in that time. But there it is.”

McGill thought for a moment. “ So you have no especial suspect? No clue?

Lemuel shook his head. “ None Inspector. It is almost as if… as if a Phantom entered the Cathedral, then the Confessional, killed the Monsignor, then disappeared. There was no blood except within the Confessional. No one saw anybody with blood on them, though I daresay any blood from the eye would have been caught by the divider between priest and penitent. As you doubtless know, there would probably not be very much blood anyway.”

McGill nodded. “Yes indeed. But I would have thought there would have been another person waiting to confess.” Lemuel smiled a touch more openly.

“ Inspector, it was approaching lunchtime! Both penitent and priest would be ready to leave things until after two o’clock” McGill smiled.

“ Yes I suppose so. Is there anything else you can tell me, Commissaire?”

Lemuel shrugged again and spread his hands.

“Helas, no. You have everything we have my dear Inspector. I wish you luck!”

Lemuel rose and extended his hand again. McGill shook it, and turned to leave.

Dupont had opened the door, standing to one side to allow McGill and Farr to exit.

As he reached the door, McGill turned back.

“ Commissaire, one thing I forgot. Where would the Monsignor’s papers be?”

“ I have no idea. Somewhere in the Cathedral? At his lodgings?”

“And where might they be?”

Lemuel laughed. “ Inspector, only the Cathedral would know such a thing!”

As McGill and Farr made their way out of the building, Farr was about to speak, but McGill shook his head slightly. Farr took the hint and the pair walked out into the wan sunshine that had broken through the clouds.

They walked some yards and McGill glanced at Farr.

" What were you about to say?"

Farr took a deep breath and exhaled.

" Sir, that man doesn't care in the least what has happened. He never even went to Blythe-Hill's lodgings."

McGill nodded. "Exactly as we thought. No one cares. It's not their problem – or at least it's someone else's problem. It's all too neat, isn't it?"

Farr humpfed. "Yes sir. Do you believe it?"

McGill shook his head. " Not in the least. I'm beginning to think it might be an enemy after all – an enemy of the Monsignor." Farr glanced at him.

" An enemy, sir?" McGill turned to look at Farr.

"Yes an enemy. Even though we think it wouldn't be the Germans, it's really quite strange that no one wants to do any proper investigation. It's almost as if friend Gerald was some kind of pariah."

"Maybe between the political aspect and the Church side of things, no one wants to get on the wrong side of somebody else. Powerful forces at work sir." McGill nodded.

"Let's go and have a look at the Monsignor's lodgings. I don't expect we'll find much, but it might tell us something."

The pair traipsed back to the Cathedral and went in search of Monsignor Moulin. When they found him, McGill asked to see where the Monsignor was living. Moulin was startled by their reappearance and even more so by their request.

"But monsieur, everything has been removed! He is, after all dead. Someone else is living in his rooms now."

"So he lived in the Cathedral precinct? Was that usual?" Moulin shuffled a little uncomfortably.

"Well, Monsignor Blythe-Hill was an important man. He requested accommodation and the Bishop granted him a set of rooms nearby. But obviously only while he was doing work for the Cathedral."

"Obviously," said McGill drily. "What happened to his belongings? And his papers?" Moulin spread his hands.

"I arranged for all his belongings to the stored."

"And where are they stored."

"We gave them to a storage company. They will go back to his family."

"In that case tell me where they are and a letter to enable me to inspect them." Moulin bowed slightly and said "Wait here." He slipped away.

McGill and Farr stood and waited for Moulin to come back. He didn't take very long, and proffered a paper with an address and a letter written in French and signed by him. "Voila!"

McGill took it. "Thank you," he said and turned away and headed for the main entrance. Once outside he stopped and looked at the address. " I should have asked him where this was." Farr grinned.

"I didn't want to be with him any longer either sir!" And they both laughed.

"Let's ask Watkins. I suspect this is not in the centre at all. He might get us a car." They walked back to HQ and got to Watkins just as he was standing up.

"Again!" he said.

"Just shows how hard we are working," said McGill. He handed Watkins Moulin's paper. "Any idea where this is?" Watkins took the paper and read it.

"Hmm it's about five miles out. You'll need transport."

"Can you get some for us?"

"Your best bet is Julius. He has his own vehicle. He's due back shortly."

"Where is his lair in this labyrinth?"

"He's taken over an office in the basement. There's a couple of men there as well. I'll take you down." Watkins stood up. " Oh by the way, I've located that Gunner Crowall for you. He'll be here in the morning." McGill nodded. What Crowall would think about being carted off to Amiens HQ didn't bear thinking about.

Watkins and the two detectives took the stairs to the ground floor, then down through another door and set of stairs to what presumably had been staff quarters. There was a set of four windows looking into the corridor they were in. There was a door in the middle of the windows which Watkins entered without knocking. It took them into one room with a door leading into the other. Two soldiers, a sergeant and a Captain, leapt to their feet as Watkins entered.

"Stand easy," he said. "The Colonel not back yet?"

"No sir," said the Captain. "Shouldn't be long though."

"These gentlemen will wait for him. Make them comfortable." And he left.

"Yes sir" shouted the Captain after him. He looked at McGill and Farr, and exhaled.

"Um, would you like some tea?"

"That would be excellent – thank you." The sergeant stepped outside the door and stopped a passing private, who looked none too pleased to be given the job. In the meantime, the Captain had moved a couple of chairs out of what was Julius' office to be in the front room with them.

"I might be able to help."

"No I'm afraid not. We're actually after the Colonel's car." The Captain laughed.

"You've about as much chance of that as I have of becoming Commander in Chief!"

Moments later there was a knock at the door, and the sergeant let the private in with the tea. McGill thought for the umpteenth time that the British Army actually worked through the tea being doled out at all times of day and night.

They were halfway through their teas when the door banged open and a fairly red faced Colonel Julius stomped into the room. The Captain and sergeant leapt to their feet, but Julius told them to sit with a growl. It was only then that he spotted McGill and Farr, which surprised him.

"You better come through. And you better bring your chairs." Minutes later they were all seated in Julius' office with the door shut.

"Do you have something?"

"Yes and no. We want to borrow your car to go to look through the Monsignor's belongings and papers. And we're pretty sure there's no German connection to the murder." Julius nodded.

"Well that's something. But only pretty sure?"

"Yes, we're not certain yet. Blythe-Hills papers may give us something."

"So where are they?" McGill passed the letter across. Julius read it. He reached for his cap which he had placed on his desk.

"I'll come with you. Something might mean something to me when it wouldn't to you."

"Fair enough." McGill and Farr rose and followed Julius out the door.

They made their way out to the back of the building, where McGill remembered that cars were generally parked and maintained. He spotted the vehicle in which they had come to Amiens, complete with driver busy topping up the fuel. Julius rapped his knuckles on the bonnet and the driver stuck his head round the side, saw Julius and hastily finished pouring.

"Are we going far sir? Should I put a couple of cans in the back?"

"No it's only about five miles each way, Geordie. Here's the address. Do you know it?"

"Yes sir. Lots of stored goods there."

"That's it. Off we go." Everybody got in and the car started immediately.

"Very impressive," said McGill.

"Geordie's been with me since ninety six. Wonderful mechanic."

Getting the car out and onto the road from Amiens was not the easiest journey it had ever taken, but Geordie was a skilled driver as well as mechanic, and they reached the storage depot within twenty minutes. There were a series of enormous sheds as well as open space, all surrounded by wire fencing and barbed wire that had seen better days. There was a queue of lorries waiting to get in but Julius instructed Geordie to drive past and find the main office. There was a brick two storey building which looked as if it was in charge, and they drew up outside.

Julius jumped out and pushed open the door, with McGill and Farr hurrying to keep up. Two men in dirty blue overalls stood behind a partition and Julius thrust Moulin's letter at the first. He read it twice, then beckoned the three men. "Suivez-moi."

He took them through the back of the brick building and into one of the enormous sheds. There were another two dirty blue attired men at the door, and after a brief discussion, one of them pointed down the cavernous shed. They trailed down with the aisles being counted off as they walked. Towards the middle of the shed, the group halted and a large tin chest could be seen under some smaller bags. These were removed and the chest pulled out. The storeman checked a label, nodded, and stood back. McGill moved to where there was a catch in the middle of the chest, flicked it open and raised the lid. Farr had reached across and took it from McGill, moving the lid all the way back on its fulcrum until the back edge was on the ground.

There was a plethora of clothes or varying type on the top. McGill carefully removed them without disturbing the folds, and passed them to Farr to be stacked to one side. He ran his hands round the lining and across the inside of the lid. He worked methodically down until he came across two boxes. One was clearly a writing table top, slanted to allow easy writing, the other more like a treasures box. Taking the latter first, McGill opened it. Inside were cufflinks, shirt studs and some other items of male jewellery. He closed it and passed it to Farr. Removing the writing table, he closed the lid of the chest and placed it on top. He opened it to find several letters. Julius leant over and took a handful, sorting through them. McGill handed some to Farr and took a few himself. They were silent for a spell as they quickly read them. Julius sighed as he handed his bundle back to McGill.

"Nothing there." McGill had come to the same conclusion. Farr was still reading but McGill placed the letters he held back into the box. He was holding it with his left hand and used his right hand to replace them. He let them go, then stopped, his right hand hovering over the letters. He put his hand into the box once more, then took it out.

"What the hell are you doing?" asked Julius. McGill ignored him and moved his left hand so that his middle finger was vertical beside the wood. He then moved his right hand in the same way but inside the box.

Julius stared at McGill's hands. " My God! A hidden drawer!" McGill's right hand was clearly sitting higher than his left. He removed the letters and lifted the box, looking underneath and all around. There was no catch or even an apparent crack anywhere. There was a small key at the front which locked and unlocked the box. McGill shut the box, then locked it and withdrew the key. From the configuration of the keyhole, the key would only fit in one way. McGill carefully re-inserted the key and, maintaining pressure on it in a forward direction, slowly turned it.

Suddenly the key went further into the box. It wouldn't turn any more and McGill pushed harder. There was a soft click, and a flap at the side sprang open. All five men stared at the box. Farr was the only one who could see into the cavity that had been revealed. He tentatively put his right hand into the space and drew out some papers. They all stared.

"My God," said Julius. "How did you know about that?" Not waiting for an answer, Julius took charge.

"Right that's obviously what we were looking for. Let's get this all put back and head back to Headquarters." McGill shut and locked the writing table and Farr opened the lid of the chest. Between the three of them they shoved everything back into the chest and signalled to the storemen that they had no more need of their services or the chest. The three left the others and headed back to the car.

Farr still had the papers in his hand and split them between Julius and McGill. He reached into his pocket for his notebook and pencil, ready to receive what words of wisdom might come his way. He looked expectantly at the other two as the car set off back to Amiens.

Julius quickly scanned what he had then waited impatiently for McGill to swop papers. Once perused, they both sat and thought.

"It must be code," said Julius. McGill shrugged. " You would have to ask why he had these hidden when they appear so innocuous."

"More importantly these are obviously papers that have been given to him as they are not in his writing."

"Perhaps he was supposed to pass them along, but in that case why didn't he have them with him in the confessional? Or was he supposed to deliver them somewhere later? I don't understand what was happening here."

Julius looked out the car window as they came back into Amiens. " I'll have some of our codebreakers have a look. There must be something in them. It makes no sense otherwise."

"Yes, and if there is, which way were they supposed to be passed? To us? Or to the Germans."

" I know this isn't how we would pass information to him for onward transmission. Maybe it is innocent after all." McGill shook his head.

"I can't believe that. Let's see what your code people come up with." By now they were turning into the road behind HQ, and a few minutes later they were back inside the building. Julius went off to his office and McGill and Farr made their way back to Watkins, and told him what they had found.

"Julius is right. We never put anything in writing, it was all word of mouth. It might be something coming from the Germans, but I've never seen anything like that and as you say why wouldn't he have had it with him in the confessional? This is looking more dubious all the time."

"I agree. But I don't think we'll get anything solved tonight. Perhaps a good night's sleep will give us all a better perspective in the morning. We'll go after the French ladies in the morning too. We'll go and get something to eat then grab a lorry back to the camp. Care to join us?" Watkins shook his head.

"All this is putting my regular work far to the rear of where it should be. I better get on and see what I can catch up with."

"Suit yourself." McGill and Farr went down to the sergeant's mess and had a healthy meal with beef and suet dumplings that filled them both. No sooner had they stepped outside than a lorry with the driver shouting about going to the camp drew up. McGill and Farr jumped into the back and were soon back inside their chalet. Both fell asleep almost as soon as their heads hit the pillows.

CHAPTER THIRTEEN

The next morning the truck they hitched dropped them back at HQ. They quickly climbed the stairs to Watkins desk and there, trying to disappear, was Gunner Crowall in front of it.

"Crowie" shouted McGill happily. "How are you?" Crowall turned at the sound of McGill's voice, saw him and leapt to his feet. He rushed forward and grabbed McGill's hand.

"Inspecter! Thank the Lord yer 'ere. Honest, I never done it!" McGill roared with laughter as Watkins looked aghast.

"Crowie you've nothing to worry about. Myself and this gentleman here, Major Watkins, just want some information." Crowall stiffened and looked furtively about. He whispered urgently to McGill. "Inspecter! I can't go about tellin' tales! 'Smore 'n my life's worth!" McGill laughed again and shook his head.

Crowall looked offended. "T'aint no laughin'matter!" McGill stifled another guffaw and assumed as serious a face as he could.

"Crowie, I wouldn't for one instant ask you to betray a confidence. We're just looking for some information about No Man's Land. It's for King and Country." Crowall looked mystified, and turned his head from McGill to Watkins, who nodded back at him.

"Oh. Well. I supposes 'as 'ow that would be orright. Wadyer want ter know? And 'oos 'e?" pointing at Farr.

"That, Crowie, is my sergeant. Sergeant Farr." Crowall looked at Farr's dark and saturnine face. He muttered to himself so only McGill could hear. "Gives me the bluidy creeps!" It was all McGill could do to prevent himself from laughing again.

Watkins stood and pointed at the door near him.

"We should talk somewhere more private." Watkins led off and opened the door near his desk. Crowall looked at McGill who nodded and they all went through the door and up the stairs to the private room. Crowall wasn't overly happy but stuck close to McGill.

Once they were all in the room and seated, McGill spoke.

"Crowie, it's really good to see you again, and if you can help us with this, I'll make sure you get promoted." Watkins eyes opened wide but otherwise he didn't move a muscle.

"Suppose I wanted to get information from here, and I mean this town, to the other side of the German front line. How would I do it." Crowall looked at him as if he was mad.

"Yew jokin' Inspecter? Whatcher want ter do that fer?"

"Don't worry about that. Just tell me if it's possible and how would you do it." Crowall made a face.

"Well, for a start yew need ter get from 'ere ter our front line. 'Tent that easy."

"All right, suppose you only had to get from here to say three miles behind our lines."

"Ar well, yew'd need papers. And yew'd need ter get a train." McGill glanced at Watkins. Farr was filling his notebook with hieroglyphs.

"So who might get those papers?" Crowall thought for a minute.

"Werl, an officer I supposes. Need ter be 'igh up like ter be able ter get them." McGill couldn't see that being the solution.

"Somebody else."

"Padre," said Crowall instantly. Of course thought McGill as Watkins and Farr stiffened.

"So a Padre could get papers and go up to the front?"

"'Course. Bringin' sucker ter the troops, iny? Any time." McGill could see that Farr was thinking deeply.

"Very good Crowie that's a big help already." Crowall almost glowed with pride.

"Now, our Padre is just behind the lines bringing, as you say, succour to the troops. How does he get from there through No Man's Land and behind the German lines?"

"Why's 'e gotter do that then?"

"Because he wants to get information from here to there."

"Na, why's he gotter get to the other side of the saussge eaters's line?"

"How else would he get it into their hands?" As he said it, McGill suddenly understood what Crowall meant. "Crowie," he said excitedly, " You mean he doesn't need to go all the way across."

Crowall sniffed. "'Coursenot.'E can meetup in the middle somewhere." Watkins and Farr stirred. It was so simple.

"Right, so, he just has to get through our lines and have a set rendezvous."

"Werl, that's easy enuff. I does that every night, nearly."

"Yes but you're on our side. Our men let you through the wire."

"Wot makes yew think that? I 'as ter go all over the place. 'Harf the time they 'ent gotta clue where I's come 'n gone from." McGill sat back, stunned. He glanced at Watkins and Farr, who were equally astonished.

"Do you mean to say, no one knows where you go in and out? Don't you get challenged?"

"Huh! More 'n me lifes werf ter get challenged. Those crazy ba… crazy sojjers shoot anyfing. They don't see me, not on yer bluidy life!" McGill was silent for a moment. He knew Crowall was exceptional, but why would the other side *not* have equally exceptional people.

"Crowie, you are a marvel. Major, I want Gunner Crowall immediately made up to Corporal." Crowall glowed with self-righteous rectitude for a moment, then his face fell.

"Beggin' yer parden Inspecter, but if it's orl the same ter you, I'll just stay Gunner, if'n yew don't moind."

"But why would you do that? Don't you want promotion?"

Crowall shook his head. "Not on yer loife! Some bluidy officer – beggin' yer parden sir – will want me ter take charge o' summat. And that 'ent no good ter me!" McGill roared with laughter while Watkins looked most discomfited. Even Farr cracked a smile. McGill clapped Crowall on the shoulder.

"Crowie, let's go and get a drink!" Crowall grinned.

"Now thet's more loike it!"

McGill and Farr with Crowall sticking close to them headed for the nearest bar.

"What's your poison Crowie?"

"They got French Brandy 'ere?" McGill nodded judiciously.

"Then oil 'ave a large 'un." McGill ordered three large brandies. Once lined up on the bar, McGill raised his to Crowall.

"Crowie you have done us a good service today. Bottoms up!" McGill drank about half his glass, and put it back on the bar, as did Farr. Crowall's was already there and completely empty by the time they did so.

"Another?"

"Ooh no, no, I only ever 'as one. Yer got the toime?" McGill pulled his watch out.

"About half ten."

"Can yers get me back? I's gotta job on ternight." The three walked back to HQ and sought out Watkins, who waved a hand and two hard looking MPs appeared and stood either side of Crowall.

"Take him back," said Watkins. McGill shook hands with Crowall.

"Take care of yourself."

"Yew too inspecter." Crowall leaned in close and whispered to McGill." Don't yew tek any snash from none of them bastards." McGill looked solemn and whispered back.

"I promise I won't."

Once Crowall had been escorted off the premises, McGill, Watkins and Farr made their way back to the private room. Watkins passed his hand across his brow.

"I see why you thought he would be useful. Now we know how they were doing it."

"Yes, and more importantly we know there's another man involved who either is a priest or masquerades as one. Did you not get anything from Blythe-Hill about how he communicated with the other side?"

"He said he didn't know, he simply passed the information. We had no reason to disbelieve him." McGill sighed.

"So he could have been one of the people who were earlier at confession. Though I suppose the clever thing would be to keep the other man well-hidden and simply provided with information when the time was appropriate to move it across." They sat silent for a moment or two, then McGill got to his feet.

"Come along Don, let's go and find a little old lady."

CHAPTER FOURTEEN

It didn't take them long to find the address they wanted, and McGill plied the knocker vigorously.

The elderly lady who opened the door was clearly fearful of the two men in front of her. McGill, tall and large, Farr small and viciously dark.

"Madame, please do not be alarmed" said McGill. " We only wish to ask a few questions of Madame Houlibert."

"It is I."

" May we come in?" The old lady shuffled to one side to allow the detectives into the narrow hall. Once inside she shut the door and squeezed past McGill and opened a door to the right. The room was bright and elegantly furnished, in contrast to the darkness of the hall.

"Please, sit." McGill and Farr sat on the sofa and Farr took out his notebook.

Madame Houlibert sat in a large overstuffed armchair, complete with footstool before it. She primly drew her legs up to place her feet on the stool.

"Madame, I am Detective Inspector McGill of Scotland Yard in London. This is my Sergeant, Detective Farr." The old lady nodded in understanding.

"We understand you were in the Cathedral at the time that Monsignor Blythe-Hill was murdered." She nodded again.

" Can you tell me firstly when you arrived in the Cathedral please."

" I go to be there by half past ten in the morning."

"And how often do you go?"

"I go every day. Not to confess you understand – just to pray and feel serene."

"Serene?"

"Oui. I am as you see a nervous person. But in the Cathedral, I am not." McGill nodded.

"But on that day you went to confess?"

"Oui. I have little to say you understand, but there is always something." And she smiled a beautiful smile which lit up her face and proved how beautiful she had once been.

"Can you tell me who you saw while you were waiting for the booth to be empty and who you saw when you left." She thought for a moment.

"Bon. When I arrived there was a man – I think English – and a lady I took to be a nurse." Wilson and Anne Lincolnshire thought McGill. "I had to wait some minutes but I had my prayers and comfort to seek so I waited without any concern. After some time a young lady I know as Madamoiselle DuLacque came out and hurried away."

"You know her?"

"Ah oui. She is well known. She does not have a good reputation, but Monsieur, she is the soul of goodness." A prostitute? Thought McGill. She must be very good if this old lady thinks well of her.

"She does good works?"

"Absoluement. Not only does she give money, she works in the shelter for the needy and dispossessed. Were it not for her particular…..trade…. she would be a saint!"

"I see. Anyway, she hurried away and you went into the confessional?"

"Non. I was still praying and the Englishman and the nurse were before me. The Englishman rose and went in. I continued to pray and feel the serenity about me." McGill sat and thought for a few moments.

"So after the Englishman came out, the nurse went in?"

"Non. She was still praying. After some minutes I decided I would go, but before I could rise, a young man came quickly from the side and went straight in."

"Did you know him? If you are there often, had you seen him before?" She shook her head.

"I do not know him but I have seen him before. He always seems very nervous – no, not nervous, we say agitee."

"Agitated?"

"Oui c'est ca."

"And how long would you say he took to confess?"

"Not too long. More than five minutes less than ten."

"And when he came out – what time would that have been?" The old lady shrugged.

"Monsier L'Inspecteur when I am with my God I do not count the time!" McGill smiled at her.

"I'm sure not – but do you know for example what time you left after your confession?"

"Ah oui. It would be around eleven thirty – a little before."

"Going back a bit, so the young man had gone into the confessional and it was just you and the nurse still waiting."

"Oui. But then another, older gentleman came and sat behind me." Allain, thought McGill.

"And then, when the young man left, you went into the confessional?"

"Oui."

"And you knew the Monsignor's voice?"

"Oui. I had confessed to him before." McGill heard a small cough from Farr, and he glanced at him. Farr indicated he wanted to ask a question and McGill signalled him to do so with an imperceptible nod.

"Madame," said Farr. "Had you seen any of the people before that day? Or were there regular people you know of who confessed to the Monsignor?" The old lady thought for a moment. She shrugged.

"I know Madamoiselle DuLacque. I had seen the *agitated*" - she stressed the word, pleased with herself – "Young man. I have seen some people but none of any consequence. There was an Irishman once I think."

"What made you think he was Irish?"

"I heard him pray. It was not an English accent. It was, I think, Irish."

"Would you recognise the young man or the Irishman again?" Madame Houlibert smiled.

"I am only old monsieur. I am not senile!" McGill smiled at her.

"Indeed not Madame. If you ever see either the Irishman or the agitated young man, would you please let us know? We can be contacted though a Major Watkins at British Headquarters. And now, I think we have all we need. Thank you." Farr shut his notebook and they all stood. The detectives were politely shown out and the door was shut.

The detectives walked along the road, heading back towards Amiens HQ.

" That's her excitement for the month I would say sir. Lovely old lady though."

" I agree. So what have we learned?"

" Firstly that no one has conducted any proper interviews. No word of a Madamoiselle DuLacque or of the young agitated man. To be fair if they asked her ladyship anything she would have confirmed Blythe-Hill was still alive when she left, that no one else was there. So none of the investigators would have bothered too much about previous penitents." McGill nodded.

"Not our way, but as we have said all along nobody wants anything to do with this. We are only here so that friend Gerald's brother can be assuaged. So what else?"

"It's possible the young red-haired man is another link in the chain with O'Leary." McGill nodded.

"Yes – and that fits in with Blythe-Hill being fed the latest piece of disinformation. I expect he had set it up so that someone came to confess within an hour or two of his receiving information. It wasn't every week, but that wouldn't matter." They walked on, deep in thought.

"So we know Allain and the nurse – who we assume was Anne Lincolnshire – were the last two to see or rather hear Blythe-Hill alive." Farr nodded.

"We better go and see if Julius has managed to get anything out of those papers. I'm still not convinced, but you never know." They made their way back to HQ.

Watkins was as ever reading a file but looked up as they approached.

"Anything?" asked McGill. Watkins shook his head sadly.

"Not so far. What about you?"

"The Monsignor was almost certainly still alive up to very nearly twelve noon. On the assumption Anne Lincolnshire didn't stick a bayonet in him, someone else must have entered the confessional and somehow managed to get him close enough to the partition to be able to stick the blade through his eye."

“I still don’t see why.”

“Neither do I.”

“What’s left on the agenda for today?”

“I think the other French lady in the first instance. She was before Madame Houlibert so possibly not any help but we need to eliminate her.”

“Do you have her address? Oh, how silly of me! Of course sergeant Farr will have it!” McGill grinned.

“Every man needs his Farr!” Farr looked slightly embarrassed, but flicked his notebook open at the relevant page.

“She’s at..” he started.

“Don’t tell me!” said McGill. “We’ll just go there! But not until after lunch!” The three of them went down to the officer’s mess and ate a hearty meal. By the time they finished a messenger had arrived to take Watkins away and McGill and Farr were left to their own devices.

“Shall we go and find that other French lady then sir?” McGill thought for a moment.

“No, I don’t think we will. We’ve been given a lead from Crowie about a priest. That priest as we have already said is a definite member of this ring. We need to find him, or at least have some idea of where he might be hiding.”

“He could hide in plain sight in the Cathedral sir,”

“He could. In fact he might even *be* a priest for all we know. I think we should go back and see Monsignor Moulin. I’m not sure he will be any help but at least we might have some more information, which, at the moment, we don’t really have.” McGill stood followed by Farr and they set off for the Cathedral again.

It didn’t take them long to get there and they asked for Moulin. They were told he was on a mission for the Bishop. Somewhat non-plussed at the turn of events, the pair were standing in the centre of the nave wondering what to do next, when a young priest approached them.

“Gentlemen, you are looking lost. What can I do for you?”

“You’re English! How extraordinary!”

“Not really. I asked to be sent to France when the war started. I felt the calling to bring something positive to this whole dreadful war.”

"Well I better introduce myself. I'm Detective Inspector McGill from Scotland Yard, and this is my sergeant, Detective Farr. We're here to investigate the murder of Monsignor Blythe-Hill." The young priest didn't seem in the least surprised.

"And I am Father Philips. I know it is Monsignor Moulin who is in charge of the situation. He is, as I expect you know, away on behalf of the Bishop. But I may be able to help."

"Is there somewhere we can go to talk which is more private?" Philips pointed to one side where a door was let into the wall. Once through, they found themselves in a corridor leading down beside the main Cathedral. After ten yards or so, another door led off into a side chamber. Philips led them through, turned, and shut the door behind them.

"Well gentlemen, what would you like to know?"

McGill was silent for a moment, wondering how to approach the sensitive subject of a potential traitor.

"Father Philips, I take it you were not here in the Cathedral when the murder took place?"

"No I was on retreat. I only came back the day after the murder."

"Where was the retreat?"

"In the Pyrenees, near Lourdes. It is wonderfully calming after the madness here."

"I can imagine. We have interviewed the priests who were here, and none of them saw anything – you obviously were not here and therefore could not either. But tell me, have there been any new arrivals or departures over the last say six to eight months?"

Philips thought for a moment.

"I was the most recent arrival of a *permanent* appointment and that is more than three years ago. But we have priests coming and going all the time."

"Any that have left since the Monsignor was murdered?" There was a pause.

"Two in fact. One was very old, he had come here some six months ago to do some research in our library. He had finished his work and had been due to leave on the day he did for some time." Philips was silent for a few moments.

"The other was rather different. He was not officially a priest here in Amiens at all. He was sent here by the Curia to investigate….. certain matters." Philips paused again. "And he left the day after the murder as well. It was not a planned departure but we were told he would be returning after reporting back to Rome."

"I see. What was his name?"

"Father Plessis."

"What sort of a man was he?"

"Older than me, very fit I would say."

"Was he here all the time or did he go away from time to time?"

"He was here most of the time but he used to go away for a couple of days every couple of weeks – perhaps slightly more often." Ah thought McGill.

"And what was he investigating?" Philips hesitated.

" We were told it was in connection with some irregularities in our accounts. I was not privy to the actual investigation."

"How long was he here?"

"About eight months." McGill thought for a moment.

"Before he came, was there another similar priest here? Youngish and fit, who used to disappear from time to time?" Philips looked down at his feet, then raised his eyes and looked at McGill, with a puzzled look on his face.

"Yes. There was a priest who came from Alsace originally. God forgive me, I never liked him. He was supposed to help me, amongst others, but he was more a hindrance than a help. After a while, we just got on and did what we had to do ourselves."

"So after a while he left. Was there a gap between him leaving and Plessis arriving?"

" No. Just a week." McGill looked at Farr who had been taking notes, but looked up at the last words.

"I don't suppose there's a picture of either of them anywhere?" Philips shook his head.

"No I'm afraid not."

"Last question. Do you know how Plessis left? And if so are you sure he was going to Rome?" Philips thought for a moment.

"No. Actually, no. I have no idea how he left. I just assumed he went on the train. I can ask if anyone else knows."

"And Rome?" Philips shook his head.

"Again, he just said he had been recalled. We had no reason to doubt him."

"So in fact any information about what Father Plessis was doing was entirely from himself. Letters did not come to the Bishop for example?"

"I don't know." I bet they never did thought McGill.

"Well, Father, thank you very much. Can you give us a bit more of a description of Father Plessis?"

"Brown hair, broad shoulders, about five feet nine inches tall. Large hands I noticed. Quiet spoken. Had a strange way of moving, I'd say. Almost like gliding." McGill's brain tingled with a memory of slipping and falling about in No Man's Land in November. Of Crowie telling him to slide and glide rather than lift and lower his feet. He's our man, thought McGill. We just need to find him.

"Anything else?" Philips thought briefly and shrugged.

"Couldn't tell you his eye colour. He didn't have any scars or anything."

"Well that's all been very useful Father. Thank you."

"Any time Inspector. It makes for a little excitement."

"I don't think I'd call murder a little excitement, Father." Philips made a deprecating gesture and smiled.

"No, I meant talking to you. Our lives are very circumscribed I'm afraid." McGill nodded.

"Thank you anyway, Father."

"I'll take you back to the entrance."

McGill and Farr followed Philips back along the corridor and out into the Cathedral. Moments later they were back outside.

"Think he's our man sir?"

"Oh for sure," and McGill told Farr about being in No Man's Land with Crowie. They walked back to HQ, only to find Watkins had gone off somewhere. Morosely they made their way to the sergeant's mess and ate what was on offer. With nothing else to do, they had a whisky each then took a truck back to the camp.

CHAPTER FIFTEEN

McGill woke with a start. He scrambled for his watch and struck a match to see the time. It was just before 5am on the morning of 21st March. Something had disturbed him. He strained his ears and thought he could hear guns rumbling. The match guttered out and he lay back, still craving sleep. After a few minutes he threw back the covers and swung his legs over the side of the cot. He shook his head. Farr was still asleep on the other side of the room. Nothing seems to disturb him, thought McGill.

He listened intently and could just make out the sounds of the artillery. It seemed worse than usual, but he decided to ignore it.

He dressed quietly, then opened the door carefully and stepped out into the grey and overcast morning. The rumble was louder now, and he looked automatically to the East. He could see a continuous glow, jagged and unbroken, stretching right across the horizon. As he stood watching the display, other doors in the compound opened. Men stumbled out of their huts, pulling up their braces and looking East. My God, thought McGill. It looks like hell.

He made his way to the mess and joined a line of men waiting patiently for sustenance. His trusty mug full of hot sweet tea, he looked for a place to sit. Finding none he went back outside to watch the show.

Men around him were talking quietly to each other, their eyes never leaving the fiery bank that never waned or wavered.

A Sergeant beside him pointed East. In a dull, resigned voice, he said "That's a major battle starting." Men had now begun going about their normal business of the day, but McGill stood and watched.

Quite suddenly, a gap appeared in the inferno. McGill couldn't judge how big it was, but it was significant enough that there were now two quite distinct lines, bursting and cavorting along the horizon. He wondered the significance.

An hour later, Farr appeared at his side, and nodded at the blaze of fire. "Theirs or ours sir?"

" Must be theirs. We'd have known if we were about to mount an attack."

" Is that going to affect our investigation sir?"

"I doubt it. Unless the Hun achieves a break through."

Suddenly there were shouts and stamping boots around them. Loud voiced Sergeants and burly soldiers cajoled and pushed the men standing around back into their platoon positions. McGill caught the arm of a Captain.

"What's going on?"

"We don't know, but that's not an every-day morning barrage. We've had orders to cancel all leave and prepare to move towards the front."

"So it's a major attack?"

"Looks like it." The Captain paused a moment. " What do you make of that gap in the line?"

"I was about to ask you the same question! Any ideas?" The Captain shrugged. "The only thing I can think of is that they are moving men up in that gap."

McGill suddenly remembered what Haig had said. If he was right, the Germans would be pushing overwhelming numbers of men through the gap and then breaking left and right to cut off the British. They would have no option but to retreat or surrender. McGill glanced at Farr, who was transfixed by the sight.

"What do we do now sir?"

" I suppose we had better keep after the people we haven't seen yet. Who is next on the list?"

Farr consulted his notebook. " A man called Allain. Lives a bit further out, according to the information we've been given. We'll need some transport I think sir. We'd better go to the regimental guardhouse and see what they can do for us."

The pair turned and headed for a larger building about 400 yards from where they had been standing. As they passed by other huts and soldiers drawn up in ranks, McGill marvelled at the fact that thousands and thousands of men were being fed and moved around apparently with ease. They stepped up onto the duckboards at the HQ building, and climbed the three steps to the main door. It stood open with junior officers and NCOs coming and going, and McGill and Farr had to join the queue that was entering the building. Inside, two Sergeants were taking names and handing out orders from a box that stood between them. McGill saw a Major standing to one side looking on, and approached him.

"Good morning Major. I'm.."

"I know who you are." The voice was clipped and frosty. "Why are you here?" Taken aback by the brusqueness, McGill hardened his face.

"I need transport out to Avenue des Deux Temples. Anything going that way will be fine, if we can hitch a lift."

The Major snorted. "There's a flap on and we need all the transport we can get. But give me ten minutes and I'll see what I can do." The Major turned away and went through a door to the back of the building. There were no seats available and McGill and Farr stood against the wall, watching the press of soldiers moving in and out.

The Major reappeared soon enough clutching a piece of paper. He handed it to McGill.

"This is a movement warrant for the two of you. There's a truck going out in the direction you need. I'll send a man with you to show you where the truck is. But you'll have to make your own way back." The Major pointed at a soldier on the other side of the room. "Show him that order and he'll take you to the truck."

"Thank you." The Major acknowledged the thanks then turned away to attend to a messenger who had just arrived. A small bag of letters and papers was handed over, and the Major loosened the string that held it closed. The messenger stayed standing in front of the Major, who was going through the contents.

McGill and Farr had crossed the floor to the soldier the Major had indicated, and McGill passed the paper to him. He glanced at it.

"This way sir," and he headed out the door, closely followed by the detectives. Neither of them wanted to get separated in the throngs of men.

Back in the building the Major continued to sort through the packet. At one of the last letters he paused, then reread who it was addressed to. He turned it over, read the senders name, then strode to the door. He looked out over the scurrying troops and sighed.

"Not going to catch up with him through this lot. It'll have to wait until he gets back." And he stuck the letter from Scotland Yard in his pocket.

By then McGill and Farr had reached the lorry they were to hitch a lift with. Their guide spoke to the driver, who indicated the detectives should join him upfront. No sooner were they settled than the driver let the clutch in and they carefully drove out towards the main gate. Once on the road they were unable to travel much faster as long lines of troops were marching and countermarching, impeding progress.

After a while, as they made their way, a memory stirred in McGill. " I think I know this road" he said to Farr.

"Really sir? Were you out this way when you were here before?"

"I think so. I recuperated from Trench Fever somewhere nearby." Farr said nothing, but McGill's eyes darted everywhere, a growing realisation that they were near the house where Isabelle de Bonnefoix lived. " I walked along here with her!" he said excitedly.

"Who's that sir?"

"Isabelle! Isabelle de Bonnefoix! She looked after me." Farr said nothing but looked towards the grand houses they were passing, careful not to mention McGill's enthusiasm. Not a bad place to be ill, thought Farr.

"Stop!" said McGill. The truck screeched to a stop and McGill leapt out and ran towards the house. Farr spoke to the driver. "Are we near Avenue des Deux Temples?"

"Just round the corner sir." Farr slid along the bench and dropped to the ground. He slammed the door and waved. The driver accelerated away.

McGill was already at the front door hammering at it. Farr followed in his footsteps to the house.

"Open up!" shouted McGill. The door was jerked open by a man with one arm. To one side of him stood another one armed man holding a cudgel. The two men's eyes widened then they smiled.

"Monsieur McGill!"

"Rene! How wonderful."

Hovering behind was the maid, Marie, who rushed forward and threw her arms around McGill, tears streaming down her face.

" Monsieur monsieur! You came! I could kiss you!" So she did.

Farr's eyes were open wide as he took in the scene. He thought a lot of his superior, but was taken aback by the joy with which McGill was greeted.

Marie was clutching McGill's hand, tugging him towards where McGill knew Isabelle's study was. As they approached, it opened. Isabelle stood there rooted to the spot. McGill took in her loveliness, then stepped forward and hugged her.

"My Alan, you came! Oh my darling, I feared you would not!"

CHAPTER SIXTEEN

Farr was astonished. He had never thought of McGill as an emotional man, but he was clearly very moved by the reunion. Farr wondered what the "You came!" meant. Marie was still in floods of tears and the butler and footman were beaming happily. Farr took in the fact that each man had one arm, one a left arm the other a right arm. He wondered about the story behind that, and he tried to think what he should do. He looked from one to the other, until Marie seemed to pull herself together, and started to usher him away, followed by the two one armed men. Glancing back towards Isabelle and McGill, she took them through a door and downstairs into the kitchen, wiping her eyes but clearly full of joy.

" Eh bien!" She sniffed." Monsieur I am sure a cup of tea will be good!" And she set to work.

Upstairs, McGill and Isabelle clung together silently.

" I didn't think you wanted me," said McGill. " You had Marie tell me to leave."

Isabelle drew back to look at him, curiously.

"How did you manage to get here? It must have been difficult."

" No no, we got a lift in a truck from Amiens. We were going to interview a suspect nearby. And then I saw your house and had to see you."

Isabelle's face took on a puzzled frown.

"You didn't know where to come?"

"No, how could I?"

"And you are here as a detective again?" McGill realised Isabelle was looking perplexed.

"Yes. The murder of the Monsignor in the Cathedral." Isabelle pushed herself away from McGill.

" So you did not come for me?" she said frostily. It was McGill's turn to be confused.

"Well I did as soon as I saw the house."

"Only that? Not what was in the letter?" McGill didn't understand what Isabelle was saying.

" What letter?" Isabelle stared at him.

"What letter? What letter? The letter I sent you!"

" I've had no letter." They looked at each other, realisation dawning on both of them.

"You never received my letter?"

"Isabelle, I swear to you, I have received no letter. What did it say? Did you ask me to come?" She looked at him for a moment more, then burst out laughing and launched herself into McGill's arms again. McGill felt even more confused, but hugged her anyway.

"Oh Cheri, then chance has played a great game. Let us sit and I will tell you all."

Downstairs, Farr was being plied with tea and cake, while all three of the members of the household talked nineteen to the dozen, mostly in French so that he understood nothing. Marie translated some of it, but Farr could get the general gist of the excitement and happiness that all of them were showing.

Finally, Farr managed to get a word in.

"So this is where the Inspector recuperated?"

" Ah oui," said Marie. "We all loved 'im from the moment Madame brought 'im home so ill and weak. But, ma foi, what a beautiful figure! And so 'andsome too!"

"Well you all certainly appear to have enjoyed his company – especially Madame!"

Marie looked at him slightly sideways.

"'E 'as told you nozzing?"

Farr looked puzzled – at least in so far that he could. "No,what was there to tell?" Marie looked astonished.

"Nozzing? Nozzing from ze letter?" Farr looked even more puzzled.

"What letter?"

"Ze Inspecteur, 'e receive no letter from Madame?"

"Not that I know off." Marie slapped her thighs then clasped her hands to either side of her face.

"Oh, mon Dieu. I hope zis will be all right! Come wiz me – quickly!" Farr stood as Marie headed up the stairs and followed her.

Upstairs, McGill and Isabelle were sitting side by side in her study, each holding both hands.

They gazed into each other's eyes for a short while. Then Isabelle sighed.

" Mon Cheri, you cannot know how wonderful it is to see you again. I have thought of you so much since that day I had Marie send you away. I was wrong. I should have tried to hold you."

"Darling Isabelle, I ..." She held up her hand.

"Un moment. I have words I must say. When you have heard them, if you wish to leave then you must." Puzzled, McGill started to speak again but Isabelle cut him off, a look of uncertainty and fear on her face.

"Non – listen! I wrote to you because I needed to tell you what had happened. I could not let myself keep silent. I needed to let you know that I was carrying your child, that I did not expect you to do anything, but you had a right to know..." McGIll leapt to his feet.

"A child? My child? You are pregnant?" Isabelle smiled.

"That is what it usually means..."

"You are carrying *our* child?"

Isabelle lowered her eyes as she saw the wonder on McGill's face and smiled inwardly. It would be all right.

"Oui," she said quietly. McGill sat down again like a sack of potatoes, and took Isabelle's hands in his once more. He gazed into her eyes for a moment, then dropped to one knee in front of her.

"Isabelle, will you..."

"Non non, you don't have to, I only wanted that you should know." He leapt to his feet again.

"For God's sake Isabelle, don't you know I love you and want to be with you forever? You've appeared in my head a hundred times in the last few months. Can't you tell I love you?" She looked at him carefully.

"I can" she said gravely. Then burst into tears as McGill smothered her with kisses, and they laughed and laughed. McGill pulled her to her feet, and swung her round, as Isabelle shrieked and chided him, and McGill crowed "She loves me! She loves me!" All of a sudden McGill stopped and made Isabelle sit down.

"Darling you must take care of yourself," he said gravely. " I understand ladies with child must be very calm and serene." Isabelle laughed at McGill's manly stereotype, and stroked his face.

"Mon cher, I am well and strong. And yes, I do love you." McGill kissed her tenderly, and Isabelle sighed with joy.

Outside the study, Farr and Marie were listening to every word. As the last words were spoken Marie punched Farr hard on the shoulder in glee. Farr wasn't sure how to react, but he smiled and allowed himself to be hugged by Marie. I could get to like France he thought.

" Eet is fine," she whispered,nodding. "Zere will be a new master in zis 'ouse, and a new babee!" Good God, thought Farr. Who'd have guessed? Whatever would the Super say?

CHAPTER SEVENTEEN

Whilst McGill and Isabelle gazed into each other's eyes, and talked quietly of all that had happened since they had parted, Farr was taken back to the kitchen by Marie. He had a hundred questions, which he started to ask and which Marie answered happily. He learned all about McGill being picked up off the street and brought back to recover. How tenderness had grown between the two. How – and here Marie became a little vague – McGill said he was leaving next day, and, well, he had done. She, Marie, had been instructed to send him on his way.

"And HE,"she said waving her hands," Pouf, imbecile, he leave! Mon Dieu, could he not see? Ah!"

Farr was working things out in his head.

"So that was when the baby…"

"Oui oui," said Marie impatiently, reddening somewhat. "I sink Madame mean it to happen. The old master –pah! Degeuelasse! No love, no joy. But Monsieur L'Inspecteur – oof!" and she shook her hand in the universal sign for something special.

Farr had never seen McGill in that light, but supposed these things happened. He was a good boss, for sure, and a man's man, but he was also clearly loved by this entire household. Whatever would the Super say, thought Farr again.

Upstairs, the lovers had fallen silent, Isabelle overjoyed by the fact that her child – *their* child – would have its father. McGill was simply overwhelmed with joy. He decided he must be in shock, or dreaming. Within a few short months he had risen from being a mere Constable – and pretty miserable at that - to being a deliriously happy Inspector with a wife and child.

"Isabelle, we will have to go. I am investigating the murder of Monsignor Blythe-Hill, and I …" Isabelle placed her finger over McGill's lips.

"I know you must leave. But you must promise to come back."

For answer, McGill folded her in his arms and murmured "With all my heart."

Downstairs Marie decided that food was required. She started banging pots and pans onto the range and rushing in and out of the cold larder bringing various plates and dishes. Farr had never seen so many different meats and cheeses. He offered to help but Marie said Rene would help. By the time she had finished there where more than twenty different things to eat, and a huge pot of soup was beginning to simmer. Marie jabbered at Rene who nodded and made his way upstairs. Politely, he listened at the door of Isabelle's study, and hearing low murmurs tapped gently to attract attention. He heard Isabelle's "Entrez!" and opened the door.

Two pairs of shining eyes glanced at him, a quizzical look on both faces.

"Oui?" said Isabelle.

Rene rattled off about lunch being ready in half an hour, bowed and quietly withdrew. Isabelle and McGill continued to sit gazing at each other, and McGill shyly stretched out a hand and placed it on Isabelle's stomach. In time honoured fashion, Isabelle placed her hand on top of McGill's and smiled happily.

Lunch was a strangely quiet yet happy occasion. They all ate in the kitchen with Marie and the two one armed men at one end of the large table and Isabelle McGill and Farr at the other.

McGill had had Marie's offerings before but Farr's eyes were out on stalks at the variety and quantity of food on offer. And the taste!

Marie watched as Farr tried first one dish, then another, then ate some more bread, all with what passed for a look of satisfaction on his face.

" Do you like my food, monsieur?" she asked with a small smile of expectancy on her face. Farr swallowed his latest mouthful, nodding and cleared his throat.

"I do! It is all delicious. My compliments." Marie's face broke into a smile as did those of the others round the table.

"Marie is a marvel," said McGill. " When I was here before I'm sure it was her food that brought me through."

"And not Madame's nursing?," asked Marie mischievously.

" Um well, of *course*," said McGill, reddening slightly. And the ladies laughed happily. Isabelle reached her hand out under the table and squeezed McGill's knee, causing him to jump a little, and redden further.

The detectives and Isabelle sat on for a bit after the meal was finished, Marie bustling about her kitchen tidying up and the other men disappearing to their usual work.

"Isabelle, Sergeant Farr and I must go. We have a suspect to interview nearby."

"Bon. When you return we can make some arrangements. But for now, bon chance!"

They rose from the table and made their way up the stairs to the hall. Farr opened the door and stepped out to give McGill and Isabelle a moment together.

"Take care my darling. We won't be long." Isabelle melted into McGill's arms and kissed him gently. There were tears in her eyes. McGill saw them and he held her face in his hands. "What is the matter?" Isabelle smiled and shook her head.

"I am just a woman in love." And she kissed him harder, then pushed him away and waved her hand. "Go!" Reluctantly, McGill turned and closed the door behind him. The detectives walked up the pathway in silence, and Farr eventually cleared his throat.

"Well, sir, quite a turn up for the books."

"Yes. Yes it is. I wonder what the Super will say?" And Farr laughed and laughed as McGill wondered what was so funny.

CHAPTER EIGHTEEN

"Have you any idea where this road we want is?" asked McGill.

"The driver said it was just round the corner, so I assume it's at the next crossroads."

They made their way further along the road that Isabelle lived on, and some hundred yards away they could see a road cutting across their path. Farr nodded towards it, and the pair quickened their pace. Once at the corner they looked in both directions, and Farr consulted his notebook.

"Number 126." They looked at the numbers and set off to the right. The numbers were declining and after about 20 houses they came to number 126. It was another grand house, not as well maintained as Isabelle's, but solid and dependable looking. They made their way to the front door and McGill used the knocker to make their presence known. After a few moments the door was opened by a maid who could not have been much more than a child. She eyed the detectives without enthusiasm.

"Oui?" McGill wished he could speak French but said "Monsieur Allain see vous play." The girl turned to allow them access and shut the door behind them.

"Suivez-moi." Oh Lord, thought McGill, what if he doesn't speak English?

The girl took them towards the back of the house and knocked on a door beside the staircase. "Entrez," came from inside. The girl opened the door and spoke rapidly in French to an elderly white-haired gentleman who was sitting reading a newspaper. He lowered it and looked enquiringly at the detectives. The girl left and Allain folded the paper and stood.

" Messieurs?" he asked.

McGill drew a breath and launched himself verbally. "Monsieur Allain, I am Detective Inspector McGill from Scotland Yard in London and this is Detective Sergeant Farr. We are here to talk to you about the murder of Monsignor Blythe-Hill in the Cathedral." For a moment there was no response and McGill feared the worst. Then Allain smiled slightly.

"You may be calm, messieurs. I speak some English!" McGill sighed.

"Thank you very much!"

"Please, sit," and he indicated a couple of well-padded armchairs, placed so as to look across the garden. He pointed towards it.

"Helas, there is no one much to help now, but it was magnifique."

" I'm sure it was sir. I assume you have lived here a long time." Allain nodded.

"This was the 'ouse of my father and my gran'father before 'im, so yes. What can I tell you? I had les Gendarmes here before."

"It's very good of you to see us like this, sir. As I said we are trying to find the murderer of Monsignor Blythe-Hill. As you say, you were interviewed by the French police, but as the Monsignor was English, it was felt that it should be investigated by the British Police." Allain shrugged, but said nothing.

" So please, Monsieur Allain, just to confirm, at what time did you enter the Cathedral?" Allain thought for a moment.

" It would be about eleven o'clock. It is my way to be there for that time. It enables me to make my confession, then to meet a friend or two for le dejeuner – the lunch." McGill could see Farr scribbling in his notebook.

"And when you went into the Cathedral, was there anyone you particularly noticed? I take it you go there on a regular basis?"

"Oui oui, every week. Helas, I have so little to confess now." Allain smiled wistfully. " There were very few people there. I noticed two ladies, one who looked as if she was a nurse, and another, much older woman. They were waiting for the confessional to be empty." A nurse, thought McGill. That would have been Anne.

"So you did not know who the priest was that was taking confession?"

"Non. I did not see him." McGill thought for a moment.

"So the two ladies confessed first and then you followed?"

"Non. The older lady went in when it became empty. The nurse made no move to take her place when she came out, so I went in."

"Do you have any idea when that would be?"

Allain shrugged. "Huh! I cannot be sure – I was not watching the clock, you know! But wait, I remember thinking it was lucky the nurse had not wanted to confess, because if she had, I might have been late for my lunch!"

"So it might have been eleven twenty or so, would you say?" Allian nodded.

"Oui, it could be. Certainly not later."

"And tell me, your confession. From what you said before it would not take long?" Allain smiled.

"Sadly, non. And my penance – pfft. Three Hail Marys!"

"And where did you do this penance?"

"I returned to the place I had been sitting before. I was quickly done, then I left. My lunch awaited!" McGill smiled.

"Yes I can see that. So the only person still there when you went for lunch was the nurse? And she made no move to enter the confessional?"

"Non non, when I left she was still praying!" Farr looked up and glanced at McGill. Yes, thought McGill, a long time to be praying on one's knees.

"And what time would you say you actually left?" Allain thought briefly.

"I was a little early for my lunch, and it is a ten minute walk to the restaurant, so no later than eleven thirty."

"And you saw no one else? No priest, no man or woman?" Allain looked surprised.

"A priest? Mais non. I know them well, and would have spoken with them. There was only the nurse when I left."

"So the nurse was the only person still in the Cathedral?" Allain shrugged again.

"There would have been others elsewhere I suppose, but in the area where I was, non, she was the only one."

"And I have to ask – you clearly were able to confess and were given penance? While you were waiting and while you were doing your penance, you saw no one enter the area, or the confessional?"

Allain shook his head. "Non – absoluement. I knew the Monsignor, I recognised his voice. When I left he was for sure alive." McGill sighed. There was nothing helpful here.

"Monsieur Allain, I thank you for your time. I doubt we will be visiting you again." Allain stood as McGill and Farr did the same.

As they reached the door, McGill suddenly stopped.

" The person who was the first person in the confessional when you went in – who was followed by the older lady. Was that a man or a woman?"

"Ah yes, a man, but young. Not a soldier, but dressed as though for business." McGill turned to Farr.

" There's nothing on him, is there?"

" No sir. He's not on the list we have."

"Monsieur Allain, could you describe him?"

"Huh! Young as I say, reddish hair. And he had a black band on his left arm."

"Not much to go on sir, and he was clearly gone before the murder."

McGill looked at Farr, then turned back to Allain.

"Monsieur thank you again. We will leave."

"Do you not wish his name?" McGill and Farr stood stock still.

"His name? You know his name?"

"Mais oui! It is Monsieur Merry. He is an English doctor." Good God thought McGill. We nearly missed that completely.

Allain took them to the front door and showed them out.

As the detectives made their way back to the main road, McGill wondered about Merry. Why had there been no mention of him? Presumably the Church authorities and the French Police had been lax and never queried whether there was anyone else in the Cathedral. They would have concentrated on who was actually there at the time of the murder, not on who was there before. But even so, Merry would have to be found and interviewed. Farr was right, he was gone before the murder. Even so.

CHAPTER NINETEEN

They made their way back onto Isabelle's road and back to her house. They were quickly admitted. It was as if they were being watched for. Isabelle took McGill into her study and Marie led Farr downstairs and plied him with tea and cakes. I could definitely get used to this, he thought.

McGill explained all about the case and how they would have to return to the centre of Amiens. Isabelle made McGill promise again that he would return and kissed him to seal the bargain. Reluctantly, McGill called down to Farr, who was also reluctant to leave. If I didn't know better, thought McGill, I'd say Madamoiselle Marie has an admirer.

With promises to return when they could, the two detectives set off on the road back to Amiens. No sooner had they covered fifty yards than an army truck swung round the corner and bore down on them. Farr stepped out into the road, hand held high to stop the vehicle. With a squeal of brakes, the driver pulled up, and leaned out of the cab.

" What you want then?"

"We need a lift back into the centre" said Farr.

"'Op in then." Farr and McGill climbed in beside the driver who immediately let out the clutch and moved off. McGill looked back at Isabelle's house to catch a glimpse of the mother of his child. There was no one to be seen. He pondered briefly about the letter but dismissed it. In times of war and disruption one letter going missing was hardly surprising.

By the time the centre of Amiens was once more in their sights, the shadows of a gloomy evening were already lengthening. Farr thanked the driver who waved a lazy salute and drove off. McGill and Farr stood for a moment, and McGill's ears picked up the continuing rumble of the heavy artillery. It was nowhere near as heavy as it had been in the morning but was it louder? Must be the wind direction he thought. They made their way towards HQ and quickly gained access. Asking for Major Watkins they were taken to him. He was sitting on the edge of his desk, hands either side, staring at the floor. McGill felt and sensed there was a tenseness and somewhat subdued atmosphere. Watkins looked up as McGill and Farr approached.

"Good afternoon. Anything to report? Julius is due here shortly." McGill shook his head.

"Nothing significant. It's pretty certain a nurse, who we assume is Anne Lincolnshire, would have been the last person to see him."

"And what do you make of that?" McGill shrugged.

"Nothing much. What she told us would seem to indicate that another person entered the Cathedral after she left. No one so far has mentioned seeing anyone else about. There was one thing though – a young man called Merry, a doctor, who left some time before, but who isn't on our list and is mentioned nowhere. We need to find him." Watkins stood and passed his hands across his eyes.

"Leave it to me. I've got other things to think about I'm afraid. It looks as if the Hun may have broken through part of the line." McGill started.

"The big push?" Watkins nodded.

"Very definitely. They attacked this morning on a very short line and literally smashed everything in front of them. Men are being pulled out of one part of the line and rushed towards the salient but the fighting is intense."

"Will it hold?"

"I don't know." McGill thought of what Haig had told him. It certainly looked as if the Huns were getting the luck with things going their way. And then he thought – and what would victory for them be? Getting to Paris? How would that be the end? Surely the fighting would just continue until one side or the other literally could not go on? It was a vicious, self-perpetuating circle.

"We don't know how far they have advanced. It's pretty confused as you would expect. But if they get through our rearmost defensive positions, IF they get through them, there's not much between them and us." There was silence for a moment. Watkins shook himself.

"Merry you say? A doctor? Anything else."

"Reddish hair and a black armband," said Farr. Watkins stared at him and sighed. Raising his voice he shouted "Sergeant!"

"Sir"

"Freeman, find out where a doctor by the name of Merry is working could you? These gentlemen wish to interview him"

"Do you want me to have him picked up sir?"

"No no," said McGill ." If you could just locate him and we'll do the rest."

Saluting smartly, Freeman about faced and headed out of the room. Watkins sighed again and waved a hand.

"You better go and get a bite to eat. This could be a very long night. I'll send Freeman to you when he gets the information." McGill nodded and he and Farr left Watkins who had returned to staring vacantly at the floor.

They headed silently for the Sergeant's mess. McGill remembered the times he had been left waiting there before, waiting for information or for a particular person to appear. They got tea and a sandwich then sat at one of the long trestle tables that were less crowded than McGill remembered them.

"Bit of a turn up," said Farr.

"Yes. Whether or not Blythe-Hill was killed by a German may shortly have no significance," said McGill morosely. They munched in silence for a few moments.

"So what do you think Merry knows?"

" Can't see it can be anything but…" McGill stopped with his sandwich half way to his mouth. "Wait a minute. What time did Watkins say the information had been passed? Nine o'clock?" Farr nodded. "So someone went to confession at nine to give it to him and sometime after that someone turns up to get the information *from* Blythe-Hill. I wonder.."

" Are you thinking Merry sir?"

"I am. We can be pretty sure it wasn't any of the people mentioned by Allain – the old lady and Anne it would not be. So it had to be someone who was there before, and who did his best not to be remembered as sitting about. Hence practically forgotten. And we've pretty much eliminated everyone else for the murder, and none of them struck me as spies. The only one we haven't seen or heard about is Merry."

"Sir, should we be looking at that? Is it not the murder we need information on?"

"Yes, yes it is, but Merry could be the link. We know he couldn't have killed Blythe-Hill, unless he sneaked back. That's always possible, I suppose. It's much more likely he has something to do with O'Leary and the ring. We have to rule him out anyway, so if we can get anything of any use to Watkins then we should."

CHAPTER TWENTY

Freeman stood in the doorway of the sergeant's mess. McGill and Farr were easily spotted as they were the only people not in uniform. He strode through the room. Farr saw him first.

"Sir." McGill looked up and Farr nodded in Freeman's direction. McGill turned round just as he arrived at the table.

"Found your man sir. He works in the hospital at Rue St. Leu."

"Thank you sergeant. We're on our way." McGill and Farr both took final gulps of their tea, and stood up.

"It's a bit of a walk sir, about twenty minutes from here."

"Any chance of a lift?"

"Doubt it sir. There's a real flap on." McGill sighed.

"Oh well, a walk will do us good as the saying goes. Have you directions?"

Freeman unbuttoned his breast pocket and took out a piece of paper. On it was written the address and rough directions of how to get there. McGill and Farr strode off doing their best to keep to the directions. It wasn't always easy as they were frequently stopped and asked to "go round."

It took longer than expected but eventually they reached Rue St. Leu. The old building looked depressed. There were stretchers being taken in and bandaged soldiers coming out. McGill and Farr dodged between the scurrying porters and got as far as a desk manned – it was the only appropriate word - by a formidable looking nun. Before McGill could even speak she had risen to her feet and pointed towards the doorway. She let forth a stream of French which neither of the detectives understood. Her meaning was clear though.

" I'm sorry," said McGill in a loud voice. "I don't speak French. I'm looking for a Doctor Merry." The nun rocked back on her heels. She shook her head.

"Merry? Non." She sat down and continued to speak to other people.

McGill placed himself squarely in front of the desk.

"Sister, if you don't help us I will have you arrested!" The nun looked at McGill with loathing, and reiterated " Non." McGill reached into his back pocket and withdrew a pair of handcuffs. There was sudden silence in the hallway. Farr turned to see what was behind them. There was a solid phalanx of men, doctors and patients alike.

"Sir" McGill glanced behind and fixed the nun with a severe look.

" I only want Doctor Merry," he said in a loud voice.

One of the doctors took a step forward.

"Monsieur may I assist?" McGill and Farr turned to see an elderly man in a white coat with a stethoscope around his neck.

" We are looking for Doctor Merry." The man shook his head.

" I regret 'e is not 'ere. 'E told us 'e 'ad been transfert. Most inconvenient."

"He's left? Where has he gone?" The doctor shrugged.

"When did he go?"

" Ce matin"

"This morning? Today?"

"Oui"

"Where does he live?" The doctor took a pad from his pocket and scribbled on it. He tore off the sheet and handed it to McGill.

"Is that near here?"

"Go left, then two streets." McGill and Farr strode through the people standing watching them and headed off in the direction indicated. Within ten minutes they were in front of the house which was where Merry lived. There was a middle-aged woman coming out of the house, wrapped in a nondescript shawl.

McGill stepped forward. "Madame – excuse me. I am Inspector McGill. We are looking for Doctor Merry."

The woman shrugged. "Il n'est pas la."

"Not here – pas la?"

"Non"

"May we see his room?"

"Quoi?" McGill sought a word in his head.

"Chambre?" The woman waved her hand and said "Pfft" before walking off leaving the front door open. Stepping inside, McGill and Farr found themselves in a building that clearly housed a number of people. There were coats and hats hanging in the hall and a row of keys dangling from a board, numbered one to six.

"I'll take one two and three " said McGill. "You take the others Don. Sing out if you find Merry's" Farr collected his three keys and set off up the stairs. McGill looked about. Room one was on the ground floor. He collected the key and unlocked the door. Inside the room was what he would expect from a young man. Clothes were scattered about, and some papers on a table by the window. McGill sifted through them. It was definitely not Merry's room.

He relocked the door and collected keys two and three, and started to climb the stairs. Half way up he heard a shout from Farr, so he skipped past the first landing that had rooms two and three to find Farr on the second landing with room four lying open.

"This was his sir,"said Farr. "There was a letter addressed to him at the back of one of the drawers." McGill took the letter while Farr continued to open and shut doors and drawers. McGill glanced about. Merry had clearly left in a hurry, but most of his kit had been removed. There were some unwashed clothes in a pile in the corner, but all the clean clothes were gone. McGill looked at the envelope. It was addressed as Farr had said to Merry. It had been crumpled up and then clearly stuffed away in the drawer. He took the letter out, unfolded it and began to read.

" The Rectory
Deeping St.Mary
Lincolnshire
1st November 1917

Julian,
I hope this letter finds you well. It doesn't sound as if you will be home any time soon. I do hope you have not been too shocked by the atrocities committed by the Hun. I know you

had wonderful memories of your time In Germany before the war, but you *must* see all that will have changed. This is no time for forgiveness, and that is a terrible thing for a Minister of God to say. As you know I have never liked the Germans, and was hurt and sad when you went off to Heidelberg all those years ago. The Kaiser is a preening, arrogant bully who must be brought to heel. Your admiration for German mores and works is much misplaced. I'm sure by now you will have learned appearances are deceptive. I'm certain some of your friends from those days are amongst those raping and killing Belgian nuns. May God bless you and keep you safe. Your mother joins me in wishing you well in your chosen profession. Your Father Tobias Merry"

Well, thought McGill. Not a very loving epistle. Now we know. Young Merry hated what his father felt. He went to Germany to defy him and probably ended up being seduced by all that was good there. I suppose to many people Germany appeared strong and great as we appeared to falter. McGill shook his head. There are many in our land who wish us to fall.

Farr had finished checking the room and turned to McGill.

"Interesting letter sir?"

"Very. Our young man had clearly been turned towards Germany by the antipathy shown by his father – a clergyman no less, with no Christian charity for the Germans. Unless I'm much mistaken Merry was an easy win for the other side. Being a doctor will have made him an easy touch for the likes of Blythe-Hill, who by all accounts could charm anyone. It wouldn't take a lot of persuasion to start running the odd innocent errand, graduating to more dangerous and traitorous acts. He clearly disliked the letter and shoved it to the back of that drawer. When he left today, he had probably forgotten about it. "

" So Blythe-Hill was giving him information which somehow Merry then got back to the Germans." McGill nodded.

"Exactly. I don't know about you but all this is making me feel sick."

"I agree sir. Treason is a very dirty word."

"At least Watkins will be pleased to know of another member of the ring."

"But why didn't he already? Did Blythe-Hill not tell him?"

" I regret to say that I don't think he did." The detectives looked glumly at each other.

"So Blythe-Hill really was a traitor," said Farr quietly.

"Yes – along with Merry. We better head back to camp and get some sleep."

CHAPTER TWENTY ONE

The next morning it was more out of a sense of duty than in the hopes of getting any more useful information that McGill and Farr made their way to the house of Madamoiselle DuLacque. A smartly dressed maid – the classic French maid – answered the door and, once McGill had introduced themselves, showed them into a sumptuous drawing room, heavily laden with silk and brocade. The detectives remained standing and a few minutes later an extremely attractive woman, beautifully dressed in a luxurious, smart style entered the room. She crossed the floor and held her hand out to McGill.

" I am Francine DuLacque." McGill shook her hand. Francine sat down and indicated the detectives should do the same. Once seated – and with Farr ready with his notebook – McGill leaned forward.

"Madamoiselle, thank you for seeing us. As I'm sure you must know we have been asked to look into the murder of Monsignor Blythe-Hill. You were one of the last people to see him alive." Francine nodded gravely.

"Yes I believe so. When I left he was alive." McGill nodded.

"We are aware of that. At least two people heard him after you left – and the murderer as well, we assume. I wanted to ask you about anyone you saw while you were waiting to confess and when you left. What time did you arrive at the Cathedral?" Francine thought for a moment.

"It would have been some time after ten o'clock - there were quite a number of people praying, so I took my place and waited."

"When you entered the confessional, how many people were still waiting?"

" A gentleman and Madame Houlibert, as well as a lady I took to be a nurse." So far so good, thought McGill.

"So Madame Houlibert came in after you? We have spoken to her already."

Francine nodded. " Yes I saw her arrive just after ten thirty."

"How do you know that was the time?" Francine smiled.

"Because that is her time, every day!"

"Might it not have been different that day?"

"Non," Francine answered shortly.

"Very well. So people ahead of you confessed and then you were next in the queue. Who was the last person before you?"

"I do not know. It was an elderly lady with a shawl over her head. She hurried away as soon as she came out. Usually people do their penance first, but she did not." Farr flicked back some pages in his notebook. There was no mention of such a lady. He sighed inwardly. No one wanted any involvement that was for sure.

"So this lady left and then you went to confess. I take it you knew the Monsignor's voice."

"Oh yes, I go every week to him."

"Excuse me for asking, but I take it he absolved you?" Francine smiled bitterly.

"Oh yes. He is harsh, which is good for my soul."

"And did you do your penance in the Cathedral?"

"Non, it is not a simple thing, my penances. It goes over the week until I see him again."

"So you hurried away? Like the other lady?"

"I did. I do not think she would have had as much to confess as myself." McGill thought for a moment.

"Do you know who entered the confessional after you?" Francine shrugged.

"I do not."

"Did you see anyone else coming towards the area where the confessional was as you were leaving?"

" Not exactly coming towards it, but nearby. As I left there was a young man with red hair beside one of the columns."

"And he was standing to one side as though waiting?"

Francine thought for a moment. "Yes, though I think he had just lit a candle."

McGill glanced at Farr who imperceptibly shrugged. A moment later, McGill stood up, closely followed by Farr.

"Madamoiselle, thank you for your time. Madame Houlibert has told me you do much for the refugees and dispossessed. I congratulate you." Francine smiled sadly.

" I try Monsieur. It is something I can do. It is never enough."

Once back on the street Farr consulted his notebook. "We could try for Wilson sir." McGill sighed.

"Yes we must. That young man would presumably have pushed past him to get to the confessional if all we have been told is true. I'm not sure it matters but we need to be sure." The pair walked on as Farr desperately read the street names.

"Right here sir and second left." They arrived in front of a large non-descript building. The front door was open and men dressed as soldiers and others in civilian suits were scurrying in and out. McGill stopped an English soldier as he tried to sidestep the detectives.

"What is this building?"

"Railway headquarters."

"With English people?" The soldier laughed.

"Not the *French* railways. It's the building where all the tracks and trains are dealt with that go to the front. They're a different gauge." McGill marvelled again at the complexity of the war. He had never thought about the trains that took men and munitions forward, even though he had had dealings with them the previous year.

Once inside the building McGill asked the Captain on the desk where he could find Wilson. A private was detailed to take them up two flights of stairs to a large room, which might have been some sort of factory before the war. There, on tables pushed together, were dozens of maps, all stuck together to give a plan of where the fighting was in front of Amiens. The detectives could see spidery lines snaking all around the map and men with clipboards erasing some and adding others. The soldier took them to a well moustached man who was leaning on one of the tables, clenching a pipe between his teeth. The pipe was unlit, which was just as well thought McGill. Wilson looked at the two detectives and then stood back from the table. "What do you want?" he asked.

McGill explained who they were, and Wilson indicated a door off to the side. The three men made their way towards it and Wilson ushered them through. They found themselves in a small room with glass windows looking into the room with the maps. Wilson took himself behind the desk and indicated two chairs for McGill and Farr.

"So gentlemen, what do you have to ask me?"

"Mr. Wilson, we are as I said here about the murder of Monsignor Blythe-Hill. I believe you were one of the last to at least hear him alive." Wilson crossed himself.

" I believe I was. I knew his voice. He was quite definitely alive when I left."

"From our enquiries it appears you were the fifth from last person who confessed that day to the Monsignor. Who was before you and who after?" Wilson thought for a moment.

"Before me was a very attractive French lady. She left quite quickly, not doing her penance in the Cathedral. After I had left the confessional, a young man brushed past me and dived inside. He yanked the curtain shut behind him. It was very rude behaviour for a house of God." That all hangs together, thought McGill. But why wasn't the red haired youth on their list?

"Can you just tell me who was still waiting when you left?"

"An old French lady and a woman I took to be a nurse." McGill nodded. Allain had entered the confessional after Wilson had left. There was nothing new here. Wilson clearly had nothing to do with the murder.

"Can I just ask you about your job here? I understand this is where the railways for the front are managed?"

"Yes, I am in charge of them. I was in charge of the engineering side of the LNER before the war," he said proudly.

"A wonderful railway, sir! And the map out there," he nodded in the direction of the tables on the other side of the windows. "I take it that it is constantly changing?"

"Absolutely. It is updated twice a day as information comes in as to what has been destroyed and what track has been laid or re-laid. We also have to make sure we have the engines and carriages available to run on the tracks. The attrition rate is very high. We have more than fifty thousand pre-war railwaymen out here. "

"I can imagine. These maps are secret information I take it?"

"They are. We have a guard on this at night. During the day it's only people working for me that get up this far."

"And this information would be of use to the Hun?" Wilson thought for a moment.

"Yes,"he said dubiously. "Only up to a certain point. Although the tracks closer to Amiens don't change very much, and hence would be more worthwhile to destroy, those nearer the front are forever being blown up. I'd be pretty sure the Germans only need to look through their binoculars to see those tracks and set their artillery sights on them."

"But still useful information for them?"

"Yes," said Wilson with more certainty.

"Had you ever had dealings with the Monsignor outside the Cathedral?"

" I had as a matter of fact. We had a few convivial evenings together."

"Did he ever ask any favours of you?" Wilson looked shrewdly at McGill and tapped his pipe on his desk.

"Interesting you should ask that. About two years ago he visited me here and asked if I would take on a nephew of his. Some story about him not being fit for service but still wanting to serve. It turned out the boy was an engineer, even though quite young. I was able to use him." McGill and Farr sat very still for a moment.

"Is he still here?" McGill asked casually.

"No. Funny thing, he disappeared the day after Blythe-Hill was murdered. Damned inconvenient. I was about to send him to the works outside Amiens." McGill sighed inwardly. Hell! He thought.

"Well please give us all his details and we'll see if we can find him for you sir."

"I'll have Marchant dig them out for you. His name was Barber." Wilson rose and opened the door. He shouted "Marchant!" closed it and sat back down.

The three men sat silently for a few moments and then there was a knock at the door "Come!" said Wilson. A bespectacled older man stuck his head round the door and asked what Wilson wanted. Wilson told him and the man disappeared.

"Would you mind very much if I went back to my maps? There's a flap on and we have lost quite a lot of the forward track."

"Not at all – please carry on. We heard the bombardment yesterday morning. It must have destroyed much of your hard work."

"Actually we're not sure. Communications have been exceptionally poor since the attack."

"Would that mean there might have been a breakthrough?" Wilson smiled.

"There's no chance of such a thing. Both sides can't make any progress. The only hope is utter exhaustion on both sides." McGill remembered what Haig had told him about the final German effort. I hope he's right about the tide being stemmed, thought McGill.

Moments later Marchant reappeared with a piece of paper. He made to hand it to Wilson who waved towards McGill. He took the paper. Charles Barber, and an address in Amiens. If he was a bad 'un he wouldn't be there anymore. Wilson had risen and indicated they should all leave the room. Once back in the map room, Wilson shook hands with McGill and turned towards the maps where much redrawing was going on. McGill and Farr clattered down the stairs and soon found themselves back outside.

"I don't like that sir."

"Not in the least. We can be certain that all happened before Blythe-Hill was turned. I suppose if the information was relatively low down, Watkins' lot would just let it go. Real information to lend credibility, not much harm done. On the other hand, if Watkins didn't know about it…." Farr nodded. "I suppose we better check out Barber's address. There might be something there for us, but I doubt it."

CHAPTER TWENTY TWO

As the detectives made their way towards the address they had been given, McGill wondered if anyone at the Cathedral had known Barber. It would certainly make sense. Blyth-Hill was fast turning into the main conduit for all the information that was being gathered in and around Amiens. I wonder if he had genuinely had a change of heart, or if in fact he only did it to save his skin thought McGill. And if that's the case, did he tell the other side that what he was being fed was not true? "God I hate this stuff" he said out loud.

"I agree sir. Give me a good old fashioned murder on our own patch any day!" They walked in silence to where they had been told that Barber lived. A robust looking woman was fighting a losing battle with a broom on the front doorstep. She looked up as the detectives approached.

" We are looking for Mister Barber."

"Moi aussi!" said the woman. "'E go – poof!" and she made the sign of an explosion with her hands. "'E 'as not pay me!"

"I'm sorry to hear that Madame. May we see his room please? We are detectives."

"Ah, bien! You catch 'im you bring me moaney!" She leant her broom against the doorframe and led the way up the stairs. Reaching under her jacket she produced a heavy keyring with a large number of keys. She extracted one, and unlocked a door. She stood back and pointed a hand into the room. "Voila!"

McGill and Farr sidled past her and into the room. It had been cleared out. McGill turned to the woman. "Have you taken anything away that was here?" She shook her head.

"'E leave like zis." Farr was already working round the room, opening drawers and looking into the cupboard. All empty. He stopped in front of the grate and bent down to look at the ashes. McGill continued to look about the room. There was nothing. Farr looked up at McGill and shook his head. " Nothing here sir." Farr stirred the ashes a bit with his pencil, and extracted a tiny bit of card.

"Looks like he destroyed his papers sir."

"Hmmm. That will make it almost impossible to get him. He might have changed his appearance too. No, I didn't think there would be much here but at least we know he must be using other papers." Farr stood and the pair made their way back outside with Madame reminding them to get her money.

"Can we get a picture of him somewhere do you think sir?"

"Not impossible I suppose. I'd think though the best we could do is get someone to draw us a picture. God knows how we would get it to people to enable them to look for him. I think we better go and tell Watkins what we know. He may be able to help." They set off back towards HQ, stopping en route to get something to eat.

When they found him, McGill and Farr sat down on the chairs in front of his desk. Watkins looked at them expectantly.

" We need to tell you a little story." Watkins listened patiently as McGill told the story of Barber and the red haired man. Slowly Watkins face went white.

"The traitorous reptile! I knew nothing about that."

"Well they must have been on board before you turned him, but he ought to have disclosed them both to you. I have to say that in fact he was still on the Hun's side rather than ours." Watkins was white with anger.

" It means he's betrayed us all. If he wasn't dead I'd kill him with my bare hands." There was silence for a moment or two.

" So where does that leave us?"asked McGill. Watkins pushed himself away from the desk he had been sitting on and started to pace in front of it. "We need full details on both Barber and Mr.Merry. I'd almost bet Barber isn't actually English. He's destroyed his papers in the name of Barber, or at least we think he has. I don't suppose for a moment Wilson undertook any exhaustive checks on him. If the man was an engineer and knew what he was doing, Wilson would be delighted to take him." Watkins was still pacing.

"There's two possibilities, McGill. Either his sympathies still lay with the Germans or he had actually come over to us. From what you say, I suspect the former is practically certain. In which case the Hun *know* that what they have been being fed is rubbish. Haig's disinformation is both useless and self-defeating. The Germans know we are under strength and that the trench system we have taken over from the French is inferior. They'll go through us like a knife through butter. That appears from what I know so far to be the case. This could be a real disaster."

"And on the other hand?" Watkins shrugged.

"If he *was* working for us why don't I know about Barber? And Merry? Why did they both disappear? Why are the Germans apparently ten miles into our territory?" He shook his head. "God what a mess!"

"At the very least we know the Germans didn't kill him. Why would they? If he was still feeding them good useful information there would be no reason. If they knew he was working for us, they wouldn't kill him, because that knowledge was useful too. No we need to look for someone else entirely and a completely different motive for the murder." Watkins groaned.

"And here you are looking for a murderer when thousands are perishing at the front and we are staring defeat in the face! And something else just came to me" said Watkins bitterly. "Our oh so charming Monsignor was forever going round hospitals and into bars to bring the soldiers succour, as he put it. I bet he was! And I bet they told him plenty that would be of interest to Ludendorff!" McGill took a deep breath.

"Just as well someone killed him then." They were all silent for a moment.

"I need to tell Julius," said Watkins. "This is potentially a complete disaster."

"You need to try to find Barber and our red haired friend. Can you get a description of them out?"

"Yes I'll send an artist round to Wilson's lot and then circulate it to all MPs. It's unlikely he could get out of Amiens. It's a strictly controlled area."

"Ask for a chap called Marchant. He had Barber's details." McGill thought for a moment.

"Remember Braintree? Remember how he got away? Barber could do the same." Watkins groaned.

"You do like making my life difficult." McGill smiled.

"Only when I have to! The good thing is it would probably have to be a murder. Huh! Good thing! Listen to me! It's unlikely there would be an odd dead body lying around to swap identities with, like before. At least you've got two people to find."

"Two?"

"Yes – Barber and the elusive red-haired Man." Watkins groaned again and set off to find Julius to tell him the bad news. McGill and Farr made their way to the Sergeant's mess to get some tea. As they sat stirring their mugs, Farr wondered what their next moves were to be.

"We've done the first part of our job, even if the higher-ups didn't want to hear what we had to say. With that out of the way we can concentrate on the actual murder rather than its overtones. Any ideas Don?" Farr shook his head.

"As you said before sir, it could be something in the Monsignor's past."

"Or it could be a Tommy who found out he was a spy and decided to do him in. I'm not inclined to believe that. If Watkins didn't know about him, it's unlikely anyone else did. We need a lot more information on his background and who his contacts were. I'm not in the least hopeful though." They stared lugubriously into their cooling teas.

McGill felt a tap on his shoulder and looked up to see the Major from the front desk standing beside him.

"There's an old lady looking for you. Says she has information." McGill sighed. An old lady? Who could that be? Quickly finishing their teas, the pair followed the Major out to the main entry hall.

There, clutching her bag fiercely and an umbrella almost as large as herself, stood Madame Houlibert.

CHAPTER TWENTY THREE

McGill could see she was in an agony of self-doubt, clutching her bag and umbrella as if her life depended on them. "Madame Houlibert! How wonderful to see you again!" The old lady acknowledged the words, but still stood like a terrified statue. Glancing about the hall, McGill remembered there was a room towards the back which could be used as a private room. Taking her arm, he gently coaxed her with him towards the room. Opening the door, he could see that it was empty. He ushered her in and sat her down. Once seated she visibly relaxed.

"Madame, I see you must have important information. But first, you should have something to restore you. What would you like? I fear we probably only have tea, whisky or beer."

Without hesitation Madame Houlibert said " Whisky." Although surprised, Farr left the room. McGill went to the door and locked it.

"So we are not disturbed." She smiled gratefully and started to sort herself out, laying the bag and umbrella on the floor at her feet. There was a gentle knock at the door. McGill unlocked it and let Farr in with what looked like a large double whisky. He placed it carefully in front of the old lady as McGill locked the door again.

Raising the glass, Madame Houlibert said "Sante" and downed it in one. Although surprised neither of the detectives showed any emotion on their faces. The glass was carefully put back on the table.

"Bon" she said. "Monsieur L'Inspecteur, you asked that I should tell you if I saw the Irishman or the *agitated* young man." Hell's teeth, thought McGill. Protect me from little old ladies.

"I did."

"I have seen the young man." McGill and Farr were stock still.

"Madame, may I bring someone else to hear what you have to say?"

"If it is important, yes." McGill passed the key to Farr, who quickly set off to find Watkins.

"Where did you see him Madame?"

"I saw him on the street. But he was not dressed as before and he was growing a beard."

"I have to ask Madame – it was definitely the young man from the Cathedral?"

"Absoluement."

"And he was dressed how?"

"He had on an English soldier's uniform." Oh hell thought McGill.

"And which street was he in?"

"I had gone to see my daughter. She lives in Rue Sainte Honore."

"Madame, I believe the young man's name is Merry. Did you see what he was doing there?"

"Non non," said Madame Houlibert. "He was doing nothing there."

"I don't understand."

"He was only walking in the street." Oh hell thought McGill again.

"So you didn't see him doing anything?"

"Mais oui. He went into a house." I could kiss you, thought McGill.

The door opened gently and Farr and Watkins came into the room. McGill pointed to Watkins.

"Madame, this is Major Watkins, a colleague of mine. We have been looking for Mr. Merry."

"Eh bien, you have found him!" Watkins and Farr, who had not been privy to the first part of the conversation, both started, as McGill smiled benevolently at the sweet little old lady who was undoubtedly one of the bravest people McGill knew. Gently he asked her to repeat what she had told him.

"And Madame," McGill asked as she finished her tale." Can you tell me the number of the house in Rue St Honore."

"Rue Sainte Honore? Mais non! That is where my daughter is living. He walked around the corner and another and *then* into Rue Maubeuge."

"So you followed him?"

"Mais oui" she said with a shrug of her shoulders. "It is clear you needed more than just that I should see him!" McGill marvelled at what Madame Houlibert was saying. If only everyone behaved like her, he thought. No criminal would ever escape!

"I see. So you saw the number of the house in Rue Maubeuge?" She nodded her head vigorously.

"Oui,"she said, "I don't know in English." Farr whipped his notebook from his pocket and placed it in front or her, together with his stub of a pencil. She bent over the notebook and wrote. As she straightened up, the three men strained forward to see.

It was the number 11.

McGill, ever the perfectionist, pointed at the writing. " So to be clear, you saw the young man with red hair, going into number eleven " and he pointed at the number " Rue Maubeuge."

Madame Houlibert's confidence had grown as she had told her story, helped, McGill was sure, by the jolt of whisky she had consumed. Now she raised her hands and smiled.

"Exacte!"

"Madame, you are very brave and very wonderful. And I thank you from the bottom of my heart. Is there some service I can do for you?"

She thought for a moment. Then, with a huge twinkle in her eye, she said "I would like a very large and *very* handsome soldier to walk me home! Oh – and to kiss me on both cheeks at the door of my house! My neighbours will be sooo jealous!" McGill laughed and looked at Watkins and Farr, who were both slightly shocked.

"Major can you arrange that?"

"Yes, yes I can," and he made his way out of the room to find a suitable candidate.

McGill chatted to Madame Houlibert affably, enquiring after her daughter and discovering she had three grandchildren. By now the whisky had brought colour to her cheeks and strength to her voice. There was a knock on the door, which Farr opened to reveal Watkins with a simply enormous sergeant with blonde hair and a handsome and well featured face. Madame Houlibert looked at the man and smiled.

"Yes he will do!" She picked up her bag and umbrella. With a slight hesitation she handed the sergeant her umbrella, who took it with a small bow. He offered her his arm, which was more like a leg of mutton. Madame Houlibert, with a smile of utter bliss, took it. She nodded to McGill and then Watkins.

"Merci!"

"Now Madame," said the sergeant, "I will walk you home." The two of them went off arm in arm, Madame Houlibert almost with a spring in her step.

McGill, Farr and Watkins were silent for a moment after the pair had left.

"So," said Watkins. "What's the plan?" McGill considered briefly.

"First thing is get a couple of reliable men to go and keep watch on the place immediately, along with a couple more who can be runners." McGill spoke to Farr. "I wish I had Cole here."

"Who's Cole?" asked Watkins.

"The best watcher you could ever meet. But we haven't got him so we'll just have to make do. You'll need to make sure they aren't spotted. I would say we will want to raid the place tonight, which probably means we'll need to go and do a recce ourselves. If you get the watchers organised first, we can pop along a bit later once we have had a chance to lay some plans for later." Watkins nodded and set off to find some of his own MPs that he could rely on.

Just as he was leaving the room, McGill called out. "Watkins!" He stuck his head back inside the room.

"Is that Rue Maubeuge where O'Leary lives?" Watkins shook his head.

"No that's elsewhere." Watkins left and McGill and Farr pondered where they were. There were distinctly two strands which had separated. The first was the spy ring, which, with a bit of luck, they would close down that night. The second was the actual murder, and here they were no further forward. McGill grumbled to himself. I'm doing Haig's dirty work again, he thought. Even fewer people will care about the murder now they know what Blythe-Hill was up to. Every one of them will be pleased he is dead.

It didn't take Watkins long to return. " Julius is trying to get through to Haig to tell him what we know. I suspect he may have to drive over there as the telephones are very bad today. We still don't even know how far through the defences the Hun have penetrated. I daresay we'll know more tomorrow."

McGill grunted. "By then we might all be learning German!" Farr looked horrified, almost the first time McGill had seen emotion enlivening his face. But Watkins looked deadly serious.

"Don't joke about it McGill. If Haig gets these next few days and weeks wrong, we might have to!"

In sombre mood the threesome went in search of some non-descript coats and hats for their scouting mission.

CHAPTER TWENTY FOUR

It was almost dark by the time they got to Rue Maubeuge. The houses were all of a large and imposing size, with large gardens behind them. Vegetables had clearly been planted to add to people's food consumption, though the front gardens, which mostly surrounded short curved carriage driveways, had been left as gardens with flowers and grass.

Number 11 was no exception. It did have the look of not being occupied but when Watkins had a word with the men he had despatched earlier, he was assured that at least two people had been seen moving about inside and no one had left. McGill and Farr took a side road and walked in a square to enable them to come out at the back of the house. There was a small stream which delineated the end of the garden and the start of the next property across.

McGill, Farr and Watkins met up again at a small café not far from the house in the next street. McGill ordered brandies for them all. There was a cold wind blowing which cut through the less than robust coats they were wearing. Brandies drunk, the three started to plan their evening raid.

Watkins decided he wanted more men on watch now, so Farr was sent to tell one of the runners. McGill thought they would need at least ten men for the attack, and all would need to be armed. Watkins opined he had some seriously excellent shots and muscle available to him. Not a surprise, thought McGill.

"What about O'Leary? We should pick him up too?"

"Yes," said Watkins. "I'll organise a detail to do that as well. We should co –ordinate the raids at say 8 o'clock?"

By now Farr had returned and Watkins rose and said he was off to collect his men. " Bring us back some side-arms please," said McGill. Watkins grinned. "I'm looking forward to shooting these bastards"

"Not before I talk to them, if you don't mind!"

"I'll do my best. Will you wait here?" McGill pulled his watch from his pocket. It would probably take Watkins a couple of hours to get his men together and briefed, and then they would want to wait until later at night before going in. Ideally the occupants might be eating and distracted.

"Might as well. There's not very much we can do. We know Merry is in there and someone else. It might be O'Leary I suppose but unlikely. We've no idea where Barber is. Let's hope we can take at least one of them alive. They probably won't know much. This might just be one ring of many." Watkins shrugged and went off. McGill and Farr settled down to wait. Every twenty minutes or so Farr went to talk to the watching men, and came back each time to report no change in the situation.

Two hours after he had left, Watkins arrived back at the café with ten large MPs. All were heavily armed. The eyes of the clientele and the barman were large and concerned but Watkins spoke to them in French and told them to be calm. A couple of the men made to leave but Watkins raised his voice.

"No one may leave until I say so! It will not be long." He placed two revolvers on the table in front of the detectives and a box of cartridges. McGill and Farr loaded the guns, then divided the remaining cartridges between them. Watkins was checking his watch. At ten to eight, he nodded at McGill.

"You're in charge from now."

"Right! Detail one man to remain here until the noise starts, to make sure no one leaves. After that they can go and the man can join us." Watkins pointed at the largest of the MPs, who nodded in return.

"Let's move." The British filed out of the café quietly, making their way towards Rue Maubeuge.

As McGill and Farr made their way through the streets deserted because of the curfew, they could hear the artillery hammering away. They didn't know if the tide had been turned and it sounded closer. The platoon tramped along behind them, their boots ringing on the cobbles. They'll be gone – they can hear us coming a mile off thought McGill. They reached the front gate of 11 Rue Maubeuge. The large house sat squat and forbidding, with little light showing.

A narrow vennel ran beside it to the back of the house. McGill looked across the garden space at the door and turned to Watkins.

"Right. In exactly two minutes I want you to hammer on this door, and if there is no reply break it down. Keep out of any line of fire, but I want the door broken open and I want no one getting out this way. Don, you come with me. And Sergeant, you're with me too."

McGill led off down the vennel, Farr following and the Sergeant bringing up the rear. Not far along there was a door in the fence that ran down the side of the vennel. McGill tried it quietly, but it was locked. They continued down and came to the small stream that ran behind the house and across the pathway. There was a low wall along the bank. McGill jumped off the path and onto the wall, then down into the garden of the house. The other two did likewise. There were no lights showing from the house. McGill motioned for stillness and silence, and carefully made his way towards the back of the house. He pulled the revolver from his pocket and glanced behind to see that Farr had done the same. The noise of arms cocking and a bolt being worked sounded incredibly loud.

A moment later and there was a massive racket from the front, followed swiftly by the sound of timbers splintering. Two shots rang out. McGill tensed and crouched. Almost immediately lights started to come on from neighbouring houses, and McGill could just make out the back door opening and a figure leaping through. McGill raised his revolver.

"Stop!" he shouted. The figure hesitated then raised his arm and fired blindly. McGill felt rather than saw a body push past him followed by a grunt, and then crashing shots which whined past him. He fired and felt the kick of the revolver with satisfaction. The figure from the house staggered and fell to the ground.

There were whistles and running feet, then torches and the Sergeant putting a hand on McGill's shoulder.

"All right sir?" McGill nodded and looked down. Farr lay at his feet, right arm extended holding his gun, looking as if he was still pushing aggressively forward. McGill dropped to his knees swiftly followed by the Sergeant. Farr's eyes fluttered and he groaned. His eyes shut again.

"Sergeant get a doctor!" Without a word the Sergeant raced towards the back door of the house, from which more MPs were now emerging, surrounding the other figure lying on the ground, rifles at the ready. Watkins was bending over the figure and removed the pistol from the dead fingers. Farr groaned again. Torches were being shone on him now and McGill could see that there was blood oozing from below his right shoulder. He turned him so that he was lying on his back. He tore some cloth from Farr's shirt and padded it over the wound. Farr groaned and opened his eyes. Seeing McGill bending over him he closed them again. A soldier appeared and placed a coat under Farr's head. There was little else they could do but within a few minutes a medical orderly arrived. He quickly probed the wound, then tore Farr's shirt apart.

" There's material in the wound. We'll need to get that out, but otherwise it's fine. The bullet can be got out quite easily." The orderly put a gauze pad over the wound and bandaged as best he could. Moments later two soldiers appeared with a stretcher and carefully lifted Farr onto it. They set off to where the door in the fence had been. Another soldier kicked it open and the stretcher bearers disappeared into the vennel. McGill went to join Watkins standing beside what he could now see was the corpse of a man he didn't recognise.

"Who is that?" he asked.

"No idea." The pair stood staring at the dead man, and McGill reached down and went through his pockets.

"Not much here. These say his name was Bonjean." Watkins took the papers and held them up to the light.

"I'm no expert, but these don't look right to me. We'll get our French friends to have a look. They'll be very interested in something like this, as opposed to a murder no one cares about. Pity he's dead - I'd have enjoyed putting him in front of a firing squad."

"And I'd have enjoyed interrogating him," said McGill. " Do you know where they will take my Sergeant?"

"Probably the officers' hospital in Avenue de la Gare – it's not far from the main station" McGill nodded.

"Yes I remember there was a hospital around there. Thanks."

McGill went into the house and started to search through it. The front door lay dangling, smashed beyond repair. Watkins had left a couple of guards at front and back, but as McGill opened doors, he became aware of a keening sound from one of the rooms at the front. He opened the door to find Merry curled in the foetal position with two extremely large and well-armed MPs standing over him. After a moment Watkins appeared. He indicated Merry.

"What did you do to him?"

"Nothing sir! The moment we came through the door he ran in here and curled up. He's been making that noise ever since."

Watkins kneeled down and roughly pulled Merry's arms aside. Merry shrieked and curled up again.

"Oh hell," said McGill. "We won't get anything out of him tonight."

"No," said Watkins. "Take him back to HQ and lock him up. Give him food and drink and we'll see him in the morning." Watkins straightened up and allowed the two MPs to lift Merry bodily and drag him out of the room. No sooner were they gone than a young MP appeared at the door, panting.

"What is it?" said Watkins. The young man extended his arm proffering an envelope. Watkins snatched it and tore it open.

"It's from Julius. O'Leary got away. Shot two of my men in the process."

"Damn" said McGill. "That's twice. Maybe we'll be third time lucky."

"IF we *get* a third chance. We better search this place properly." The pair split up and started going from room to room. There was nothing anywhere that suggested the people in the house were anything other than ordinary French people, suffering the privations of the war with a grumble but with good cheer.

They ended up on the first floor. Watkins had done the top floor

"Found anything?" he asked.

"Not so far, but there's a couple more rooms to check."

The pair went into what had the appearance of a small library with shelves of books all round. Watkins glanced about and went out. McGill looked over the rows of books, and decided they would all need to be gone through in case there were any letters or papers secreted in them. He turned and went back into the corridor. Watkins was just coming out of the next door along. McGill took several paces and joined him.

"Nothing here." McGill glanced into the room. It was a small bedroom with a bed, side table and a chair. As he glanced about, something niggled in his brain. He stopped and looked round again. He slowly backed out of the doorway, as Watkins watched him curiously.

"What?"

"I don't know. There's just something…." McGill turned to the left to look along the corridor, then right, back towards the door to the study. He strode towards the door, and looked into the study again. He went back into the corridor and turned left towards the bedroom door. He paced the space in between the two doors. " Watkins, please stand right at the side of the study door". Watkins obliged, and McGill turned and looked at him. "Right, take three steps forward." Watkins obliged. McGill entered the bedroom and looked in the direction that he knew Watkins was. He shuffled in and out of the door a couple of times looking towards Watkins, a slow grin brightened his face.

"There's a hidden room! It's not very big but there's definitely a shortfall between these two rooms!" Watkins and McGill changed places and Watkins performed the same choreography as McGill had. A smile spread over his face.

"Got it! But how do we get in?"

"At worst we can knock a hole in the wall, but I'm certain the access should be reasonably easy to find." They joined forces in the bedroom. There was only a blank wall, and no apparent join anywhere. In the study the wall was covered by a built-in bookshelf. McGill felt down one side and Watkins the other.

"There's something here," said Watkins as he picked at the wood of the bookcase. McGill joined him and ran his fingers down the side.

"Yes I can feel some sort of gap…" McGill stood back and looked at the bookcase. It was quite ornate at the sides and at the top, with a sort of gargoyle hanging out into the room. McGill started pushing and pulling it, but to no avail. He ran his hands all down the decoration on either side – nothing moved. Stretching up, he moved his hands along the top as far in as he could. Turning, he spotted the small set of library steps and brought them to the side of the bookcase. He climbed up and started reaching towards the back wall. His hand encountered a knob. He grinned then pulled it in all directions. Finally, he pulled it up and there was soft "click." One side of the bookcase moved ever so slightly away from the wall. Stepping down, McGill put his hand into the larger gap now visible and pulled. Without a sound, the whole bookcase slid away from the wall. There, in the middle, was a plain, flat door, which completely blended into the wall. There was the very faintest outline. If you weren't looking for it you would never see it.

"You'd never see it even if the bookcase was open," marvelled Watkins. There was no keyhole. McGill studied it for a moment, then pressed gently on the door. There was no discernible noise but it opened slightly, enabling McGill to pull it fully open.

The pair stood contemplating the room they had revealed. There was a telephone, a desk, several filing cabinets and masses of papers everywhere. Watkins whistled.

"This will take some time to go through. I'd better get a guard on it and then contact our friend Julius." McGill nodded.

"Yes. There ought to be something here to latch onto. I'll leave you to it just now. I want to see that Farr is all right. I'll see you in the morning about young Merry. And see if the Frenchies can tell us anything about those papers." Watkins nodded and McGill shook hands with him. He made his way back out into the street through the front door. It was pitch black outside but he could still hear the sound of artillery off to the East.

CHAPTER TWENTY FIVE

McGill made enquiries and sure enough Farr was in the hospital near the main station. He made his way there, and finally found a person who knew what had happened to Farr. He had had an operation. The bullet and the cloth fragments had been removed and the wound cleaned. McGill was told Farr was sleeping now but he could be visited the next day. Satisfied, McGill set off for the camp and his bed for what remained of the night.

Next morning McGill was in front of Watkins' desk by 7:30. Watkins was already there, looking if anything worse than the day before. He found Watkins in almost the same position as when he and Farr had left him the last time in HQ. He had a worried frown on his face and he looked as if he hadn't slept.

"You don't look too bright," said McGill. Watkins looked up and sighed.

"Neither would you if you had seen the reports from the front line. We're falling back everywhere."

"Doesn't sound good. Has Haig thrown in the reserves?" Watkins shook his head.

"He hasn't committed them yet. It's a very confused picture, and it's not actually clear what's happening. He doesn't want to commit too early and find he's sent them to the wrong place."

McGill nodded and sat in one of the chairs.

"It's not getting any better," grunted Watkins, "The Hun have taken back all the territory we had won since 1916. In just three days!"

"So I'm guessing they are into open country now."

"They are. We are having to fight with little or no cover, and using old trenches that have mostly fallen in over the last two years. Haig is pulling men from all over the sector but he is still holding back the bulk of the reserves. According to Julius, he is looking for some kind of break in the fighting to be able to launch a counter attack." McGill didn't really know about fighting wars, but he did know, from his time as a beat policeman, that the best form of defence was attack. He supposed that was what was meant.

"We need to talk to Merry and find out what he knows."

"Agreed." Watkins picked up his swagger stick, and the pair made their way down the stairs to the ground floor, then through a narrow door which led on to steps to the basement level. Staff stairs, thought McGill, below stairs. At the bottom was a flag-stoned corridor. There were a couple of MPs one at either end who saluted as Watkins appeared.

"Where's my prisoner from last night?" Another MP appeared from behind a column.

"This way sir." They walked down a side corridor and stopped outside a heavily studded wooden door. Watkins turned to McGill. " Wine cellar" he said as the MP unlocked the door.

Inside, although it was gloomy, it was remarkably un-dusty and warm. There was a camp bed and a table and chair, as well as a chamber pot. The remains of a meal were on the table where Merry sat. Wild eyed, thought McGill.

"What am I doing here? Why did you break into my friend's house?"

"Your name is Doctor Julian Merry and you have been spying for the Germans" said Watkins.

Merry's eyes widened. " No! It's not true. I'm no spy!"

"Well why did you disappear from the hospital and your room? And what were you doing in your "friend's" house? And why are you in a soldiers uniform?" Merry was silent for a moment. He's trying to think of a plausible answer, thought McGill.

"I just needed to get away. You have no idea how ghastly working in that hospital is."

"Oh, I think I do. So why did you go to that house?"

"The owner is a friend of mine."

"And what is his name?" Merry hesitated. Without any sign, Watkins brought his swagger stick down hard across the plate on the table, smashing it and creating an enormous crashing noise. Merry jumped to his feet, shaking all over. "Emile! " he shouted."Emile Bonjean!"

Watkins stood in front of Merry, almost nose to nose. Very quietly he said "No it's not. The French have confirmed the papers we found are false. That means he is a spy and so are you."

"NO! I don't know anything about that!"

"So tell me about Monsignor Blythe-Hill," said McGill

"What?"

"Blythe-Hill – the Monsignor you confess to." McGill could see Merry was worried by how much his tormentors appeared to know.

"Yes! Yes! He is my confessor!"

"No he isn't. You must know he is dead. He gave you information to pass to the Germans. That's spying as well." Merry had turned white and was shaking even more violently. "Maybe you killed the Monsignor. Either way you'll be shot or hanged."

Merry's eyes widened and suddenly he sat down hard, covering his face with his hands. "Oh God! Oh God! I can't bear it! I've done nothing!"

"I'm very afraid to say that you have. Let's go back to the beginning. The last time you were at Confession, the Monsignor was there and you talked with him." Merry slowly lowered his hands and stared at them on his lap.

"Yes he was alive when I left him."

"And what did he tell you?" There was a pause, then a deep sigh escaped Merry.

" He told me about the poor condition of the trenches where the British had taken over from the French." McGill and Watkins relaxed. Merry would talk now.

"And you knew where that was?"

"Yes. There was a map in that house in Rue Maubeuge where all the trenches were marked."

"So you admit you were carrying secret information to the enemy." Merry sighed again and then, very quietly, said "Yes."

After that Watkins took over and there was a long list of information that Blythe-Hill had given Merry to take to Rue Maubeuge. Once or twice Watkins almost took a sharp intake of breath, but managed to stifle it. It was clear Blythe-Hill was working for the Germans all the time and had never turned back to the British. With every sentence, Merry hammered another nail into his own coffin.

Watkins kept at him. "Going back to your French friend Emile. Was it always to him you gave your information?" Merry nodded his head.

"Yes, but sometimes there was another man there." McGill stiffened. He could sense Watkins' excitement.

"And who was he?"

"I never heard his name."

"Why was he there?" Merry shrugged.

"I assume to hear what I had to say."

"Can you tell me anything about him, anything at all?" Merry thought for a moment.

"I'm sure he wasn't French or English. I just had a feeling he might be Irish, but I don't believe I ever heard him speak." Bloody O'Leary thought McGill.

"But in general it was Emile to whom you gave information?"

"Yes"

There was a pause. "Did you ever meet a man called Barber?" Merry looked confused.

"Barber? No. Why would I meet him?"

"He might have been in the house delivering information to Bonjean – or whatever his name is. Or you might have seen him in the Cathedral."

Merry shook his head. "No, in the house I only ever met Emile and the other man – no one else."

"And elsewhere – you never met him?" Merry shook his head emphatically. Watkins looked at McGill.

"So tell me ," said McGill. " Why did you do it? I've read the letter from your father." Merry's lip curled.

"He never understood me. He wanted me to turn out a little Englander like himself. But we are in a new world now. We English will no longer stride the world as if by divine right. If you had been with me in Heidelberg when I was doing my medical training, you would have had your eyes opened." McGill glanced at Watkins. There's no hope for this boy, he thought. I doubt he'll last the week.

"One last thing. Who told you to get out?"

"A priest I didn't know came to find me. I assumed he had been sent by Blythe-Hill." God save us, thought McGill. The priest again. How perfect.

They left him there. There would be other questions to ask as more information came in, but for now they had everything they needed. The pair slowly climbed back up to where Watkins's desk was. They slumped into the chairs and McGill voiced his thoughts.

"There's no hope for him, is there?" Watkins shook his head.

"Julius will take him away and he'll never be seen again. I've no idea what will be said to his parents, but I doubt they'll be told the truth." There was silence for a few minutes, both deep in thought. McGill shook himself.

"Right, we have work to do. We need to make Rue Maubeuge look as if it hasn't been attacked and we need some men there to pick up anyone who turns up. We're still missing Barber, and he might appear. I don't think O'Leary will go there. He will know the ring is smashed. We need to get his description and picture out to all points of egress, and to all your MPs. The access roads to the city will already be manned, and the station is well guarded. I have to say I doubt we'll get him. He's too wily, and he has a half day's start on us. If he gets back to Ireland we'll never get him. By the way, how sure are we his name IS O'Leary?" Watkins guffawed.

"We're not. That's just the name we were able to pick up from his papers one day when there was a check going on."

"I should be able to check what name he had when he was trying to get into England. And I could do with speaking to my Superintendent to bring him up to date with what's happened." Watkins nodded.

"I'll get Rue Maubeuge fixed and some men stationed in the house – no uniforms. And I'll get a call organised to your Super. What's his name?"

"Truman." Watkins laughed. "It would be!"

McGill went down to the mess and ordered himself a meal. Within half an hour Watkins joined him and told him his call was booked for 2pm. Watkins ordered food as well, and the pair sat quietly while Watkins ate.

"You really dislike all this, don't you?" said Watkins.

"Yes," said McGill. " It makes me feel unclean. Back in London you know where you stand. People steal for money or murder for money or love. Treason doesn't enter into it. I'm glad we have been able to tell Haig what the position is, even if it doesn't help him. But I would much rather I had solved the murder and all the rest had nothing to do with anything." Watkins nodded.

"I know what you mean. But I've seen the results of treachery on both sides. Believe me, you soon get cynical and weary with it all. I just hope after the war we can get back to decent values."

"Haig told me he believed everything would change." Watkins sighed.

"I really hope not everything."

They made their way back towards the HQ telephone exchange. It buzzed with activity and the click of telephone plugs being pushed in and pulled out of connections. There was a small room to one side of it which was used for private conversations, and they waited patiently. An MP came up and told Watkins he was wanted elsewhere, and he left McGill to await the call. Just before 2 o'clock one of the switchboard girls smiled at McGill.

"Your call sir. Please just go through and pick up the earpiece." McGill did as he was told and after some moments he heard an English voice saying he was being put through to Superintendent Truman. After a few crackles and screeches, Truman's voice came on the line, shouting as he always did when using telephones.

"McGILL! How are you getting on?" Quickly McGill told him about Farr, but kept the information about the spies to himself.

"So how did he get shot?"

"Can't tell you that sir, I'll just say Sir Douglas will be very pleased."

"Well that's odd but good I suppose. What about Blythe-Hill's death?" McGill explained where they were and why he wanted the information on Anne Lincolnshire, as well as anything else there was on Blythe-Hill.

"Yes I got the request from Farr. There's a man on the way with what we have already. He should be there later today. Don't worry too much if there's nothing to be done. I never expected anything. We are only being forced to do this to keep a rancid politician happy."

"I know sir. But I rather think if my idea is sound we might at least find out what happened." Truman grunted.

"All right, get on with it. Oh by the way – a letter came for you from a French woman…." McGill interrupted him.

"I know sir. I'm going to be a father!"

"So I gather! I took it upon myself to open it and read it. I didn't know if it had anything to do with the murder. Anyway look after yourself. One sergeant down is not too bad. One inspector down is one too many! So no eloping with Madame!" McGill grinned to himself as he disconnected the call. Just like Truman, he thought, as he set off back upstairs.

CHAPTER TWENTY SIX

Watkins had reappeared.

"How did it go?"

"Fine," said McGill. "There's a courier coming with a couple of files for me later today. I'm guessing they will get to you if I'm not here. I want to go and see Farr, but I'll be back later."

"I'll hang on to them. Should I keep the courier as well?"

"Yes why not? We might have something we want to send back. By the way I need to send a telegram to a Superintendent Morrison of the River Police. Can you arrange that?" Watkins nodded and pointed McGill back to the switchboard. "Ask for Sergeant Webster."

McGill turned and went back down into the switchboard area." I'm looking for Sergeant Webster." A hand shot up to one side. McGill squeezed in between the rows of operators until he was standing behind Webster. " I want to send a telegram..." and before he could say anything else, Webster shoved a form and a pencil at him, and pointed to a small clear space nearby. McGill placed the form on the desk and addressed it to Morrison at the River Police. He thought for a moment then wrote.

"What name on manifest at Albert for escapee if any? McGill." He passed the form to Webster who glanced at it and placed it at the bottom of a small pile of similar forms. Oh Lord thought McGill. This is going to take time. "I'll be with Major Watkins when the reply comes back." Webster nodded, already working on the pile and finishing one even before McGill moved away. Extraordinary thought McGill. Not a word.

McGill turned his thoughts to the other missing men, Barber, O'Leary and the priest. He felt rather than knew that Barber might be the easiest to catch, if easy could describe any of it. They had more on him than on the other two. He had no idea where they should look for Barber. He had erased his traces extremely well. There was no clue at his lodgings or his place of work as to where he might go. The information on him

was very sketchy and McGill was beginning to think that in fact
Barber was a false name. If that was so and he had reverted to
his real name or some other name, then there was much less
chance of catching him.

McGill thought about the way everyone needed passes and
papers to be able to move around. His mind drifted back to
when he had been in France in November. Then, a lieutenant
had been able to change identities with another when their train
was blown up. Maybe Barber could do the same? All it would
need would be another body with papers to explain why they
were where they were. He shuddered. There were plenty of
dead bodies that could be used.

McGill went in search of a tea, and collected a second for
Watkins. He took them carefully upstairs and placed them both
on Watkins desk. Watkins nodded gratefully as he continued to
read a file. He handed it across to McGill.

"See what our friends say about Bonjean." McGill scanned
the file quickly. The French denied all knowledge of such a
man. The papers were false and were in fact not recent. McGill
glanced at Watkins. "Can we learn anything from the body?"

"It's at the morgue at the main hospital."

"Did Julius learn anything yet from that room?" Watkins
shook his head.

"Not yet – at least not anything we didn't know already."
McGill sighed.

"The betting would have to be he was a German." McGill
pulled his watch out. "We probably have a couple of hours until
I get my telegram response. We could go and have a look."

"You go. I need to catch up a bit here. Besides if the
telegram gets here sooner I can send someone to get you."
McGill collected the now empty mugs and took them back to
the mess.

McGill stepped out into the sunshine that was trying to cheer
up the dark buildings of Amiens. It was a short walk to the
main hospital and he stepped out briskly.

Once there, he went in search of the morgue. It was
underground along a corridor that could have done duty as a
bomb shelter – and probably would if the Germans got much
closer. There was a set of swing doors at the end that were

being pushed backwards and forwards as people came and went. Inside the door, there were two MPs, who immediately barred his way. McGill pulled out his warrant card and explained why he was there.

"Just wait here a minute sir. I'll go and get Doctor James for you." McGill stood to one side of the doors with the other MP, who scrutinised anyone coming through. A few minutes later a thin bespectacled young man appeared with the MP following him. He looked curiously at McGill.

"You want to see the body of the man shot last night in Rue Maubeuge?"

"That's right. And any clothes he had." James nodded and pointed the way to a side room. There were two sets of double doors, and as the pair passed through the temperature dropped more. James walked along a wall of solid doors, checking the name tags. He stopped at one and swung the door open. He reached in and pulled out a trolley. McGill looked down on the face he had last seen on the ground behind Rue Maubeuge.

"There you are," said James. " One pistol round and two rifle bullets in him. He would have been dead before he hit the ground." McGill studied the body. There was no tattoo or anything on the body. "Nothing on his back?" he asked.

James shook his head. " No. No distinguishing marks. A few bruises from where he fell but that's all." McGill continued to inspect the body carefully. There was nothing here to suggest he was anything other than a Frenchman. If that were the case, why the false papers?

"May I look at his clothes?" James reached under the trolley and pulled out a bag. McGill took it and went towards a metal table nearby. He upended the bag and carefully went through the clothes. They appeared to be very ordinary and what any Frenchman would wear. McGill looked at the jacket and shirt. One bullet through the front, one almost side on and the third into his front as well. He shoved the clothes back into the bag, and handed it back to James.

"Nothing I'm afraid," he said. James shrugged, placed the bag under the trolley again and started to push it back into the space.

"Wait a minute," said McGill." Did you check his teeth at all?" James looked surprised.

"His teeth? Why would I do that? He was shot."

"Are his teeth French?" Light dawned on James' face.

"Ah, I see. You think he might not be." McGill nodded and James pulled the trolley out again. " He's still stiff but I can probably get enough movement to see." James reached across and picked up a horrible looking bit of equipment which he stuck in Bonjean's mouth. There was a slight tearing sound and the mouth opened a bit more. James stretched and picked up a small dental mirror which he carefully put between the jaws of the instrument. He moved his head up and down and side to side, then stood up and pushed the trolley slightly so that the light fell fully into the mouth. He repeated his head movements and swung the mirror around inside the mouth. He took the mirror out, and stuck his finger inside, rubbing it around the inside of the mouth and teeth. He disentangled the instrument holding the jaws open. They stayed that way. James waved at them. "Don't worry about that when the rigor wears off they will just shut again." James wiped the instruments he had used on his apron and put them back where they had come from. He smiled at McGill.

"Good idea, Inspector. Those teeth have not been looked after by a Frenchman in my opinion. The French have a particular way of crowning teeth, which our friend here doesn't show. On the other hand, what I'm seeing could have been done anywhere in Holland, Belgium, Germany, Austro-Hungary or Switzerland. Definitely not further East – it would be much coarser - and not likely to be Italy – they use much more gold. So our man is not, in my opinion, French. Although," and here he gave a little deprecating gesture, " I suppose he could have had work done while he was visiting those countries. As I say, I'm no expert."

"You may not be an expert Doctor, but what you have told me is extremely useful information. Thank you." McGill shook hands with the doctor and left as James put the body back in the refrigerator.

Once back in Amiens HQ, McGill trotted up the stairs to see Watkins. He was fairly certain his telegram would not have been replied to yet, but at least he had something to share with Watkins. McGill sat in one of the chairs in front of Watkins, who had seen McGill coming towards him and had sat back in his chair.

"But soft, what light through yonder window breaks?" he asked. McGill shook his head. "I'm guessing that's from some poem, but in reality not much!" He proceeded to tell Watkins what he had discovered. Watkins put his hands in front of him and started to count off.

" So – one, we are pretty sure Bonjean is not French and is possibly German. He is also the main conduit for information coming *from* Blythe-Hill. Two. Merry was simply a courier, who got information from the Monsignor and took it to Bonjean. Three – O'Leary and Barber were primary sources of intelligence delivered to Blythe-Hill for onward transmission. Four – we have no idea where O'Leary and Barber are. Five – we don't know those are their real names. Six, there's another man somewhere who is the actual courier to the other side and about whom we know nothing, apart from the fact he either IS a priest or masquerades as one. And seven, we have no idea by whom or why Blythe-Hill was murdered. Have I left anything out?"

"No I don't think so. We need to fill in each number with a bit more detail, but I would say that was pretty much it." Just then a soldier appeared and handed Watkins a telegram. He glanced at it then handed it to McGill. He took it and tore it open. There were just two words.

"Sean Delaney." McGill passed the telegram to Watkins, who read it then passed it back.

"I'm not sure that helps us very much. I've put information out about O'Leary and I can add Delaney to it, but I would think he will be calling himself something completely different now that both those names are compromised." McGill nodded, sighed and sat back in his chair.

"When the next courier or set of information doesn't turn up when it is supposed to on the other side, I think they will send someone to find out what's happened. So Rue Maubeuge becomes more important. Did you get the door put back?" Watkins nodded.

"Yes, and I've got three good men stationed in the house. If anyone appears, we will definitely get them."

"So our main lines of inquiry now are to try to find O'Leary and Barber – and the priest." They sat silently for a moment or two.

"Where would a murder first be reported?"

"French or English?" McGill though for a minute.

"English. A French person would obviously go to those incompetents at Police Headquarters. They'd never tell us for a week even if we asked. "

"The Adjutant General's Field Headquarters."

"And where is that?" Watkins pointed upwards.

"One floor up." McGill was pleased to hear it and stood. The last thing he wanted to do was return to the trenches somewhere.

"Coming?" Watkins stood and the two men headed onto the landing and one floor up. As they walked up, Watkins told McGill that the whole of the second floor was set aside for the Adjutant General and his staff.

"These are serious people," said Watkins. " They control the Provost Marshall's office. They are the ones with the power of life and death behind the lines. Cross them and you won't live long. Hundreds of deserters have found that out to their cost. We MPs are subject to their authority." McGill shook his head. He didn't agree with shooting people whose senses had been destroyed by the incessant pounding of the guns and endless attacks and counter attacks.

"You aren't though – you're answerable to Julius and Haig."

"That's true. But I still wouldn't want to get on the wrong side of them."

There were three smartly turned out RMPs who recognised Watkins and saluted. Watkins saluted back and then asked for a Colonel Chetwode. One of the soldiers disappeared through a door, and a few minutes later a Major appeared who smiled at Watkins and indicated that he and McGill should follow him.

The trio made their way through an ante-room and into a corridor where doors led off on both sides. The Major knocked on a door and, not waiting for an answer, walked through followed by Watkins and McGill. Watkins threw an impeccable salute at the moustachioed Colonel behind a desk. McGill could see that the window behind the Colonel looked out over the back of the building into the park that housed the vehicles and workshops of Amiens HQ.

"Hello Watkins. What can I do for you?" Briefly Watkins explained who McGill was, what he was doing in Amiens and why they had come to see the Colonel.

At McGill's name, Chetwode's eyes narrowed and he looked hard at McGill. Once Watkins had finished speaking, there was silence for a moment.

"McGill eh? You were here last year I recall. Bit of a carry-on with some dead man who we couldn't identify."

"Indeed sir. Turned out to be a Lieutenant Braintree." Chetwode nodded. Then his face relaxed.

"Smart bit of work that. Pity you never found the murderer." McGill felt the Colonel's eyes boring into him.

"No sir, sadly not" McGill's features hadn't moved at all. Chetwode continued to look at him for a moment, then looked away.

"So, why are you here today? What do you want of me?"

"Well sir, you may have heard of the action last night in Rue Maubeuge. We captured one man and another was shot. But elsewhere another man who we wanted to capture managed to escape and there are two more men who disappeared earlier. We are convinced we do not have their real names, but in any case they have ditched the papers they were using. We are, however, also convinced they will need to find new identities to enable their escape. We have already put out descriptions but it would be really difficult to catch them with those alone."

"So what would you have me do?"

" I fear sir, they may take over another identity from someone they murder."

Chetwode stared at McGill in astonishment.

"You think they will kill someone just to steal their papers?"

"I do sir. Remember these men are already facing the firing squad, so one more murder will make little difference to them." Chetwode shook his head.

"How low this war has made us sink. Put that way, I can see your logic."

"All I ask is that if any murders come in we get to see them immediately. The papers will have been stolen but we might get a name from something else. If they are in a rush they might not take letters or other things."

"The minute anything is reported I shall make sure Watkins is advised. With a bit of luck you'll get to it with our own people."

"Thank you sir. It's all we have I'm afraid."

McGill and Watkins left the second floor and headed back down to Watkins' desk. There was little they could do except wait. Watkins pulled a file from the stack on the right of his desk, read it, and placed it on the pile to his left. After some minutes, a sergeant placed another three files to Watkins' right and removed those that had been on his left.

"Great system you have here," said McGill. Watkins glanced up.

"The problem is the right hand files never stop coming!"

"I have the same problem." Watkins worked quietly for a time and McGill let his mind drift to Isabelle and what their life would be. He wouldn't be a kept man. He would want to continue at Scotland Yard. He realised that could create problems but he felt sure that something could be worked out. He was just starting to focus on his child – on *their* child he reminded himself - when another sergeant appeared and saluted.

"There's been a murder sir." Watkins looked up.

"Do you know if the man's papers have been stolen?"

"They haven't sir. He was a Gunner Fleming. He got in a fight in some bar and someone pulled a knife." Watkins and McGill relaxed and Watkins waved the sergeant away.

"There'll be a few of those," said Watkins.

Ten minutes later the same sergeant appeared and went through the same rigmarole. But to the question about the papers he replied "They have!" Watkins and McGill immediately stood and followed the man out of the building where a small group of MPs led by a Captain were standing. The Captain saluted then pointed along the street. The group set off and within ten minutes found themselves walking into a dark dead end street. There was an estaminet around the corner. Perfect thought McGill. Drunk reels out of the estaminet, our friend puts his arm round him and walks him down the lane for a piss, then kills him. The soldier's body lay face down to one side of the street, two ugly, bloody bruises on the back of the man's head. Watkins quickly knelt down and turned him over. He rifled through all the pockets. In the trousers with a dirty handkerchief he found a letter. He handed it to McGill and continued going through pockets. McGill looked at the Captain.

"Nip off to the estaminet and see if anyone saw anything please." The Captain called one of his men and set off.

McGill held the letter and looked at the addressee. It was Private Horatio Sprott. He took the letter out of the envelope and started to read.

"Dear Horry." McGill couldn't read any more. He carefully put the letter back in the envelope, just as Watkins stood up.

"Got it? His tags have gone but I know his regiment from his flashes."

"Yes. We're finished here I think. We'll have a quick word with the Captain then head back." The pair set off for the corner where they could see the Captain and his man talking to someone. The Captain turned to Watkins.

"Can't really make out what he's saying sir. Do you speak French?" For reply, Watkins let out a long sentence which had the Captain glowing with pride. The Frenchman replied and Watkins spoke again.

"He says he saw the two going into the alley. They were both drunk."

"Were they both in Soldiers uniforms?" Watkins translated and the man nodded vigorously.

"Oui." So whoever it is has a uniform already thought McGill. Watkins thanked the man, and he and McGill started to walk back to HQ.

"We'll need to find out what Private Sprott's orders were. That might be our best chance," said McGill. "We're really lucky this happened so recently." For answer, Watkins stepped up his pace. In short order they arrived back at HQ. Instead of heading for his desk, Watkins turned left at the top of the stairs and opened a door onto a scene of chaos. This was the room where marching orders were written and sent out. They crossed to a desk which was somewhat quieter than the rest, where a Major was sucking greedily on a cigarette. Watkins told him what he wanted to know and the Major shouted for a sergeant who appeared running across the room. The Major explained the information he needed and the sergeant ran off in a different direction. Less than a minute later he appeared with a file, which the Major took and opened. The sergeant turned and ran off again.

"That lot are on leave until tomorrow, but with all that's going on they will be going back up to the front shortly." McGill and Watkins looked at each other. Whoever it was had jumped from the frying pan into the fire. He wouldn't be able to run away from the regiment without getting shot as a deserter. The sergeant suddenly appeared and handed the Major a piece of paper before darting off again. The Major read it, stubbed out his cigarette and said "Sprott's been sent on compassionate leave. His wife's just had a baby. He's got a travel warrant to get back to London." McGill and Watkins turned and ran for the door, Watkins shouting "Thank you" over his shoulder.

McGill knew that the trains left every few minutes for the front, or Etaples, where the enormous hospital was. The newly arrived troops were assembled there before being sent forward. Direct trains for Boulogne or Calais were relatively few and far between and were for people being sent on leave or for officers heading to London to consult with others.

Watkins told McGill to head straight for the station, while he rounded up some of his men. McGill peeled off and headed for the place he knew so well from the previous year.

CHAPTER TWENTY SEVEN

When he got there he could see that little had changed. Chaos was everywhere with thousands of troops coming and going. He sighed to himself. How on earth was he going to find someone when he didn't even know what he looked like. He made his way into the movements office which was as noisy and untamed as ever. Because he wasn't in uniform, he was able to get to the long desk and shout that he wanted to know when the next train was going to London. He learned it was in ten minutes time from platform three. Before the man had a chance to turn away, McGill grabbed his arm. "When did the last one go?"

"Early this morning." McGill smiled grimly to himself as he thanked the man. A man calling himself Sprott would be on the train in ten minutes or not at all.

As he came out of the movements office, he spotted Watkins and four MPs running into the station. McGill held up his right hand with three fingers showing and screamed "Platform three." He turned and sprinted towards the platforms, searching out the number 3.

As before there were gates across the platform but there were already many men through onto the platform. McGill pushed and shoved his way to the front and told the sergeant on duty who he was and why he was there. By then Watkins had arrived, and the sergeant immediately cleared the way for he and his four men to get onto the platform. Watkins spoke to one of his men.

"Get into the engine and tell the driver if he moves the train you will shoot him." McGill was astonished at how readily the MP accepted the order. At port arms, he jogged off to the front of the train.

"You and you" said Watkins jabbing a finger at two more of his men. "Wait here and if anyone called Sprott appears arrest him. But be careful. He's a murderer. And you" pointing at the last man, " come with us."

Drawing his revolver, Watkins started to walk down the train opening the doors and asking for papers. McGill didn't want to do anything apart from keep an eye out for what was happening. He had no weapon and did not want to tackle whoever was pretending to be Sprott without one.

By now it was time for the train to depart but clearly Watkins' man was doing his job. Not long after a couple of railway people came running up and McGill was able to explain what was going on. One of them blew three short blasts on his whistle and one long one. Within moments armed soldiers had sealed off the entry to the platform and more had spilled through to help with the search. "It's a man called Sprott!" Shouted McGill as the soldiers passed him. "And don't kill him!"

Watkins was quietly going about his business and had got through the first carriage. He was starting on the second when further along heads started to pop out of windows, as the freshly arrived troops lined up facing the doors. One or two people tried to get back onto the platform but were none too gently pushed back onto the train.

Suddenly there was a commotion from a carriage further down with shouts and yells. McGill didn't know what was happening but he saw a couple of the soldiers duck down to look under the carriages. Bloody hell, thought McGill, he's nipped out the other side. He raced to where two carriages were coupled together and jumped onto the buffers, took another step onto the buffer on the other side then jumped down. He looked towards the front of the train and there stood a soldier with a gun in his hand.

"You!" shouted the man."Come here!" McGill raised his hands slowly. It's not the Irishman, he thought. It must be the man who had been Barber.

"I'm not armed," said McGill.

"Just get over here", Barber said waving the gun. McGill had no idea what the man intended, but in the event it didn't happen. There was the explosion of a rifle being fired, and Barber collapsed, screaming, clutching for his leg. He raised himself on one arm and pointed the gun at McGill again. Before he could fire a khaki streak jumped from a window on the train and landed on him. Barber shrieked in pain and anger, and was suddenly surrounded by more troops and MPs. McGill breathed a sigh of relief, shaking slightly. Watkins came up beside him, holstering his revolver.

"You all right?"

"Never better."

"You've got your man to interrogate anyway." McGill shook his head.

"He's actually not much use to me. He won't know anything about Blythe-Hill's murder." Watkins grinned.

"He might know something about O'Leary though". McGill grinned back.

"He might!"

CHAPTER TWENTY EIGHT

Barber's wound was superficial, the bullet having passed right through. It had been the man who had launched himself from the window who had fired the shot to disable the gunman. Watkins took his name and told him he would be mentioned in despatches. None too gently two MPs hoisted Barber to his feet and handcuffed him. Each holding an arm they half-walked, half-dragged him out of the station. Once there Watkins commandeered a horse drawn vehicle. McGill and Watkins along with Barber and his guards got in and Watkins told the driver to take them to Amiens HQ. The rest of his men set off on the short walk back.

About half way there, Barber tried to throw himself out of the cart. Unhurriedly, one of his guards leant across and gripped the place where Barber's leg was wounded. He screamed and subsided onto the floor.

Once the cart reached HQ they all tumbled out and the guards marched Barber to a gate at the side of the building.

"Back entrance" said Watkins, striding up the steps. Watkins went over to the Major on the desk and scribbled two notes, one to Chetwode to tell him they had their man, the other to Julius. That done, he turned to McGill.

"Right we better go and talk to him." He led off down the back stairs and to another part of the subterranean tunnels. Watkins' two men were standing outside a heavy door, waiting for him.

"Did you leave the cuffs on?"

"Yessir. Thought it best." Watkins nodded then indicated the door should be opened.

Barber was lying on a bed on one side, trying to get comfortable. A medical orderly had ripped his trousers and was bandaging his wound.

"Out" said Watkins. The orderly hurriedly picked up his bits and left.

Watkins leant across and pulled Barber upright to a sitting position.

"Do I have your attention?" Barber nodded.

"Then let's begin. Shall we start with your real name?" The man was silent for a moment, then looked at Watkins defiantly.

"Karl Von Tobbel."

"German," said Watkins flatly.

"Ja."

"You realise you will be shot as a spy and a murderer?" Von Tobbel didn't flinch.

"Yes"

"Will you tell us what you know?"

"No. Shoot me now."

"You speak excellent English without an accent," said McGill. "How did that come about?"

"My English mother took me to England when I was very young. My father had died and my mother remarried a man called Barber. They sent me away to school and your oh so correct people made my life a misery for being German and called Von Tobbel. Eventually I adopted the name Barber and said I was English." He wants to justify himself and unload the bitterness he feels, thought McGill. If he won't talk about spying maybe be will about Blythe-Hill.

"I see. Well I am not interested particularly in your spying activities. I am here to investigate the death of Monsignor Blythe-Hill. Can you tell me anything about that?" Von Tobbel shook his head.

"I know nothing. I saw very little of him. I can tell you he was not killed by our side."

"Yes, I knew that. I have to find another murderer and motive." Von Tobbel shrugged.

"Did you know him well?"

"I only met him when I came to Amiens about three years ago. He knew my history, as he had known my real father years earlier in Germany."

"Was he a good friend?" Von Tobbel considered.

"I would say yes. I was confused about the war, and he helped me realise on which side my loyalties should lie."

"And you fed him information from the office where he found you work." It was a statement not a question, and one Von Tobbel could not disagree with it. "We know all you have done, but I want you to tell me what you can about Blythe-Hill.”

“As I say he helped me to the right decision. Other than that I know very little. I had relatively little actual contact with him once I was in Wilson’s office.”

“How did you know when to clear out?” The pause was so long McGill thought he wasn’t going to say anything.

“I received a code word in a message.”

“Who from?” There was another long pause.

“We raided Rue Maubeuge last night,” said McGill. Von Tobbel still remained silent.

“I doubt it was Merry so it was either O’Leary, Bonjean or a third man – the priest.” Von Tobbel reacted slightly at the mention of a priest. “Bonjean is German is he not? And of course that is not his name.”

Von Tobbel almost spat.”No he is from Alsace. I only know him as Bonjean.” Ah the French lands occupied by the Prussians after the Franco-Prussian war thought McGill. Hence the German teeth. But if his name really was Bonjean why the false documents? He must have another name.

“You have no idea of his real name?” Von Tobbel shook his head.

“What about the Irishman, O’Leary. We know that is not his real name as well. Do you know who he really is?” Von Tobbel shook his head again.

“And you know no reason why Blythe-Hill should be murdered or who might have done it?”

Von Tobbel laughed. “When I heard of it I thought it had been the English.”

“If that were the case I can assure you we would know who it was. The why would have been his treasonous activities.”

“Pfff. Then you still have a mystery.” McGill looked at Watkins who shrugged. McGill sighed.

“Well Herr Von Tobbel I have nothing else to ask. There may be others who wish to talk to you but for me, I will say goodbye.”

As McGill and Watkins turned to go, Von Tobbel spoke again. “ I think you are not English.” McGill turned back.

“No, I am originally from Scotland.” Von Tobbel nodded.

"Like the Irish you will wish to be free of the English one day."

"Is that why O'Leary fights for the Germans?"

"I would think so. And one day England will be reduced to the nothing it should be." McGill smiled.

"Well, you certainly won't live to see it."

Watkins and McGill went back to Watkin's desk, to find Julius sitting behind it smoking a cigarette. At the sight of the duo, he stubbed the cigarette out and rose.

"I've heard – good work. And by the way, those papers we found in Blythe-Hill's writing table. They don't have anything in them but they are used to create a code. So if we pick up anything we should be able to decode it in the next week or two. They'll probably change it by then." Waving his hand vaguely in a salute, he marched out of the room and off down the stairs.

CHAPTER TWENTY NINE

There wasn't much more to be done and both Watkins and McGill were dog tired. Even so, he felt he should go and see how Don Farr was getting on.

McGill set off to where Farr was being looked after. This hospital was not like Anne's. The wounded here were what one would describe as walking wounded, with clean bandages and pyjamas. And mostly consisted of Officers.

Farr was sitting up, pain etched on his pale and waxy face. His right shoulder and arm were all bandaged and strapped across his chest.

McGill pulled a chair over and sat down beside the bed.

" How are you feeling Don?"

" I'd like to say all right but I have definitely felt better."

McGill laughed. " Yes I can imagine."

" Did they get the bastard?"

"Yes, they got him a split second after he got you. You shouldn't be so eager! What were you doing anyway, I told you to hang back."

" We had to get him sir. There's a war to win, and I just hope this" and he indicated his arm, " will help. When I saw him raise his gun I just threw myself forward to get a clear shot at him. Didn't mean to stop a bullet."

"I'll see you get a medal. " Farr shook his head.

"I don't care sir, I'm just glad we broke the ring." They were silent for a moment.

"Do you think we can get any further on the Monsignor's murder?" McGill thought and looked straight at Farr. He didn't mention the files that were on their way.

"I doubt it. We know for sure now he wasn't killed by the Germans but there's no direct link to anyone else. All the people with any connection just want it forgotten about – the Church, the British, the French. It's seemed all along that the only people who really care about his death are us! Still I suppose that's our job really."

They chatted briefly for some more minutes and McGill assured him that the Super was looking forward to them both getting back. With a final shake of Farr's left hand, McGill set off back to HQ.

As he crossed the hall, he heard his name being called. One of Watkins' men had been waiting for him holding a large, bulky envelope. McGill thanked him and looked around for a quiet place to read. He tried the door to the room where Madame Houlibert had so delighted McGill, but it was locked. He walked back up to Watkins, who was going through some papers.

"Can I borrow your secret room for half an hour please?" Watkins pulled a bunch of keys from his pocket and selected one. With it held in his hand, he passed the whole bunch over.

"Find your way all right?"

"I'll manage." McGill stepped away from Watkins' desk and through the door that eventually led to the little turret. Once there he locked the door, and with a sigh sat at the table and placed the two files side by side.

He looked first through Blythe-Hill's. McGill moved backwards and forwards through it, looking for anything that might look suspicious. He had been in Germany for some years, and that fitted with him being a traitor. He had taught at a school in England for some years before moving to Rome for a period. When war broke out he had immediately asked to be sent to Northern France. He was formally attached to Amiens Cathedral. McGill was going over the dates, when he suddenly saw a two months gap. Turning back to his appointment to Amiens, the letter from Rome had not been addressed to him in Rome but to an address in Germany.

In the summer of 1914 he had been in Rome. He had gone to Germany at the beginning of June. He had been due to return at the beginning of July but he did not. There was no mention of where he actually was, apart from the letter from the Curia, dated 3rd. July 1914. The sneaky devil, thought McGill. He obviously thought war would result and offered his services to the Germans. It wasn't impossible he had been working for them for some time before that. After all, the brother of a Member of Parliament would hear many things of interest to a foreign power. If he had any lingering doubts, he now knew the how and why of Blythe-Hills treachery. He made a couple of notes on the information he had gleaned and turned to Anne Lincolnshire's file.

If anyone could be described as having lived a golden life, Anne was that person. Born into a rich and powerful family, she had charmed and beguiled a succession of young men. Until one day her brother had brought Gerald home to their estate for the weekend. McGill remembered the picture of Blythe-Hill. No wonder she fell for him, he thought. There had been what one would call a whirlwind romance all one summer but then – nothing. The golden couple had gone their separate ways. Gerald appeared to take to the Church and Anne – well, Anne had left the country very soon thereafter with Archie, Duke of Lincolnshire. He was twenty years older than she was but by all accounts a charming and gracious man. They had married quietly not long after Gerald went off and had immediately embarked on a year-long honeymoon.

McGill stopped reading and thought back to the two niggles he had felt when interviewing Anne. The first was about her son's birth. The second was about his death. He pawed through the papers and found a birth certificate. The boy's birth had been registered in India almost nine months from the day of the wedding. Had they jumped the gun a bit? It wouldn't matter. And the niggle came back stronger. Why had Gerald taken himself off so precipitously? Why, after being such a golden couple, had Anne left it all for an older man? And quite suddenly, McGill knew.

He flicked back and forth some more in the folder checking some other dates. Where was the birth registered? In a town he had never heard of in Northern India, well away from the big towns and Raj rule. He smiled to himself. He was sure the boy, James, when they eventually got back to England some months later, would have been described as "big for his age." He sighed. It still didn't explain the murder, but he felt he might just have a lever to prise something out of Anne.

Closing the files, he left the room, locked it and took the bunch of keys back to Watkins. He glanced up from his papers as McGill placed the bunch on the desk.

"Any luck?"

"Maybe. I don't think it's the solution to the murder but at least it's a bit of insight."

"Want to share that with me?"

"Not at the moment. It's just an idea for now. I'll let you know when I'm sure. Pop these in your safe for now would you please?" said McGill as he placed the files on the desk. Watkins shrugged his shoulders and turned back to his papers. McGill watched him for a moment then turned away. He decided he needed to spend some time outside, breathing air. He needed to leave the stench of treachery behind him.

McGill walked towards the Cathedral. He was under no illusion that the mystery would be solved there. He couldn't see that anyone connected with the Cathedral had any reason to kill Blythe-Hill. There were only two possible motives. Either someone else knew Blythe-Hill was a traitor and had killed him. But if that were the case, why not just get the Authorities to deal with him? Or it was something in his past. McGill's instincts told him it was the latter. If Julius, Watkins and Haig didn't know the Monsignor was betraying them, it was very unlikely anyone else did. And it couldn't be someone in the Church. Blythe-Hill represented no threat, even within the labyrinthine workings of the Curia. From what McGill had read in the files, Blythe-Hill was a very minor cog. He reached the park near the Cathedral and sat on a bench. The sun had set some time ago, but the air was not yet cold. McGill only had one idea and one person who might talk. And that was a big might. McGill rose and walked around the garden for some minutes, then made his mind up. He gathered himself and decided to set off into the centre of the town.

CHAPTER THIRTY

He had hardly taken two steps when he saw a Military Policeman jogging towards him. It was the man who had jumped on Barber or rather Von Tobbel at the railway station.

"Sir!Sir! Major Watkins sent me to get you!"

McGill turned fully towards the man.

"Why? Is something wrong?" The MP stopped in front of McGill and bent over, hands on knees to catch his breath. He exhaled forcibly and took a huge breath.

"Yes and no sir. We've got another body with no papers." O'Leary! Thought McGill, and set off swiftly towards HQ with the soldier trailing behind him.

When they got there, McGill found Watkins just walking down the steps with four other MPs.

"You got the message. I don't think we are as close behind this time. Looks like he's been dead nearly twenty four hours." Watkins pointed away to the left and the little group set off smartly in that direction.

As they walked, McGill asked what else Watkins knew. It amounted to nothing apart from the fact it was a dead body with no papers – or indeed anything else about its person.

"Bloody lucky. I'd just sent a man to tell Chetwode we didn't need any more dead bodies when that sergeant appeared again and did his whole thing about "There's been a murder". I almost didn't listen to him and it took me a moment or two to pick up what he was trying to say. As soon as I got it I sent Wilkinson here off to find you. I reckoned you would head for the Cathedral."

"He only just caught me. Where is the body?"

"Down by the canal."

"Canal? There's a canal here?" Watkins looked at McGill.

"Bloody big one. Goes all the way from here to Switzerland using some of the rivers and North, it goes into the Channel." McGill stopped dead. Watkins took a couple of extra paces, then stopped and looked at him, with the troops flailing about them, not sure what was happening.

"He's on a barge!" said McGill. Watkins looked at him as realisation suddenly dawned.

"Hell's teeth,"said Watkins. "He could have gone either way."

"Not only that but he could have got off at any time. We'll never catch him." Grimly, McGill had started walking again and the group started moving forward once more.

A few minutes later they reached the towpath of the canal. It stretched away in either direction with barges moving both ways. They spotted a little group of Gendarmes further along and made their way towards them.

McGill drew Watkins to one side. " How did we get told about this?"

"It was a couple of our troops who pulled the poor sod out of the water. They reported to their sergeant who told the French but also told us. Nobody knows if he's French or English, there being no papers." McGill snorted.

"No one's going to care are they?"

"We do" said Watkins.

They had reached the group and McGill stared down at the body. It was still puddling water about it, although the bulk of the water had by now run off. The man clearly wasn't English. He was wearing working men's clothes and a coloured handkerchief knotted round his throat. McGill pointed at it.

"Is that how he was killed?" Watkins knelt down and undid the knot. Once the cloth was freed, the man's neck showed where it had been tightened to kill him. Watkins raised the man's head and a short length of stick came loose from the cloth. Watkins spoke in French to the Gendarmes. They replied, and he turned to McGill.

"They are waiting for their inspector to tell them what to do."

A group of other men, who looked as if they were bargees, was growing round the body and the French Gendarmes shooed them further back. The MPs joined in, making sure there was plenty of space.

"The only thing we can do about this is ask up and down the canal if anyone is missing. Unless one of these people here recognises him, but he could have come from some way away."

"I don't think so,"said McGill. "This isn't a river. It's a canal. As such the water doesn't move very much. It's only when the locks are opened and then it's only a relatively very small amount of water compared to the canal that gets shifted. I'd say the body might be from within a couple of hundred yards at most. He might have been stuffed under an overhang, and drifted free." Watkins blew his cheeks out.

"Right. Well, we better start asking about." He walked towards the bargees and raised his voice, asking in French if anyone knew the man lying on the pathway. There was a cacophony of answers and much gesticulating, but not much information. Watkins sharply told them to talk one at a time. One of the bargees stepped forward and started to speak. Watkins interrupted him twice with questions. Keeping his eyes on the man, Watkins spoke to McGill.

"He says no one here knows him. They are all local men who know each other and this man is not one of them. So he must be from a barge that has come from elsewhere. There has only been one barge in this basin like that. The "Roseanne" which came in two days ago and left yesterday night. The controller here would know where she was going."

" Where do we get the controller?"

"He's at the office a couple of hundred yards further along. I think we can leave Monsieur Roseanne there to the French." McGill nodded and the British contingent moved off in the direction indicated to the office of the controller.

Within five minutes they were entering a small brick built building. There was a podium to the right of the door with a large red-faced man sitting behind it, shuffling papers, as two bargees argued with him. There was much shaking of heads and slapping of surfaces, but after a couple of minutes one of the bargees extracted some money from a pocket and threw it at the red-faced man. Without a word he handed one of the bargees a token, and they both stormed out. Watkins started to speak but the fat man held up his hand. Sliding off the seat, he picked up the coins with much huffing and puffing, hauled himself back onto the seat and said "Messieurs."

Watkins explained they were interested in the barge Roseanne and where it was going. The fat man reached below his lectern with some difficult and extracted a clipboard with several sheets of paper on it. He flicked back one page then ran his chubby finger down the list.

"Abbeville."

"Ask him what the cargo is and if he knows how many people on board"

Without waiting for Watkins to translate the answer came "She is empty and she 'as two men on board." Two? Thought McGill. Who the hell is the second one? The priest?

"When did she leave?"

"Helas, I did not see, but late last night."

"Could she simply go past Abbeville to the coast?" The controller shrugged.

"She should not, but it is possible."

McGill pulled his Hunter out and looked at it.

"They've had nearly seventeen hours start. What speed could they do?" Again the controller shrugged.

"Per'aps four maybe five kilometres per hour."

"What about the locks? How long does each one take to navigate?"

"Huh! From ten minutes to two hours." McGill thought hard for a minute then turned to Watkins.

"He must be heading to the coast. If he can steal a fishing boat he can get clean away to Ireland. It would be like looking for a needle in a haystack. With the tiniest bit of luck I think he could already be at the coast. His speed would be around three miles per hour and the locks would delay him at least – how many locks?"

"Nine"

"Right so that's at least ninety minutes let's say two and a half hours in total for locks plus travelling time of what?" Watkins was calculating.

"He's probably just arriving there now."

"He'd need some kind of excuse for heading beyond Abbeville – he doesn't have any papers for it."

"I'm not sure he would care. The people in Abbeville wouldn't know he was destined to stop there and he would just keep going. Would they even notice he had been through?"

Watkins turned to the controller. " Can you contact Abbeville and ask if anyone saw the Roseanne passing?" With a sigh he pulled a telephone from under his lectern and started the rigmarole of making a call.

McGill and Watkins waited impatiently. "If he's already at the coast we'll never catch him," said Watkins

"We need a car to get us there as fast as possible. Do you have an RMP contingent out there? Where is it anyway?" Watkins thought for a moment.

" Saint-Valéry-sur-Somme. It's a pretty little fishing harbour, not many boats based there though. I think we have some men not too far away."

"Well we better get on to them and ask them to keep an eye out. In the meantime can you get us a car?" Watkins pointed at one of the MPs and told him what he wanted. A telegram rated highest priority was to be sent to the place where the nearest RMP contingent to Saint Valery was, telling them to stop and detain the barge Roseanne and anyone on board. And a car and driver was to be despatched to collect himself and Inspector McGill as well as two other MPs. "Sharply now," said Watkins as the man broke into a jog and set off back along the path.

They did not have to wait very long for the call to be put through. The controller was soon exchanging pleasantries with his opposite number in Abbeville. Eventually, felicitations having been exchanged, the fat man said "Ecoutez Jean-Pierre" and explained about the Roseanne. A stream of incomprehensible French could be heard coming from the ear piece with the controller saying "Oui" from time to time. Eventually the earpiece was replaced and the controller put his hands together. Puffing his red cheeks out, he spread his hands in a gesture of defeat.

"Alors, the barge she is in Abbeville. But she leave." Watkins spoke in French to try to understand what was being said. Some words went backwards and forwards and then Watkins turned to McGill.

"She got there alright and hung about for a short spell, but then she left to go to the coast. And our friend Jean-Pierre said he didn't know the two men, but he *did* know Francois Dragan who usually was in charge. The two on the boat told him that

Francois had been taken ill, and they had been told to make all speed to the coast to pick up a cargo."

"So we can be sure he's at the coast by now I take it." With that they heard the parp parp of a horn and the car that had been ordered by Watkins drove into the cul de sac that ended with the controller's office. The car swung round reversed once and was then pointing the right way to head off along the road.

McGill, Watkins and the two other MPs jumped in and the car took off almost immediately. The driver leaned back and shouted "Where to sir?" and Watkins shouted back "The coast!" With a crunch of gears and a whine from the engine, they were soon heading towards Abbeville. "How far is it?" asked McGill.

"Around fifty miles to Saint Valery. The problem is we have no idea where he might be going along the coast." They sat silently as the car gobbled up the miles.

Just under two hours later, they were at the outskirts of Saint Valery. They could see the last lock ahead of them which would let boats down into the actual harbour and thence to the sea. There was a quayside with a train track and cranes dealing with cargo and quite a number of barges moored alongside.

"Drive slowly along here," commanded Watkins. The car slowed and they all leaned out to see the names of the barges.

"There she is sir," said one of the soldiers, pointing. Sure enough there was the Roseanne tied up beside one of the cranes. The driver stopped the car as close as he could to the barge, pulled on the handbrake and turned off the engine. The silence after the noise of the journey was almost deafening, rapidly replaced by the noises of a busy dock. All five men got out of the car and Watkins drew his pistol. The MPs worked the bolts on their rifles and they all spread out along the dock, covering the length of the barge. The driver handed McGill a revolver. "It's loaded sir." McGill gratefully took it and checked there were six bullets in it.

There was no light on the barge. Watkins stepped out onto the small deck at the back. The door which led below decks was shut, and he stood looking at it unsure how to proceed. McGill joined him on the deck and they both stared at the door for a long moment. McGill motioned Watkins to stand to one side.

He glanced behind him to make sure there was no light immediately to silhouette him, then kicked the door in and rolled to the other side.

Nothing happened. One of the MPs handed Watkins a torch, and he carefully pointed it into the small living area, keeping his body to the side. McGill ducked his head quickly into the space and out again, then stretched across and took the torch from Watkins. Diving into the space he just missed the small fixed table and found himself underneath it. Flashing the torch all around, he could see there was nobody there. "It's all right," he said, "No one here." Watkins came down through the shattered hatch, one hand holding the top of the cabin. McGill had got to his feet and was already looking to see if there were any papers anywhere that could give some clue to where O'Leary might be heading. Watkins joined in, searching cupboards and bunks to no avail.

"There's nothing here," he said.

"No" said McGill. "We better get up top again and see what we can learn from anyone round about." The pair clambered back out of the hatchway and onto the dock. Across the other side of the railway track there was a worker's café, and Watkins strode off towards it. The MPs and McGill followed him. By the time they were all in the café, Watkins had learned that the Roseanne had docked just over an hour before, and that two men had got off and headed towards the town itself.

"Do you think they might have a contact here?" asked McGill.

"I wouldn't be surprised. I don't think this was on the spur of the moment. They clearly had this all planned." There was a narrow cobbled street which led up the hill to the main part of the village and the five men set off to climb it. As the group rose past the old fishermen's cottages, McGill thought about what O'Leary was trying to do. Obviously there was going to be a boat of some sort to pick him up. What kind of boat? Could they get a hold of any Naval patrols? Once they got to the top of the hill, Watkins questioned a couple of men standing at the corner of a cross roads as to where each road went. One went along the coast, one went inland and one led down to another little village and harbour.

"Which way do you think McGill?"

"Unless we are completely being misdirected, he wouldn't come out this way unless he was going to try to get out of the country. So it has to be either further along the coast or this other harbour. I guess we could look at the harbour and then potentially go further along the coast, but my view is we will only get one chance. If he's not down at this harbour, I'd say he's away."

"I agree. Come on men," and Watkins strode off down the path followed by McGill and the four MPs.

It took them about twenty five minutes, but they found themselves on the other side of a headland from Saint Valery. There didn't appear to be a harbour as such, more like the sides of a narrow river with some small boats moored alongside. The group clattered along the side, quickly checking the boats as they passed them. None had anyone on board. When they had reached the final boat, it was clear that O'Leary and his companion were not to be found. There was a small path leading off along the shore. "Do we take it? He can't be behind us."

"Yes "said McGill. "Leave two men here in case he's somewhere about." The remaining four strode off along the path. After a few minutes, a large building could be seen with a light showing. McGill speeded up and by the time he reached the entrance he was almost running. He made sure his revolver was cocked ready. The door was slightly ajar and he pushed it fully open with his foot. Cautiously, he stepped into the building where a single storm lantern was casting a flickering light across ships chandler's goods in profusion. The far end of the building was open to the sea which could be seen rippling with silver threads. Bobbing in the shallow waters was a small skiff with two men on board. The sail was starting to rise up the small mast as the skiff swung in the breeze. McGill ran forward, revolver at the ready. He saw the sail fully raised and the skiff was beginning to move steadily away from the shore. By the time McGill was standing on the beach, the skiff was already some yards offshore. The man at the tiller turned to look back. The wan light from inside the building glanced across his face. McGill instantly recognised the face of the man from the top of the gate at the Albert. It had the same look and the same arrogance, but also something else. Surprise? Satisfaction? O'Leary raised a hand and waved in what McGill could only describe as a friendly fashion.

McGill raised his pistol and fired two shots. Watkins fired just after. The two MPs unslung their rifles and dropped to a kneeling firing position. By now the boat was nearly a hundred yards away and the rifle shots crashed out. O'Leary had ducked down below the transom, but the other man, still beside the mast, threw his hands up and crumpled into the bottom of the boat. Watkins grunted and lowered his revolver, indicating to the two kneeling men to cease firing.

"We won't do much damage now. It's bobbing about too much and it's too dark. We'd best get back and get the Navy onto it." By now the boat was more than two hundred yards away and almost invisible. The sail could be seen pulling away into the dark. Watkins holstered his revolver and McGill stuck his back in his pocket. The MPs stood up and slung their rifles across their backs. Dejectedly, the group set off back to the village. Forty minutes later they were trudging into Saint Valery. As they walked back down the steep cobbled road towards the dockside, McGill could see there were several more MPs milling about. Watkins walked towards them as a Captain peeled away from the group and saluted him. Watkins told him what had happened and asked where the nearest Naval establishment was. The Captain told him there was an observation station on the other side of the river at Le Crotoy. Watkins told the Captain to take charge of the Roseanne and asked how to get to Le Crotoy. He was told there was a small rowing boat that plied backwards and forwards but the owner would have retired for the night. Watkins told the Captain he was commandeering the rowboat but he would bring it back. Signalling to McGill and one of the MPs they let themselves down the side of the dock and into the boat. The MP handed his rifle to Watkins, and, the lines having been loosed, ran out the oars and set off across the narrow strip of water at a goodly pace. Within minutes they were bumping against the wall on the other side of the harbour beside some weed covered steps. The MP shipped the oars and McGill grabbed a ring set into the wall and tied the painter to it. Gingerly the three men climbed the steps avoiding slipping on the green slime. As they reached the top, two Naval MPs stood with rifles raised. As soon as they saw Watkins, they sloped arms and saluted, who saluted back.

"Can you take me to your CO please."

"I'll take you sir," said one of the men, turning round and leading off along the harbour wall. The other man stayed where he was, clearly on guard.

Minutes later they arrived at a small building which had probably been a store of some description. Inside was an open space where several sailors were sitting. There was a door at the back of the room and Watkins strode towards it. He knocked sharply and waited for the call to enter. Once it came he opened the door and walked in followed by McGill. Sitting behind a desk smoking was a middle- aged Naval Lieutenant, with greying beard and moustache. McGill summed him up instantly as a passed-over officer who his superiors had simply wanted to shuffle off somewhere. There was a whiff of drink and looking more closely at him McGill could see the reddened face and the start of broken veins. Seeing Watkins, the Lieutenant sat up a bit straighter but didn't stand up or salute. McGill was fairly sure a Major in the army was senior to a Lieutenant in the Navy, but he supposed both Watkins and the man sitting would know the score.

Taking a final drag on his cigarette and stubbing it out, the Lieutenant extended his hand and said "Lieutenant Commander George Wells, at your service." Watkins shook and said "Major Henry Watkins. This is Detective Inspector McGill of Scotland Yard." Wells' bushy eyebrows shot up as he stretched across to shake McGill's hand.

"Scotland Yard? What on earth are you doing here?"

"I started out looking for the murderer of a Monsignor in Amiens Cathedral, but it's rather grown arms and legs."

"And an arm is out here – or a leg?"

"After a fashion. Just now we need the Navy to stop a small boat that set sail from the other side of Saint Valery. There are two men on board. One is an Irishman who we know as O'Leary. We don't know who the other man is, and in any event he has been at least wounded, or perhaps killed. What have you available nearby to go after them?"

Wells scratched his head and reached for another cigarette. Having lit it, he exhaled and sat back in his chair.

"The best bet would be to send a message out to one of the patrols offshore."

"How would you do that?" Wells looked at his watch.

"We send a message by Aldis lamp every four hours out to an inshore vessel which then transmits it on to the rest of the patrol. They're about fifteen miles out but we only signal about four or five miles and then it's passed on. The next one is due in about an hour." McGill was surprised at the extent of the coverage and asked "Do you have much to report normally?" Wells laughed bitterly.

"Not much. But every now and again someone like you turns up. The main problem here is sheer boredom." He took another deep drag on his cigarette then reached into a drawer in his desk and pulled out a bottle of Pusser's Rum.

"Care for a tot while we wait?" McGill pulled his enamel mug out of his pocket, and Wells picked two small glasses out of the same drawer and placed them on the desk. McGill put his mug beside them and Wells carefully poured three equal measures. Raising his own, he said "Ourselves" McGill took a sip and murmured "Ourselves." Watkins lifted the other glass and murmured "Death before dishonour." Wells set his glass down and clearly thought better of pouring himself another tot. Wiping a hand across his mouth he pulled a pad and pencil from another drawer and set them on the desk.

"Right. What do we need to get them to do?" The three of them debated the final version but with ten minutes to spare they had:

"Urgent. Arrest small boat sailed from Nor Nor West of St Valery approx. two hours ago. Two occupants one wounded. Making for Ireland probably. Report."

Wells raised his voice. "Chief!" The door opened and a grizzled navy blue clad petty officer stuck his head round the door. "Yessir."

"Get this sent from the lamp immediately we have contact."
The PO took the paper and left. McGill glanced at his watch.
Five minutes to go.

"Think another tot wouldn't go amiss" and Wells splashed
three more into the glasses and McGill's mug. Wells'
disappeared almost immediately, McGill and Watkins being
more careful, aware it was supposed to be drunk with water.

"Let's go and see it all happening." Wells stood up for the
first time since he had been joined by McGill and Watkins.
They left the building and turned sharply round the corner and
up a set of stone steps. At the top was a flat area with a large
lump of equipment, manned by the Petty Officer and a rating.
Wells moved the trio to the rear of the equipment. The Petty
Officer handed Wells a pair of binoculars and raised another
pair to his own eyes. Far out to sea, McGill suddenly saw a
couple of bright blinks and the Petty Officer, eyes glued to his
glasses, said "Acknowledge and standby." The clack of the
cover to the light being opened and closed sounded loudly in
the light breeze. There were more stabs of light out at sea, and
then the Petty Officer said, "Message starts" and slowly read
what had been composed, waiting for each word to be
completed before saying the next. At the end he said "Message
ends." There was a brief acknowledgement and the Petty
Officer retrieved the binoculars from Wells. They all trooped
back down into the station.

"We'll get a report every four hours "said Wells. "The patrol
has some fast motor boats in it so they'll probably send two off
in the direction we gave them, and the patrol itself will follow
in their wake. Two hours start won't get them more than about
ten miles ahead. I wouldn't expect to hear anything at the next
exchange but by the next one we should know. What are you
going to do for the next few hours?" Neither McGill or Watkins
had any idea.

"I suppose I better report to Julius what's going on. Do you
have a telephone?"

"There's one in the Post Office in Saint Valery." Good grief
thought McGill, no wonder Wells looked so bored. He had
certainly cheered up as the rum and chat had done the rounds.

"At least we can row back."

"We'll have to come back later. Can we get the car here?"

"Yes," said Wells. "It'll take more than half an hour but the road itself is grand. It follows the railway line that runs up this side of the Somme as well. Another tot before you go?" Watkins and McGill declined, gathered the RMP who was chatting with his opposite numbers and carefully stepped down into the rowboat, which had been diligently guarded by the two Naval MPs who had first greeted them at Le Crotoy.

It was still dark as the boat was tied up, but its owner had appeared and was demanding loudly that he should receive payment. McGill rummaged in his pocket and took out some of the money he had been given. He removed two bills from the wad and handed them over. The boat owner was immediately mollified and shook hands with McGill, expressing his thanks. Watkins went off to find the Post Office to contact Julius, and McGill looked for the car, which was further away, parked by the canal. Picking up the MPs that had been left behind before, they all walked back to the car. The driver was bundled up asleep but came awake as soon as Watkins shook him.

"We need to get round to the other side of the estuary, place called Le Crotoy. We should be getting a message at the Naval Station there in the next few hours. It should take just over half an hour to get there." The driver gave himself a shake and got the car started at the second attempt. Climbing aboard, McGill decided he would shut his eyes and try to sleep. The others tried the same and, although not entirely successful, they all managed to doze. The driver took it slowly to let them have some peace. Forty five minutes later they had arrived back at the Naval Station. Light was beginning to appear over to the East but the sea still appeared ink black. McGill came to as the engine clattered to a stop, and looked at his Hunter. There was still a couple of hours to wait for the first response, so he shut his eyes again. He was woken by a knock on the window. It was the Petty Officer. "The CO says report due sir." Groaning and grumbling, the car's occupants stretched and reconfigured themselves as they limped stiffly onto the road, stamping feet and swinging arms. The sun wasn't visible as there was a low cloud, but at least it was technically daylight. The PO had set off up the steps followed by the rating. Wells came out of the door and pointed up the steps. McGill and Watkins trotted up behind Wells. The tableau from before was repeated with the PO handing the binoculars to Wells. After a short while there was a flash from the gloom, and the procedure unfolded again. As the lights flashed from the sea, Wells grunted. " Nothing yet" and he handed the binoculars back. "Better go and get some breakfast."

"Are you still on duty next report?" asked McGill. Wells barked a laugh.

"We're all on duty all the time here. We get relieved every seventy two hours."

"We don't get relieved" said Watkins drily. Wells barked again.

"Come on we'll go and get something to eat." The three walked up the street a short way and into what had been a hotel but which now was a place where troops who were not badly injured were able to recuperate for a short spell. Wells greeted several of the patients and all the nurses with a serious twinkle in his eye. The three men passed through to the back of the building and into what had been turned into a mess. Without missing a beat, Wells collected a plate and made his way down the line of food, collecting a very full plate and being handed a mug only half full of tea at the end of the line. McGill and Watkins followed on, and joined Wells at a table that looked very much as if it was specifically reserved for him. Wells was already tucking in manfully. After several mouthfuls, he reached inside his jacket and extracted a hip flask. Raising it towards McGill and Watkins, who shook their heads, he filled the mug to the top. Stirring it once he then slurped a huge couple of mouthfuls and smacked his lips. "Can't beat a good cup of tea," he said jovially. Can't be much tea left in it thought McGill. Watkins appeared a little preoccupied, and once breakfast was finished, he dipped his head at McGill to get him to join him away from Wells and anyone else.

"What did Julius have to say?"

"Haig is going to a meeting of all allied commanders in chief tomorrow, at Doullens. While we've been doing our best with spies, the Hun have retaken Albert and Royes, and cut the main railway. They're within twenty five miles of Amiens.

Haig hasn't committed all the reserves yet, so they are planning to counter attack within a couple of days."

McGill was taken aback. "How have they done it?"

"It's a new kind of attack, a sort of storming all-out battle on a very short front. They concentrate massive artillery and guns and troops and smash through and just keep going. There are pockets of our men they have left behind and another wave follows up. So it appears they have taken thousands and thousands of prisoners." McGill remembered what Haig had told him only a few days before about the attack that was coming.

"I suppose in the scheme of things us trying to get O'Leary is very small fry."

"I'd still like to get him though," said McGill. "I don't like people being murdered for any reason."

There was nothing for them to do until the next report was due. Wells apologised and said he had some matters to attend to, but they were free to stay in the sanatorium. Watkins went off to get his men together and to get them some food, which was easily done, and McGill sat, exhausted, staring out of the window towards the sea, desperately waiting for the next report. Watkins joined him after a little while and the pair sat silently, dozing a little, for the next few hours.

Ten minutes before the next report was due, the Petty Officer came and collected McGill and Watson. When they got to the Aldis lamp, Wells was already there, patiently waiting for the PO to hand him his binoculars. Although it was fully daylight, the gloomy bruised clouds were still hanging low and it felt like winter. All eyes were strained to catch the first flash. When it came it was not straight ahead as it had been before but off to the West and faint. "Acknowledge" said the Petty Officer. The clacks rattled out, followed by more flashes from seaward." "We've to standby" said Wells. There was a gap as the inshore boat moved further towards the land, then the flashes of dots and dashes began in earnest. The rating spoke each word as it came and the Petty Officer said "Copy". He wrote it in a book. It took some time but eventually the rating said "Message ends." " Standby" said the PO and the blinds clacked. He passed the book to McGill.

"Vessel Fleur be Valery intercepted. One dead occupant. Boat close hauled heading towards English shore. No sign of anyone else aboard. Dead man no name. Orders" Hell thought McGill. He's got onto another boat somehow and he's deliberately sent the boat he was on in the wrong direction. He passed the book to Watkins, who read the message. Watkins sighed.

"That's that then. We can safely say the ring is no more, but it leaves a nasty taste that O'Leary got away."

"I agree" said McGill. He turned to the Petty Officer. "Tell them no orders but thank you for your efforts." The message was repeated and the rating clacked the blinds up and down. There was an answering flash or two from out at sea and then it was finished. McGill felt very flat as he walked back down the steps. He turned and shook Wells' hand.

"We did our best," said Wells. "Just sorry your friend jumped ship. We'd have had him otherwise."

"I know," said McGill. "That's twice I've missed him. If I ever come across him again I don't intend there should be a third time." Watkins shook hands with Wells too, and then they all clambered into the car again and set off back to Amiens.

CHAPTER THIRTY ONE

By the time they reached Amiens HQ it was after lunchtime. Amiens had been overrun with refugees from the German attack, and simply getting the car back to base had taken a herculean effort. They'd had no lunch though the breakfast had been substantial. McGill and Watkins made their way to the mess and picked up sandwiches and teas. Sitting morosely munching, they both felt deflated. Though the ring was smashed, there was much work still to be done in connection with the house in Rue Maubeuge. The dead man on the boat was almost certainly the final traitor, who O'Leary had warned and taken with him on the barge. Someone had spoken French to the canal controller at Abbeville. It might have been O'Leary, but it was more likely it was the dead man. McGill shrugged inwardly. It made no difference now. Information on him would have been good but the chances were slim to non-existent.

"So what do we do now?" asked Watkins.

"I can't see we can do anything else. Julius and his lot will be crawling all over Rue Maubeuge. Something may come out of it, but I'd be surprised. My job is still to try to find out who murdered the Monsignor. I've got very little to take me forward, but I suppose I ought to try." Watkins stood up.

"I better go and see what's happening. There's that meeting at Doullens tomorrow which hopefully might help matters. Will I see you later?"

"Possibly. I have a few things I need to tidy up apart from the murder." Watkins nodded and turned away, which McGill stared into his tea for a short while longer.

He needed to see Isabelle and to try to make arrangements. He had no idea how things would work but he did know he wanted to marry her. If it meant he would have to leave Scotland Yard and live in France then he would. With a sigh he rose and thought the best thing would be to go to see Farr before he did very much else.

As he walked, McGill thought of all that had happened in the last few days. He was sure Farr was all right and was being taken care of. He decided he would use his new insight in respect of Anne Lincolnshire in an attempt to solve the murder. He would visit Farr later, but the other matter to be tidied up was weighing on his conscience. The treasonable aspect of Blythe-Hill had taken over every other side to the murder, and he felt it was time for the murder to take centre stage again. He made his way through the scores of refugees and troops that were streaming through the city. There was a sense of urgency which had been missing for some time in their movements. He knew the Germans were relatively close, and everyone was doing what they could to stem the grey tide.

McGill stood outside the stairs leading to the basement hospital for a moment then set his shoulders.

He was quickly ushered into Anne's presence. She was behind her desk, sitting quietly, fingering her watch.

" Ah Inspector, how nice to see you again. And where is your Sergeant?"

" A small wound received in the line of duty – but he is being well taken care of." Anne lowered her head, clasping her hands. " I am glad."

The two looked at each other for a moment, then McGill spoke.

" Did Blyth-Hill know James was his son?"

Anne studied her clasped hands carefully. The silence dragged for a moment or two. Then she raised her head and smiled.

" No," she said quietly. "How very clever of you. But he never knew. I told Archie though, before we married. I couldn't lie to him." McGill nodded.

" So why did you kill him?"

Anne paused again. She smiled sadly to herself, then started to speak quietly, focussing on her hands.

" You have to realise my son was everything to me. His death was the end of my life. He wrote to me just before he was killed. It was as if he had a premonition. It was a terrible letter. And then he was dead. I thought I would die and in fact I had the means right here". She waved her hand at the glass cupboard in the corner.

" But I didn't. I decided Gerald had to die. I wanted desperately to live long enough to kill him, even if it was the last thing I did. My life was over anyway, so what did it matter? And I was glad when I had done it."

" What was in the letter?" Anne reached into her desk drawer and handed over a soiled piece of paper. McGill took it, almost reverentially, and unfolded it.

"Darling Mamma,

I am shortly going to the front again, and I wanted to tell you something. Not only that I love you and Pappa, of course, but that I have lived with a black cloud for many years. I feel, now, that the time has come to exorcise it.

I went to confession in Amiens Cathedral some weeks ago, and saw Gerald Blythe-Hill. You may recall he was a master at School when I was there. I hid from him in the Cathedral and went to another confessional.

But Mamma, you must believe me when I tell you he was a monster. I cannot tell you all he did, but know that we young boys all lived in terror of him. It was not so much the thrashings but what happened after them. But what could we do? There was nothing. And sadly he particularly liked me.

This has been within me since that time, and I feel, now, that it will be expunged in the heat of battle. I felt it right you should know.

Have no fears for me nor feel sad at what I have told you. Many boys in many schools suffered as much. It is all a part of growing up I suppose.

My love to you and Pappa – and wishes for you both to be happy.

Your loving son,

James"

McGill re-read the letter, emotions coursing through his body. He carefully folded the letter and passed it back to Anne. They looked at each other for a long moment. Anne spoke first.

"His own son! Can you see I had no alternative? He's damned anyway but I wanted him in hell quickly." McGill nodded.

"Why did Gerald leave you?"

"I told him I thought I was pregnant. Like a stupid flighty girl I thought he would be delighted, that we would elope and live happily ever after. What a fool I was! The minute I told him the look of contempt and hatred on his face told me everything I didn't want to know. He simply turned on his heel and walked away. I hated him from that moment. And worse, I knew he had never truly loved me."

"What did you do?"

"What could I do? I needed a man to marry immediately. And there was Archie, who had loved me since I was a little girl. When I told him he never even questioned it. I was in floods of tears at his feet, and he gently raised me. He looked into my eyes and said " How marvellous you are going to have my child." I knew it was going to be all right."

"So tell me what happened in the Cathedral"

Anne snorted. "I regret to say it was an entirely visceral emotion. It was pure hatred. A mortal sin, I know, but I'm sure God must give some latitude to mothers." She paused, as though collecting her thoughts. "It is the most extraordinary thing. It was almost as if I was being led on to do it. It was meant to happen. There was the wounded man who still had his bayonet on him when he was brought here. He should have had it taken off him before he got anywhere near here. Even then, someone else should have taken it from him. But they didn't. It was still with him when I did the ward rounds, hours later. I removed it, thinking to hand it in. But no one challenged me, and I took it back into this room. And then I looked at it for hours. When someone came in to see me I hid it. I really did mean to hand it in. Somehow it was still there, and seemed to get bigger and more brutal, and it whispered to me that I knew what I had to do. And then my resistance broke, and a terrible resolve came over me. It wasn't to kill him at first. Curiosity took me to the Cathedral. I saw Gerald, though he didn't see me. There he was looking so pious yet superior and smug." Anne almost spat the words. "I knew then he had to die. I was sure the path I had been taken along was just and necessary." She paused, and poured herself a glass of water from the carafe on her desk. She took a sip then carefully put the glass back on the desk.

"I waited until there was no one else ready for confession. I prayed – oh how I prayed - for guidance. Any sign might have made me think again, but there was none. No one saw me enter the confessional. I didn't say the usual words, I just said, "Hello Gerald." I could feel him shifting on the other side of the lattice.

"Anne?" he said. "Is that you?" And he did what I knew he would, he leaned towards the lattice to look through to see me. As his eye came towards me, I had the bayonet in my hands, and I drove it through his eye with all my strength. At that moment, I felt the great weight of despair lift from me, and I sat there for some minutes, exulting. I could see him sprawled back, the bayonet handle pointing skywards, the point obviously downwards to hell. After a time I left the confessional, and sat back in the pews. He had made quite a noise when he fell, and I expected people would come running. But no, no one did. So I sat and waited, quite certain that someone *would* come and I would be taken away. And still no one came. It dawned on me that somehow I was protected. No one had seen me, no one had heard and no one was around. After nearly half an hour, I left. I had clearly done God's will." Anne stood and crossed herself. She moved across to the cupboard. She opened it and stretched in, then closed the door again and sat back down.

"So there you have it. My confession. And now you have come for me. I have no regrets and no remorse. I would do it again without hesitation. And I have no fears of dying."

McGill passed a hand across his forehead.

" Anne, you must know I have to obtain a written confession properly witnessed, so you could still deny everything. And my masters would never prosecute you. There would be too much scandal. So I have to ask whether you will allow me to take a confession from you with a witness and will you sign it?".

Anne brought her left hand to her mouth, as though thinking. She reached for the water glass and took a deep swallow. Carefully, ever so deliberately, she placed it back on the desk.

" Yes I know, but I won't. I wanted to confess to you, because I knew you would understand. I can't have Archie hurt by all this. He has always been a brick." With that she took a box of matches from her desk drawer, struck one, and raised the letter towards the sputtering match. McGill and Anne watched the letter turn to blackened ash, and at the last moment she dropped it into her bin. McGill stretched towards the carafe and slopped a bit of water into the bin. He glanced at Anne who nodded. " Thank you."

"I will have to tell my superiors". Anne smiled briefly.

"That will be up to you. I trust you." I wish people wouldn't say that, thought McGill. It puts the onus on me. He glanced at Anne again, and thought, is she all right?

" Whatever you do, don't tell Archie. He mustn't know."

"That I *can* promise. If he learns of all this, it will not be from me." Anne breathed out. "Thank you," she said.

"Will you not let me write your confession?"

She shook her head. " No, and it doesn't matter now." Her head dipped and she jerked it back up. McGill stared at her, and stepped to the cupboard. He yanked it open. There was a small bowl sitting on the middle shelf with nothing in it. He turned to Anne who was now clutching her desk. She repeated.

" Remember, I trust you.." and she fell to the floor. McGill stared at her, her eyes still open. She took one gasping breath before it left her completely. McGill knelt and felt for a pulse in her neck. There was none. He closed her eyes and stood slowly. He wasn't religious, but he said a brief prayer. At least she's with her beloved boy, he thought. He fervently hoped that God did give special dispensation to mothers.

He looked around the room. He opened the drawer of the desk. He rifled through what was there, but found nothing of import. He opened the cupboard again. There was nothing he needed to remove. He sighed then opened the door into the ward. The nurse who had shown him in was passing and he stopped her.

" Please bring a doctor." The nurse looked at him, nodded and went in search of one. Within a few minutes a white-haired man with a bloodied white coat made his way through the beds with a puzzled look on his face.

"Yes?"

"I am Detective Inspector McGill from Scotland Yard. The Duchess has had a heart attack. I'm afraid she is dead." McGill stood back to allow the doctor into Anne's room.

The doctor kneeled beside the body and checked for a pulse, then raised an eyelid. He let it drop back. He took Anne's hands and turned them over. He glanced at McGill and carefully put the right hand down. He used both his own hands to raise the left to his eyes and examined each finger in turn. He put the hand down then sat back on his haunches, placing his hands on his thighs. He turned towards McGill and looked steadily at him, unflinchingly. McGill stared back, unblinking. The doctor stood slowly.

"A heart attack you say?"

"Yes". The doctor stroked his chin.

"And you want me to certify that?"

"Yes." McGill paused, then looked sharply at the doctor. "She was a Catholic you know." McGill could see the doctor working it all out, realisation dawning on him. He nodded and reached into his pocket. He pulled out a stained pad and scribbled a few words then signed and dated it.

"Give this to the authorities."

"Thank you. I appreciate it." The doctor nodded again, and looked at Anne once more.

"She was a great woman you know."

"I know."

"Do you want me to deal with the body?"

"I will make the appropriate arrangements." The doctor nodded.

"Very well." The doctor held out his hand. McGill took it and shook once. "Is there anything else you want to tell me?"

"No." Without a word, the doctor turned and went back into the ward. McGill looked at the paper, and carefully folded it. He took his wallet out and placed the paper almost religiously within. He went into the ward and took a sheet from one of the beds, then returned and placed it over Anne. He stood for a moment more. He turned and left the office. People looked at him strangely as he walked through the ward. The word had clearly already spread. As he climbed the stairs back to street level, his way was blocked by Julius.

"I've been looking for you. One of my men said they had seen you heading this way."

McGill took the doctor's note from his wallet and handed him the note. Julius read it, and looked at McGill with a raised eyebrow.

"So" said Julius.

"So" said McGill. "Will you deal with it?"

"Of course. And I will tell Sir Douglas." McGill nodded.

"May she Rest in Peace."

"Indeed. She won't be disturbed by me." Julius turned and walked away quickly. McGill followed him with his eyes. After a few moments, he turned and walked in the opposite direction. I wonder what he had actually come to see me about, thought McGill.

CHAPTER THIRTY TWO

McGill made his way back to where Farr was recovering from his wound. He sat beside the bed and chatted inconsequentially for quite some time, Farr still in pain but clearly in better spirits than he had been earlier.

There was a commotion at the door to the ward, and three soldiers entered, led by Julius.

" McGill!" McGill turned and saw the group striding towards him.

"Hello Colonel. What can I do for you?"

Julius addressed Farr. "Has the Inspector told you about the case?" Farr looked bemused, and Julius went on "I see not. Right McGill, with me." McGill sighed and rose to his feet.

" I didn't expect you quite so soon, but I did expect you." Julius nodded, and inclined his head towards the exit.

McGill bent and shook Farr's left hand. "Take care Don. I'll see you back in London. If you can, get out to Isabelle's house and tell her what's going on."

"I will sir. I wouldn't mind seeing that Marie again, either." McGill laughed.

"Maybe you should recuperate there like I did!"

"I might just do that sir."

Julius impatiently indicated McGill should hurry up. As they left the building, McGill asked Julius "Where to first?"

"Haig's too busy as you can imagine, but he thanks you for your work. You are not to put anything in writing until it is decided what is to happen. I've to take you direct to the Prime Minister." McGill started.

"Lloyd George himself?" Julius nodded.

"And you will only talk to him and no one else." McGill laughed.

"I've heard that before and I expect you have orders to shoot me."

"You know me too well, McGill," said Julius with not a trace of a smile.

There was a car waiting. The five of them crammed in and headed for the train station.

"What about my bag?"

"Farr can bring it on. I expect he'll be some days yet." McGill nodded. Just as well I bought my neighbour a new one, he thought.

The three soldiers were replaced by three more at Boulogne and then three more at Victoria. McGill dozed for some of the journey, but Julius in particular kept watch.

A car was waiting at Victoria and Julius and McGill got in. The three soldiers climbed in behind them. Even had he wanted to McGill wouldn't have been able to get out. It was after midnight, and a slow mist was drifting about as a wetting rain soaked the streets and buildings. The short journey to Downing Street passed in silence. As the car drew up, Julius opened the car door and let McGill step down. The soldiers quickly followed, and McGill felt as if he was being herded towards the Prime Minister's door. Two policemen stood outside, their capes glistening as the rain refused to pass over. As the group approached the door, it was opened and a footman bowed slightly. Two more footmen took Julius and McGill's coats and hats.

"We'll be here when you are finished," said Julius.

A butler appeared and indicated the stairs, leading McGill upwards. At the top of the stairs the butler turned right and opened a heavy oak door.

"Detective Inspector McGill, sir"

As McGill walked into the room, a small, bright eyed man rose from behind a desk.

"Thank you, Simms." The door closed quietly behind him. McGill recognised the slight lilt, the moustache and the high domed forehead instantly. The eyes bored into McGill, then Lloyd George passed to a side-table.

"So, you are the famous McGill," he said as he poured two whiskies. The slight Welsh lilt appeared to caress its listeners. He paused as he looked at McGill again, offering one of the glasses.

"Thank you,sir," said McGill, taking the glass and turning it in his hands. Lloyd George raised his own and took a tentative sip.

"Not as good as Haig's I'll warrant." McGill took a sniff, then a sip, and smiled.

"I see you are a connoisseur, sir." The eyes crinkled, the hand made a deprecating gesture, and the voice chuckled. "I try."

Lloyd George turned back and sat down behind the desk again. Oh I can see why they call you the Welsh Wizard, thought McGill.

"Sit down McGill. Tell me your story." So McGill took a seat, and started his tale, leaving nothing out.

When he had finished, there was silence for a moment. Lloyd George went to the sideboard again and poured himself another drink. He waved the bottle at McGill who shook his head.

As he took a swallow, he watched McGill. "So Inspector, I can see why the Commissioner thinks so highly of you – as does Sir Douglas." McGill said nothing as Lloyd George continued to weigh something in his mind.

"So it is absolutely certain Blythe-Hill was in fact a traitor?"

"It's absolutely certain, sir. Colonel Julius can fill in all the details, but his people are sure as well. We know the Germans had nothing to do with his death. For all the reasons I have given I can see no possible motive why they would anyway. O'Leary escaped. Merry was a poor young fool, and Von Tobbel had all the arrogance of the true Prussian Junker. The priest – at least we think it was the priest – was shot. He would never believe the British could overcome him, probably even as the bullets tore into him. We still have no idea who Bonjean actually is or was, though he is dead anyway. Someone may turn up at the house in Rue Maubeuge, and Julius' people may find out more. But at the end of the day the ring is smashed. The only one to escape was O'Leary." Lloyd George nodded, his eyes boring into McGill. After a few moments, he nodded.

"I agree with you. Sir Douglas has kept me informed. So that avenue is closed. You have no need to report to him. What do you think I should do?" McGill thought for a moment.

"I think you have two possibilities sir. You could tell Sir Terence he should resign or you will make public that his brother was a traitor. You'd be rid of him forever. Or you could tell him to work for you. In either event you have the facts to hold over him."

Lloyd George, in a mocking tone, said " Blackmail? That's hardly honourable!"

"I know sir, but surely the whole point of this exercise has been to neutralise him."

"Has it? I'm not so sure. Perhaps I already knew and simply wanted to be seen to be doing something. And he can be useful to me in ways you can't imagine. I should have paid attention to Haig when he said you would get to the truth." Lloyd George took another sip.

"And what of Anne? What do we say about her?"

McGill shrugged. "Died of natural causes – a heart attack brought on by a broken heart. I'm sure Julius has already secured her death certificate based on that doctor's paper. People would believe that, especially as James was her only son. A large funeral and a suitable period of mourning by the Duke."

"And Gerald?"

"Killed by a German spy, using a British bayonet to throw us off the scent. In a way it could be true." Lloyd George took another swallow. "We'd have to make up a story about why they would do that, but I'm sure it can be done." Lloyd George nodded.

"Then there's McGill. What do I do with you?"

" Me sir?"

"Yes you. Can I trust you? What you know is very dangerous." McGill felt the ground opening up beneath him, as he had done before when dealing with men who had absolute power.

" I gave Sir Douglas my word before, sir, and I believe he has never had cause to doubt it." Lloyd George laughed.

"Ah, my boy, Sir Douglas is a soldier with a code of honour. You forget I am a politician. How do I bind you in such a way that all these secrets are safe?"

"Do you feel you need to sir? My word and behaviour is not enough?" Lloyd George shook his head. "No there needs to be a bond to bind. I could never trust someone who apparently has no blemish."

McGill realised he needed some chink in his armour, so that Lloyd George would feel safe. What would he understand?

" Well sir, there is a woman." Lloyd George immediately perked up. So it's true what they say about you, you old goat, thought McGill.

"A woman?"

"Yes sir. A French woman."

Lloyd George positively beamed. I knew he would understand that, thought McGill.

Epilogue

The war had been over for several months. McGill was back investigating major crimes and cases that Sir Giles referred to as "something fishy going on." He sat staring out of the window, thinking of his daughter and his wife in their new house. Lloyd George had been as good as his word. Isabelle had been quickly brought to London and all required procedures had been waived. Haig had held the Germans, who got within ten miles of Amiens at Villers-Bretonneux. He had then attacked with spectacular results. By the November of 1918 his armies were on the frontier between France and Germany. The famous Armistice – eleven-eleven-eleven – had finally brought the carnage and misery to an end.

McGill still marvelled that someone like Isabelle should be happy to marry a mere police Inspector, and even more that she would give up her life in France. They had been married quietly the day after she arrived in England, with Farr as best man and Marie as maid of honour. Farr had in fact spent some days recuperating in Isabelle's house, and McGill was sure that another wedding would be forthcoming. Farr's normally saturnine and immobile face took on a glow when he looked at Marie. He had definitely put on weight since starting to eat Marie's cooking.

Isabelle had insisted they should have a suitable house for the man she was sure would end up as Commissioner. In vain McGill explained that Commissioner was a political appointment, not just another promotion, but with utter Gallic logic, Isabelle refused to hear such nonsense. They had moved to a charming square more convenient for McGill's work, and Rene, Marie and the rest of Isabelle's staff had removed en masse to London. Isabelle had insisted that everything would be paid for by her, but the house was in McGill's name. He was looking forward to his leave when they would travel to Isabelle's seaside house in Normandy. He couldn't imagine what his life had been before, as he thought of his present happiness. There was a knock on the door. He swung round on his chair and shouted "Come!"

The door opened and Croker's head popped round the corner.

"Excuse me sir, there's a gentleman to see you. Won't tell me his name."

McGill's heart plummeted. He fervently hoped it wasn't Simonds or that damned enigma, Colonel Julius, who had worked for Field Marshal Haig. Although enquiries had been made about O'Leary, no sign of him had been forthcoming. McGill sighed. "Better have him come in, Croker."

Croker stepped back and pushed the door fully open. A well-dressed young man stepped smartly through, and stamped to attention. He threw a crisp salute.

" Nobby! By all that's Holy! What are you doing here?" McGill leapt to his feet and grabbed Nobby's hand, pumping it up and down.

"Steady on! That's my wounded arm!" McGill dropped the hand as if it were burning and a look of concern came over his face.

"Don't worry," said Nobby. "It won't drop off! But at least I've a wound to brag about to the grandchildren!"

" Nobby, this is simply marvellous! I've thought of you often. And you never mentioned you were related to Sir Douglas."

"Well, yes, but it's not something I brag about!"

"Come and sit down and tell me what happened after I last saw you."

McGill sat back down behind his desk, and Nobby (more properly Francis James St. John Murgatroyd) took the seat in front of it.

"Croker! Tea please!"

"Coming up sir!"

"Now, Nobby, when I last saw you I was being heavily escorted away from Amiens HQ and towards your illustrious relative."

"Indeed you were! I heard some of what happened thereafter, but I daresay you wouldn't be at liberty to tell me everything." McGill grinned, and shook his head. "You'd be dead right there, Nobby. I'm pretty sure I'd still get shot if I breathed a word. Did you know Haig offered to have me arrested and shot as a spy?"

Nobby laughed. "Sounds like the old devil! Still, he didn't, so that's a blessing." He eased his arm a bit, holding it with his left hand.

McGill nodded towards it. "So how did you get that?" Nobby grinned.

"My own silly fault! You know when the Huns nearly reached Amiens at the end of March last year? Well, as you can imagine there was a bit of a panic on, and all we HQ people got shoved into trucks and sent up the line. I ended up at Villers-Bretonneux, just in time to take part in the counterattack which finally stemmed the tide. I was bloody pleased I can tell you! After having been kept out of it all those years, to get to the front line finally was like a dream come true!"

"I can imagine, even if it wouldn't exactly be the dream I would wish!"

"Well, our lieutenant got shot, and then the Sergeant – remember him? – the one who was on guard with me at HQ. Well he had a fit of the screaming ab-dabs when he was wounded. So the lads kind of voted me in to be in charge. We dug in and held the Huns off for twenty four hours, then there was a lull, and they came at us again. Fortunately, we'd been reinforced but as I'd been on the ground from the start of the action, everyone deferred to me, and had me running around telling men what to do. So there we were, doing a good job of holding them off, and even pushing them back a bit, when the order comes to advance. So I rally the lads and off we go, hopping from trench to trench and shell-hole to shell-hole. And though I say it myself we did a good job, overpowering the individual groups as we found them and holding trenches against counter attacks. Finally, ANOTHER twenty four hours after we attacked, we got the word we were to be relieved. We'd been dug in for six or seven hours and another regiment came along and leapfrogged us, which meant we could set off back to where we had started. Funny thing, lots of the Boches were dead drunk which made our job easier. So as we set off there were a few of the Hun who had passed out. We'd just left them, as there was no way we could carry them to the rear. So as I was swinging along, one of them jumps to his feet and stabs me in the arm with his bayonet. Poor chap didn't last long, the private next to me shot him through the head. Should have tied them up or something I suppose. Anyway, I got a medal and a field promotion, so I am now officially Captain Murgatroyd."

"Well well, that's some story Nobby. But tell me, how did you go from Private to Captain – surely it should only have been to Lieutenant?"

Nobby laughed. "Ah well, they decided I was too valuable as a fighting man to go back into guarding duties. So the next thing is, I'm in charge of a platoon heading towards Germany. When the Captain was wounded they made me up to Acting Captain, and it sort of stuck. And here I am!"

By now Croker had appeared with the tea, and hovered, listening to the tale. McGill pulled his old enamel mug from his drawer. Nobby eyed it fondly.

"Those were the days, eh?" he said, nodding towards it.

"Indeed they were."

"And what of you?"

"Well, I'm a married man with a daughter."

"You don't say! How did that come about?" McGill glanced at Croker, who rapidly busied himself with getting out of the room and shutting the door. A happy smile came over his face as he told the tale of Isabelle, and his new found happiness.

"Couldn't happen to a nicer chap!"

"And what about you? Is there a Mrs. Murgatroyd?" Nobby grimaced.

"There would be if Mamma had anything to do with it! Whenever I go to see the old harridan, there's always another eligible horse-faced filly staying. Really, if she would just leave it alone, I'm perfectly capable of finding my own wife." McGill laughed.

"That's what you think! We are putty in their hands. Anyway, tell me why you came to see me – or is it just a social visit?" Nobby looked at McGill keenly.

"Suppose I were to tell you I've become a Private Detective?" McGill rocked back in his chair and roared with laughter.

"No, really, I have! The family aren't best pleased, but it beats huntin' shootin' 'n fishin' any day! And as it happens, I've picked up a juicy commission from the Government."

McGill was still smirking, but his face started to fall at the mention of Nobby's new job.

"Nobby, please, don't tell me you're here at the orders of some politico."

Nobby nodded. "Sorry old chap, but I am." McGill sat, stunned by the turn of events. "No, Nobby, no, I won't get involved. Besides, I only answer to my Super and the Commissioner." Nobby reached inside his jacket pocket with a grin and produced an envelope. He took out the letter inside, and gravely handed it to McGill.

With a sinking heart, McGill took the paper and started to read.

" My dear McGill…….."

To be continued…
The final part of this trilogy, Resolution, will follow

Reprisal – Historical notes

1)   The period McGill was in France straddles the German March 1918 Spring Offensive. Known as Operation Michael, it ran from 21st March until 5th April. The facts about it, as relayed by Watkins, about Doullens and Haig's actions are all correct, as well as Nobby's subsequent statement, after the tide was turned, that many of the German soldiers were dead drunk.
2)   At Le Crotoy, although Wells raises a toast to "Ourselves", this is in fact a Wednesday Naval Toast. 26th March was actually a Tuesday, so the toast should have been "To our men" (now changed to "To our sailors")
3)   Suicide is a mortal sin for Catholics, hence McGill making a point about Anne Lincolnshire's heart attack